MW01658076

Playthang

Also by Janine A. Morris

DIVA DIARIES

SHE'S NO ANGEL

Published by Kensington Publishing Corporation

Playthang

Janine A. Morris

Dafina Books

KENSINGTON PUBLISHING CORP.

DAFINA BOOKS are published by

Kensington Publishing Corp.
850 Third Avenue
New York, NY 10022

Copyright © 2008 by Janine A. Morris

All rights reserved. No part of this book may be reproduced in any form or by any means without the prior written consent of the Publisher, excepting brief quotes used in reviews.

Dafina Books and the Dafina logo Reg. U.S. Pat. & TM Off.

ISBN: 978-1-60751-194-6

Printed in the United States of America

I dedicate this book to two angels . . .
my uncle, Webster Dub Young,
and my friend, Renesha Bowen-Smith,
who both passed away
while I was writing this book.
Love and miss you.

R.I.P

Gone, but not forgotten

Acknowledgments

First and foremost, I would like to thank God for all his blessings and mercy. I still have to pinch myself sometimes that this is me living this life. It feels like a dream to be fulfilling all the goals I set for myself as a little girl. I am completing my third year of law school and my third book will be in stores this year. I know you can do anything you set your mind to, but I still feel so blessed to be living out my dreams. God has been good to me.

I also thank God for granting me with my parents to whom I owe so much. To my amazing parents, Julius and Carolyn Morris, thank you. You guys have been a perfect example of making it happen and never giving up. I thank God that you guys raised me to have the self-worth and self-confidence that I have, and that you taught me right from wrong and loved me enough to make sure I knew I had options. Thank you for supporting me in all my dreams and endeavors and for being there emotionally, physically, spiritually, and financially. I truly don't know what I would do without you guys.☺

Ahmad Meggett, when I met you a decade ago I had no idea you were going to fill my life with so much joy for so long. You constantly push me to "keep it up" and you remain a friend that I can depend on as well as a man that I can love. From the breakfasts in bed and the instant piña coladas to the shoulder to lean on whenever I need one, you spoil me. You are beautiful on the inside, extremely handsome on the outside, you make my life magical. There is not one thing about you that I would change. You are too good to be true. I thank God for sending me the person that I feel extremely confident is my true soul mate. I hope that six more decades go by and we still have this amazing "something that we share." You still are—and I hope you will always be—"my air."

My twin brother Jason who is no longer with me in flesh but in spirit, thank you for giving me the motivation to do twice as much, enough for you and me both. To my siblings, Tashah Bigelow and Julius Morris J.R., thank you for always being there when I've needed you and for guiding your baby sister. Tashah, as you know it will always be automatic and when we don't want to deal with anyone else in this world; we always have each other. J.R., my big brother, time has flown and we have grown so much. Although life has made it where we are not joined at the hip anymore you are always there for me when I need you most, and I will always be proud to be your little "big" sister. My sister Lisa, I love you and as you said, "It's in the blood." My brother-in-law Alex, you're still my Alexy Palexy who lives in a galaxy. My nephew Hamilton, you are growing into such a fine young man. I love you so much, if you only knew just how much joy you've brought me since the day you were born. My nieces, Tylah and Leila, keep being the strong and smart little ladies you are. You are my little princesses, and you make me proud.

To my second family, Henry, Cynthia, Rashard, Rashida, and Leslie Meggett, I don't think you understand how truly blessed I feel to have you all in my life. Ma and Dad Meggett, I am always telling people about how great you two are, how much you inspire me and how much I love you both from the bottom of my heart; and I sincerely mean every word of it. You make me feel comfortable and treat me like your own child and that means a lot to me. (And Ma, thanks for supporting my writing career the way you have.) Rashard and Leslie, congrats on your new marriage and new home, all you have to do now is make the new baby . . . let's get to it. Rashida, you are the little sister I never had, and you and Sekai (K5) have made such beautiful baby twin boys. To my new nephews, Alijah and Amari Guy, welcome to the world and may you enjoy all the spoiling we will bestow upon you. To Grandma Doris, Uncle Junior and Uncle Peter, Aunt Berta, Aunt Cookie, Tanika, Troi, Candice, Kevin, Brandi (congrats on the wedding bells), and Brian—thanks for treating me like family.

To my Aunts Val, Ann, Kirby, Ruthann, Zelda, Frankie, Earline, Dorothy, and Barbara; and my Uncles Joe, Ray, Dwight, June, William, and Gregory, thanks for your role in my life and for all your support. My father is one of seven, my mother is one of ten, and all seventeen of my grandparents' children had children, some up to five. So as you know there are too many cousins to name, but to my amazing loving and large Morris and Young family, you are my five fingers that make a mighty fist. You know who you are, love you all. Lauren and Gordon Dillard, we are the YOUNGest, and we have the duty to take the world by storm.

Ebony, they say friends are for a season, reason or lifetime; I think we have ruled out a season and a reason and I'm looking forward to the rest of our lifetime of friendship. The rest of the Fabulous 5, as always, I love you chicas; Derica, Sytieya, Nicole, and Rene. I have always been selective with friends, who I keep around me because I truly believe negative people can drain you. You girls have been what friendship is all about, and I love that we are all growing as women together. I am looking forward to several more years of birthdays, vacations, girls' nights out and Secret Santa's with you ladies. Love you all. Speedy

Claxton, over ten years of friendship and I love you dearly; we can talk about anything and manage to have a blast just by going out to eat. They hate on us because they don't understand us. Ira "Bo" Miller, you are one of the most enjoyable people to be around. Where's the comedy without you? Snap, thanks for always supporting everything I do. You are a great person and God will bless you for your kid's charity and warm heart. Jacinta Claxton—I love how we always agree, great minds think alike, Sammy Martin—the ball of fun fire that you are, Mona and Marc Thompson—congrats on the baby, Karen St. Hillin, Malyka Muhammad, Kim Cutler, and Larry Davis, thanks for all the support and years of great memories; I hope we continue to make more. Tenille Clyburn, I love you, lil' missy, you make one realize true friends are hard to come by.

Alicia McFarlane and Kimberly Ginyard, I'm happy that I'm gaining more from law school than just legal knowledge, a degree, fulfillment of a childhood dream, and a piece of paper that's going to remind me every day that I'm unstoppable. I'm happy that I also gained two great friends in you girls. You're both astounding women and I'm happy to have crossed paths with you. To all my other friends, old and new, thank you for all the love and support; Martha Cuellar, Vanessa Quinones, Nadia Sang, Carl Slater, Billy Barnett, Jared Hall, Leighton Shields, Serge Thelamuque, Phun, Ozfather, Trice Palendacour, Kevin Darius, Dulani, Taneha Gillard, Brandi Monique, Jennifer Wade, Tina Chadha, Kimberly Pena, Nicole and Chrissy Begelow, Andrea Bernard—BBC, Diandra Ortiz—BBC, Summer—BBC, Taja Blain, April Debartolo, Timothy Mitchell, Samantha Stechler, and Tamanisha Miller.

To my editor Rakia Clark, thank you so much for everything. You are a beautiful person inside and out, it's a pleasure to work with someone as inspiring and understanding as yourself. To my agent Sarah Camilli, thanks for believing in me. My publicist, Adeola Saul, thanks for being the one who can be both my friend and upfront about business. Jessica McClean, thanks for all the support and guidance.

To my other author friends, Candice Dow and Daaimah Poole, you guys have been like my sisters in this. Candice, I appreciate the way we can pick each other up, motivate each other, and reignite the fires inside of us to keep shooting for the stars. Donna Hill, Nikki Turner, Tova, Zane, and Karen Quinones; thanks for the kind words and words of advice. Karen Thomas and Latoya Smith, thank you for everything. Stacey Barney, thank you for sharing your wisdom and helping to mold my versatility.

Denise Warren, thanks for keeping me and half of the tristate fit. I love you and I wish you another twenty-one years of success with Body by Denise.

Frank Iemetti, thanks for being my mentor, my boss, and my friend. You have always been someone that stands out amongst a crowd, being honest, forthright and caring, and it's an honor to know you and work with you. Nikki Smith, we meet people every day and every now and then one of them was meant to be in your life. You are good people, and I'm glad that our days at Emmis led to a great friendship. I love you, mama. Bugsy, my gained uncle, you know I love you like I've known you all my life. There is no explanation for how great a person you are other than God is in your heart. Koren Vaugn, from day one you've been my home girl and will always be. Marc McLaughlin, thanks for always looking out and all your love. Deneen Womack, what are we waiting for? lol. DJ Envy, DJ Absolut, and DJ Clue, it must be a Queens thing that makes us so real;

thanks for everything. Keisha Monk, thanks for the love; see you at BBD. To Travia Charmont, Shaila of the Kiss Morning show, Julie Gustines, Jacques Thomas, Gwynet Cowan, Hulio, Vito, Miss Jones, Ray Ramos, Toya Beasley, Talent, Lenny Green, Nema Jackson, Monse, TatWza, Randi Hatchel, Shelby Woods, DJ Camilo, Chris Nadler, Ebro (congrats), Rose Crichton, Gigi, Donyshia Benjamin, Pat Robinson, Funkmaster Flex, Mister Cee, Cipha Sounds, Angie, Ben Burnside and Ben Finley, Mark Halupa, and all the other greats at Emmis, I wish you continued success. Ife Moore, on-air in NC, thanks for all the support.

Jay Brown at Def Jam, Jeanine McLean at MBK Management, John McMann, Mike Kyser, James Brown, Cheryl Singleton, and Pia McBain at Atlantic, Karen Rait at Interscope, Sean Pecas at Def Jam, Dontay Thompson at J Records, Lisa Ellis at Sony, John Menielly, Joe Riccitelli, John Strazza, and Jeff Sledge at Jive Records. Nelson Taboada at G-Unit, Sherise Malachi, Dave House, Rodney Morandi, Patty Laurent, and Latesha Williams, thanks for everything.

Last, but most certainly not least, all my readers and supporters, I celebrate you. Carol Mackey at Black Expression, thanks for supporting me since day one. All the book clubs and the bookstores that support and carry my novels, and all of you who have picked it up and allowed me to share the thoughts in my brain for a moment in your life—I celebrate you. Thanks so much, and I hope to continue to entertain you with my stories.

If I have forgotten anyone, please forgive me. (The law books have my brain kind of fried.)

1

The look on her face expressed a clear level of discomfort. It seemed Ms. Grant wasn't prepared for the question that Jordan had asked her. Jordan, on the other hand, was poised and bright-eyed, awaiting an answer.

The young lady was sitting directly across from Jordan, alongside her colleagues. Jordan sat with only her client, Aminae Carty, who was an artist professionally known as Amina.

"I'm not sure I understand what you are getting at," the young lady responded.

"What I'm getting at is there seems to be a lack of awareness on your company's part. Amina has sold over 300,000 singles in this past month alone, without the backing of a major company. Therefore, I believe it is apparent that she is not your typical breakthrough artist, which is why I asked whether you are fully aware of her potential," Jordan said, looking directly at the three people across from her.

Amina sat in the chair, trying to look as confident as possible, but it seemed that she was uncomfortable as well.

The colleagues on the other side of the table were all employed by Def Society Records. The young lady sitting directly across from Jordan was the director of business & legal affairs,

Jill Turner. The other two faces belonged to Jill's assistant and her manager of business affairs.

"Well, yes, we are aware that Amina made strides with her career prior to deciding to join us. However, the support and funds that we plan to put behind her will take her career to another level, which may take her years to achieve on her own, if at all."

"Ms. Grant, my client and I are well aware of what Def Society Records is offering. If we didn't feel it would benefit her, we wouldn't be sitting here. However, we are also aware of how adding her to your roster will benefit you. Amina has done the hard work of generating her own buzz and awareness throughout the East and West coasts. She has a recognizable name, she has received radio airplay, and she is extremely talented. Adding her is a win-win for your company, and all we are asking is that you recognize that and not offer her the same deal you would offer someone who hasn't accomplished as much."

"Ms. Moore, I see your point, and at this time, this is all I'm capable of offering."

"Well, we are not capable of accepting this offer. However, we greatly appreciate your interest and time, and hopefully we can do business together in the future."

Ms. Grant looked surprised as she watched Jordan gather her folders and papers from the table.

"Ms. Moore, we would hate to lose out on the opportunity to work with Amina. Let me have a meeting with Shewayne, the president, and see if we can rework the budget to find a better figure to satisfy you and Amina."

"That is fine. I will respectfully hold off the other offers until we speak again."

"That will be appreciated."

Jordan stood from her chair. As she pushed the seat farther back, she realized Amina was still sitting there, looking a bit perplexed. Jordan gestured to her with her eyes that it was time to make their exit. Amina immediately jumped up to stand beside Jordan. Ms. Grant and her colleagues rose as well; they picked up their files from the table and began preparing to exit the conference room. Jordan and Amina both scooted their chairs back and began walking toward the door.

Everyone pretty much reached the door at the same time, and they exchanged words along the lines of "good-bye" and "I'll speak to you soon." Once the lobby was cleared, Amina and Jordan waited for the elevator. They stood there in silence for a few moments while the receptionist watched them wait. Once the elevator arrived, they both stepped in, and Jordan pressed the button for the ground floor.

"You OK?" Jordan asked Amina.

"Yeah. A little nervous."

"About what?"

"Well, what if they don't want me anymore?"

"Amina, I wouldn't have jeopardized your career. I told you on the way over that the goal of today's meeting was to get a better deal. I am certain that they will counteroffer with a much better deal. That offer she gave was not their best. I have known Shewayne for a long time now; I know he will send Ms. Grant back to us with the appropriate figures."

"OK. I trust you," Amina said with a shrug.

"Good. You should. I wouldn't steer you wrong."

Jordan and Amina walked out of the building onto Eighth Avenue and looked around.

"Which way are you headed? You need a lift somewhere?" Jordan asked.

"I'm good. I'm meeting some friends around the corner. Thanks."

"OK. I'll be in touch."

Jordan walked down the street toward her car. Almost there, she looked up and noticed a Starbucks across the street. She began to cross the street to go grab herself a mocha latte, but halfway across she changed her mind. She realized she didn't need the extra calories, and she needed to resist this constant urge of hers. So she turned back and headed toward her car. She walked a few feet and arrived at her black BMW X5. She beeped the alarm, opened the door, and sat inside. Once she settled in her seat, before she started the car, she reached into her bag and got out her BlackBerry. A look of disappointment came over her face when she realized that she hadn't received a call or e-mail from Jayon the entire day. She was tempted to call him and ask where her hello was for the day, but she decided against it. Instead, she just started her car and pulled out into the heavy traffic of Manhattan to try to make her way home. Surprisingly, she didn't mind the traffic; Jordan was in no rush to get home to her empty house.

2

It was the third time over the course of two weeks that Jordan had been sitting on her front lawn waiting on Jayon. The two of them had gotten so busy with work these past few months that they had to make appointments to spend time with each other. However, the times they set seemed to be difficult for Jayon to keep. The last time, he had Jordan waiting on him for almost an hour, and he said he was held up with a client at the office. This time, Jordan didn't even care what his excuse was, because nothing seemed to justify him not answering his phone or calling her to let her know he'd be late.

From up the street all you could recognize was Jordan's five feet seven, 145-pound frame slouched in her patio chair. She looked out over her garden, which she had to admit was due for some tender loving care. Her rose bushes and plants were still healthy except for a few that were wilting here and there, but there were weeds popping up and some excess leaves lying around. It wasn't hard to see the look of frustration covering her medium brown complexion. Her light brown eyes were downcast due to the frown she was wearing. Her shoulder-length hair was slicked back into a bun, and she wore a multicolored, sheer minidress with a slip underneath it and some black sandals. She was dressed for a bright and happy evening, but from the way things were looking, it wasn't going to go as planned.

Jordan slowly stood up and folded her arms. She glanced down the block and noticed the little girl playing in front of her house down the street. Sitting a few feet away were the little girl's parents. They were just sitting there watching their daughter play as they conversed about who knows what. Jordan didn't know what they were speaking of, but they looked happy. She couldn't help but feel weak realizing how she no longer had that. Her family was shattered, and she missed the hell out of her son. It was enough dealing with her ex-husband's engagement, but seeing Jason with the two of them made her sick to her stomach. Watching the happy neighbors gave her the same feeling, so she finally looked away. Jordan looked down at her feet and then back up again. She looked down the street one more time, and then she dropped her arms and headed for her front door.

Once she stepped back inside her house, she plopped down on her couch and buried her face in her hands. She sat there wondering what had happened to her and the life she had worked so hard to perfect. For the life of her she couldn't figure out where she went wrong, and every time she thought of it, she got no closer to figuring it out. After a few moments of sitting there, tears began to roll down her face. Whether they were tears of sadness or tears of anger was hard to determine. All Jordan knew was she felt like she was failing. Her home life was bad, and even things at work were bad, and she didn't know if she had it in her to fight her way back to the top anymore.

Moments later, Jordan heard a noise. She lifted her head off the taupe throw pillow she was resting on, then listened harder to see if she heard it again. As she laid there completely still, listening, she saw a figure in her peripheral vision. She looked toward the doorway and screamed. Somewhere in the midst of her panic attack, she noticed that it was Jayon. He was standing there laughing at the scare he'd put into Jordan, although she was not yet laughing back. His five feet eleven, 195-pound frame filled the doorway, and he was dressed in blue jeans, Sean John sneakers, and an Akademiks rugby.

"Where have you been?" Jordan began.

"I was at my meetings late."

Jordan scanned his outfit, and obviously enough for him to notice. "You were at meetings dressed like that?"

"Jordan. I went home to change first. What's wrong with you?"

"What's wrong with me? You couldn't call, Jayon? I've been here waiting on you . . . that's what's wrong with me."

"Why didn't you call me?"

"Jayon . . . I called your cell phone like three times."

"Oh, must've been bad reception where I had my meetings, 'cause I didn't see them."

Jordan gave him a look of doubt, a look of disappointment. It was apparent that she wanted more than anything to blurt out, "Do you think I'm stupid? Do you think you can tell me anything?" and go off on a rant. However, she just communicated her thoughts through the look on her face.

"What?" Jayon asked with a smirk.

"Nothing, Jayon. You're making it a joke, and it's not funny," Jordan said as she stood up and went to grab the remote off the entertainment center.

"What's not funny?"

"Nothing, Jayon. Forget it. Play stupid. That's fine."

Jordan sat down and pushed POWER on the remote.

"What? You in here sulking like I did something to you."

Jordan was kind of upset that Jayon found her like that. She hated to look weak.

"I wasn't sulking, Jayon. Don't flatter yourself," Jordan said with conviction, knowing dang well she was just sulking.

"Whatever, J," he said as he walked upstairs.

Jordan sat there frustrated as hell. A piece of her wanted to just break, say everything that was on her mind, including the not-so-nice stuff. But she also didn't want the drama or the argument, and she knew Jayon would say she was looking for the negative because he would think he had done nothing wrong. Jordan sat on the edge of the couch, staring at the television but paying attention to nothing on the screen. Her thoughts were all over the place, beginning with the curiosity of how she ever became so accepting of her and Jayon's situation.

Jordan could hear footsteps coming back down the stairs. She pretended that the television had her attention and that she was relaxing. Jayon came into the living room dressed in a white sleeveless T-shirt and black sweat shorts, he apparently got comfortable since he assumed their plans were shot. Jordan had assumed that he was upstairs changing. She was tempted to ask him who said their plans were cancelled, but she was aware that her attitude probably said it. After Jayon walked around for a bit doing whatever he was doing, he eventually sat beside Jordan on the couch.

"Want to watch a movie?" he asked.

Jordan paused before she answered. She wanted to say "not really," but instead she calmly answered, "OK."

Jayon put his hand out for the remote, and she handed it to him. Jayon turned to the movies on demand channel and began looking for a movie to watch.

"See anything you want to see?" he asked.

"Not yet," Jordan replied.

Jayon kept channel surfing.

"I'll be right back. I'm going to change while you find something," Jordan said as she stood up from the couch.

Jayon didn't reply, he just steadily moved through the movie listings as Jordan headed up the stairs. Jordan was trying to remain calm and put aside all of her emotions. Jayon had the ability to suppress all drama even when there was a need to address it. Jordan could admit that it helped their overall relationship from being filled with drama, but Jordan also knew that a lot of things festered between them, and that wasn't healthy. She also knew it didn't make sense to bother to bring up how late he was now that she had agreed to watch a movie with him.

Jordan opened one of the drawers to her pajama dresser and pulled out her Victoria's Secret pink boxer pajama set. She started taking off her clothes and began to genuinely calm down. Usually, changing out of clothes that she had put on to go somewhere without having gone to that place would be enough to upset her. She was feeling that way too, until she realized it could have been worse. He could've come even later or not at all. She tried to look at the bright side—they were going to spend a quiet evening at home.

Jordan hung her dress back up in the closet for another night, since it didn't get its night out. As she closed the closet door, Jayon's jeans fell to the floor. Jordan bent over to pick them up, and a piece of paper fell out along with some money. Jordan started picking the items up when she noticed handwriting on the paper. The investigator in her instantly glanced over it. Written on it was "Nicole" and a phone number. Jordan looked at the paper a few seconds longer for any clues as to where it came from. It was on a torn piece of plain white paper, and there was nothing else written on it. Jordan proceeded to return the items to his pocket while she felt herself begin to boil with anger. She knew that it seemed as if Jayon had gotten some girl's number in an attempt to "get to know her better." Just the mere thought of addressing him over this number felt so high school. Besides, she knew there were a million legit excuses that Jayon could give, like it was a business colleague or an old friend. So Jordan decided to choose her battles and let this one go, or at least save it for a later date.

Jordan made her way back downstairs, the whole time telling herself repetitively to let it go. By the time she made it to the couch where Jayon was sitting, she hadn't completely erased the negative thoughts from her head, but she was still trying.

"You ready?" Jayon said as he pointed the remote at the television to unpause the movie on the screen.

"Mm-hmm," Jordan responded.

Jayon hit the PAUSE button. "This is that movie I was telling you about with the clones. It's called *The Island*," Jayon said as he scooted back to get comfortable on the couch. "Want to make some popcorn?"

"Not really," Jordan answered.

She had been silently wishing that Jayon would stop talking to her so she wouldn't have to struggle to hide her anger.

"You don't want popcorn while watching a movie? OK, that's a first," Jayon said.

Jordan didn't reply. She just kept looking at the television screen, which was showing the opening credits. She watched the boat ride across the water on the screen, and then all of a sudden the screen froze. Jordan looked over at Jayon, and he had the remote in his hand, pointing it at the television.

"What's wrong with you?" he asked.

"Nothing, Jayon. Turn it back on."

"You are acting mad funny, and you're saying nothing is wrong."

"Jayon, nothing's wrong. I am just tired."

"Tired?"

"Yes, tired."

"OK, if you want me to believe that, I'll let it go."

Something snapped in Jordan's mind. She was tired of being nice and holding her tongue, and since he insisted, she figured she'd let him know.

"Who is Nicole?" Jordan blurted out.

"What?" Jayon asked, looking totally confused.

"Who is Nicole?"

"What are you talking about?"

"You know what, Jayon, I don't even want to talk about it. Because in all honesty, I don't know if I can trust whatever you tell me anyway."

"Where is all this coming from?"

"You show up hours after you were supposed to, acting like it's nothing, having no regard for the fact that I was here dressed and waiting for you; then I go upstairs to change and a phone number falls out of your pocket. I just don't even know what to think anymore," Jordan rambled on.

"That was a client," Jayon said.

Jordan giggled. She laughed because she was expecting something like that.

"What is so funny?"

"I just thought you would say something like that, that's all."

"Well, Jordan, how can I win then? Why'd you ask?"

"I tried not to, but you insisted on asking me what was wrong."

"Well, I'm sorry for being concerned."

"I wish you were concerned with keeping me waiting for hours."

"Jordan, I said sorry. I was held up at work. What do you want me to do?"

"Call, e-mail, something. You come in late, I couldn't get a hold of you, you didn't try to contact me, and then you have numbers in your pocket. Really, Jay—what do you want me to think?"

"It's not about what I want you to think. I can only tell you what I've told you. What you choose to think is your own decision," Jayon said as he hit the PAUSE button and the movie started again.

"It's that very nonchalance that makes me think the way I do even more."

"Whatever," Jayon responded.

Now Jordan was pissed. She hated when Jayon just shut down, when he decided that he was done talking about something. She was upset that she even broke her silence, because now she was more upset than she had been from the start, and Jayon's attitude was only going to make it harder to calm down.

The opening scene of the movie started, and Jayon was sitting with his feet kicked up on the ottoman, while Jordan had one foot up on the couch and the other on the floor. They were sitting at opposite ends of the couch, both watching the movie.

Jordan was tempted to stop faking the funk and walk her black butt upstairs. She was barely paying attention to the movie anyway, because she was still trying to lower her blood pressure. When she thought about it more, she realized that it was possible that going upstairs was only going to make it a bigger deal. She told herself not to even stress it. Jayon wanted to play innocent and play little games; two could play at that.

3

By the time Chrasey sat down and requested the drink menu, she looked up and saw Jordan walking in. She instantly smiled at the sight of Ms. Moore walking toward her in her power suit and carrying a black Louis Vuitton briefcase. Jordan had that typical look of the successful black woman, and it always amused Chrasey to think of how the world would react if it really knew she had issues just like the rest of us.

Jordan glanced around the restaurant, smiling at a few people, until she finally spotted Chrasey sitting at a table in the middle of the room. The Cheesecake Factory on a Friday night got pretty crowded, but the food and drinks were worth it. Jordan made her way to the table where Chrasey sat, and she instantly placed her briefcase and purse in the booth and walked off.

"Gotta go to the bathroom," she blurted.

Chrasey giggled and buried her face in the drink menu that the waiter had just brought over. She was beginning to narrow it down as to what her drink for the night would be, when she heard someone close by clearing their throat.

"Look at you." After debating if she wanted to squeeze onto the bench or sit at the chairs facing the bench, she muttered, "You're turning into an alcoholic." She pulled a chair out from the table.

"Ha ha ha, Missy . . . you are teaching me well," Chrasey replied.

"Where's Jordan?" Dakota asked, gesturing toward the briefcase sitting on the bench.

"She is in the bathroom."

"Oh. Well, what're you drinking?"

"I'm thinking a Mai Tai."

"I'll take that too," Dakota said.

At that moment, the waiter walked over. "You ladies ready to order?"

"Not yet. Waiting for someone to get out of the bathroom," Chrasey said.

"OK, no problem. I'll give you a few minutes," the waiter responded.

The waiter walked away and headed toward the next table over.

Chrasey followed him with her eyes. "He is kinda cute," she said.

"Stop it, slut," Dakota said.

Unbeknownst to Dakota, Jordan was walking up behind her, returning from the bathroom.

"Isn't that the pot calling the kettle black?" Jordan laughed as she wiggled into her seat.

"Ha ha ha," Dakota muttered.

"Whatever, heifers. Pick what you are getting, 'cause I am starving," Jordan said.

Jordan immediately opened her menu and began perusing the pages to see what she wanted to eat for the night. She went straight past the beef section and toward the chicken and pasta sections.

"I'm not sure what I'm in the mood for," Jordan said.

"Well, I'm getting the Navajo Sandwich," Dakota added.

"Nobody asked you," Jordan said.

"What's your problem this evening?" Chrasey said before Dakota could respond.

"Nothing, I was just joking," Jordan said, looking at Dakota.

"You better be playing, 'cause you're about two seconds from getting jumped over here," Dakota said, laughing.

"I'm just cranky. Work, that damn Jayon . . . I'm missing Jason like crazy, just going through it right now, that's all."

"You ain't called me in like two weeks. I was wondering what's been going on with you. When Dakota said we was meeting, I knew I had to come because I had to catch you while I could."

"I did call you a couple days ago at work, but when your secretary said you weren't at your desk, I didn't leave a message. My bad."

"It's cool. So what's been going on with you?"

"Well, my now ex-husband doesn't want to agree to give me custody of Jason."

"Really?" Chrasey asked. "I didn't know you were asking for it."

"I said he could have him every weekend and half the summer, but he's still not trying to work with me and, quite honestly, it's driving me crazy," Jordan said.

"Well, what is it that he is willing to do?" Dakota asked.

"He is willing to let me take him weekends and half the summer. He says it's too much change for Jason, which I see what he is saying, but either way the back and forth is unstable no matter how we arrange it."

"Yeah, that is true. I just don't want my godson being stressed out over you two's nonsense," Chrasey chimed in.

"I know, Chrase. That's why I feel so torn. My decision to let Omar have him in the first place was based on trying to do right by Jason, but I always felt guilty. I could never tell if there were some selfish reasons for that too. This time I know it's all for Jason. I do miss him, but I know it's what's best for him," Jordan said.

"Well, honestly, J, how do you know it's best for him?" Chrasey asked.

"He tells me he doesn't like Omar's fiancée, and that when Omar is at work she doesn't do anything with him. No woman is going to be making my child feel unwelcome or neglected."

"What does Omar say about that?" Dakota said.

"He just says that it's not like that. Jason keeps to himself, and she tries to bond with him and so on. Really, I don't care what attempts she has made; Jason isn't comfortable there, and he needs his mother's love," Jordan said.

"So what are you going to do?" Chrasey asked.

"I'm filing papers to get custody of him."

"Really! You're going to take him to court?" Chrasey asked.

"Well, I'm hoping he will not want to go through the trouble and just settle with me. If he doesn't, then yes, it will go through the courts."

"You think you have a good chance of winning?" Dakota asked.

"Yes, they always side with the mother unless there are some extenuating circumstances."

"Well, good luck with it. If you need some character witnesses, we got you," Dakota said, laughing.

"Whatever, miss. Y'all heifers will make me lose the case."

As they all laughed at the humor found in the not-so-funny situation, they snacked on the bread and their drinks.

A few moments later, the waiter came and took their orders. They all ordered different things so they could steal a bite from the others' plates, as they usually did. Once the waiter walked away, they began chatting again.

"So what's going on with David?" Chrasey asked Dakota.

"He is fine; he is starting his new job this week."

"He got promoted, right?" Jordan asked.

"Yeah, he is excited," Dakota answered.

"That's good for him," Jordan said before taking a bite of her bread.

As Jordan reached for a sip of her water, she saw in her peripheral view a man walking toward her table. She took a sip from the glass, and then looked up as she placed her water back down. By now, the gentleman was standing only a few inches from the table. Once it was obvious that his intention was to get the ladies' attention, they all looked in his direction.

"Hi, I'm so sorry to interrupt your dinner, ladies, but I would've never forgiven myself if I didn't come over here and at least introduce myself."

The ladies just looked back at him and smiled some.

"My name is Alan," he said.

"Hi, Alan," Chrasey said.

The guy looked at Jordan and said, "I won't be surprised if some lucky man has taken you for himself, but if by chance it's possible, I would love if you would call me sometime," Alan said as he placed a business card in front of Jordan.

Jordan looked down at it and read that Alan was a director of finance and his offices were located up the street from her own.

"Thanks, I'll give you a call, Alan," Jordan said, picking up the business card off the table.

"Sorry I didn't place it in your hand, but I didn't want you to feel pressured to take it."

"I never feel pressured to do things I don't want to do, but thanks for the thoughtfulness."

"OK, I'm going to let you get back to dinner. Nice meeting you, ladies," Alan said as he turned to walk away.

Alan walked back to the bar where two men were looking in his direction as if waiting to see if he had been shot down or not.

"I guess you scared him away," Dakota said.

"I'm just saying, how you going to put the card down on the table?" Jordan asked.

"You are always so hard on these men. You would think you were still married the way you won't give them no play," Chrasey said.

Jordan just shrugged her shoulders.

"You made him nervous; cut him some slack," Chrasey added.

"I know. Maybe we can meet for lunch one day," Jordan said, looking down at the business card. "He works right up the street from my office."

"Uh-oh," Dakota said. "I remember when you wouldn't even take a number; there must be trouble in paradise."

Jordan made a face at Dakota.

"That's true. . . . What Jayon do now?" Chrasey said.

"Nothing at all. I just don't feel like living by any rules right now," Jordan replied.

"They're your rules. Nobody made you live by those rules," Dakota said. "I used to tell you to live a little."

"I know that, and that's why I'm breaking my rules for a while."

"Well, you gotta do a lot more than pick up a business card off the table if you call yourself living a little," Dakota replied.

4

The sounds of whistles and crowd screams were coming from the living room when Jordan opened the front door. She was walking into her home with three grocery bags, her briefcase, and a Macy's bag in tow. Jordan closed the door behind her and dropped the bags by the door.

"Jayon, can you come help me with these bags?" she shouted.

She began to walk down the hall toward the bathroom. She noticed that Jayon hadn't responded, and she hadn't heard any movement since her request. She finished up in the bathroom and walked out into the living room. Jayon was still sitting in front of the television with the joystick to his PlayStation in his hands.

"Jayon, you didn't hear me ask you to help me with the bags?"

"I was coming. Where are they?"

"By the door," Jordan said.

"Why are they by the door?"

"'Cause they were heavy and I had to pee."

"OK, well, I'll be right there. The game's almost over."

Jordan looked at Jayon for a few seconds longer and then walked away. There were days she just wanted to break that damn PlayStation. She was walking down the corridor when she felt her cell phone begin to ring. She looked down at her pocket, and removed the phone from its clip. When she looked in the caller ID, there was a local number displayed with no name. She initially hesitated to answer, unaware of who it was, but she decided to answer to remove her focus momentarily from Jayon.

"Hello," she answered.

"Hi, is this Jordan?" the voice replied.

"Yes, this is she."

"Hi . . . You probably don't remember me, but we met about two months ago at the BMI Music event."

"Oh, yeah. I do. What is your name again?"

Jordan walked farther back into the kitchen so that her conversation wasn't overheard.

"Malcolm."

"OK, right."

"Well, I'm sorry to bother you after hours, but I wanted to try to get you when you weren't so busy at work."

"I actually just got home, and I wish I could say I wasn't busy anymore once I was off, but that'd be a lie."

"I understand. I know you're a very productive woman. I was hoping I could steal you away from your hectic schedule one of these days for dinner or drinks," Malcolm said.

Jordan didn't recall the person she had in mind from the BMI event trying to hit on her. In fact, if she remembered correctly, they were discussing business only. For a moment she wanted to do her normal shut down line, but she hesitated because she wasn't sure if his comments were still from a professional perspective. Besides, she could still hear the PlayStation game blaring from the television in the living room.

"Sure, one of these days sounds good to me. Why don't you call me tomorrow at the office, and we can arrange a day."

"I will call you first thing tomorrow," Malcolm said.

They both said their good-byes and hung up. Jordan began to walk back down the hall to see if Jayon had even begun to fulfill her request from over ten minutes ago. She entered the room, and Jayon was sitting on the edge of the couch with the joystick in his hand and his eyes glued on the television. Jordan took one look at him, and when he didn't even look up at her when she entered the room, she rolled her eyes and walked off.

"I'm coming," Jayon said, probably in response to her teeth sucking.

Jordan walked onto the porch, took each bag one by one, and began to lug them into the kitchen. She took the route that didn't call for her to cut in front of the television, but still, Jayon probably heard the sound of the bags rustling together. As Jordan was a few feet from the kitchen, she heard footsteps coming from the other side of the wall. She continued until Jayon was walking toward her and attempting to take the bags from her hands.

"Don't even worry about it now," Jordan said, trying to steadily walk pass Jayon.

"Give me the bags," Jayon said with attitude, as if he had a right to be upset.

To avoid the argument that was brewing, Jordan let go of the bags and headed back down the hall. She walked upstairs and went into the bedroom. She sat down on the side of the purple king-size bed and ran her fingers through her hair. Jordan knew she was no longer in a fairy-tale relationship; she knew her prince had pretty much turned back into a toad. Each day that went by, she didn't know if there was something she could do differently or if she had done all that she could do and had to now deal with the hand she was dealt.

When she forgave Jayon over a year ago for cheating on her, he was so apologetic and appeared to be sincere. She had such high expectations for what a great significant other he would be in order to restore their relationship back to what it was. That lasted all of a month or so. In the beginning, he was real sweet and caring; he would spill compliments upon Jordan, suggest the sweetest dates, and so on. However, as soon as Jordan was over his indiscretions, he stopped being so romantic and putting in the extra effort. He started to go back to Jayon the friend, the boyfriend that was more like just a homeboy. That was enough in the beginning. Hell, it was more than enough back then. When they first started, Jordan loved feeling like she had the best of both worlds, a lover in her best friend. That was fine until she realized that he wasn't that best friend after all, and he lied and deceived her just like any other man would. Once she realized that, the friend thing wasn't so cute anymore. She could no longer thrive off their friendship; she needed some romance and effort just like the next woman. Unfortunately, Jayon became less of a boyfriend, and these days, less of a friend. Lately, he was just company, and she felt like she was settling. Settling more than she ever was with Omar.

5

The restaurant was crowded, and the bar was pretty filled as well. Jordan looked around, unsure where to sit. Finally, she saw three unoccupied seats side by side. She began to walk toward the vacant seats so that she could wait for her friend Tayese to come meet her for lunch.

"Can I get you anything?" the bartender said as soon as Jordan swung her feet around to the front of the bar stool.

"Actually, I'll take a Mai Tai."

"OK," the bartender replied as she dashed off.

Jordan pulled out her BlackBerry to text Tayese and see if she was close by. As she began typing the message, an incoming call appeared on the screen. It was Tayese.

"Hello," Jordan said.

"Hey, where are you?" Tayese asked.

"At the bar inside Caruso's."

"I'm walking in right now. See you in sixty."

"OK," Jordan replied and hung up.

The bartender returned and placed her drink on a napkin in front of her.

"Thank you," Jordan said before she took her taste-testing sip.

Jordan was still sipping from the tiny straws the woman

had placed in her cup when she heard Tayese say, "You couldn't wait for me to get started?"

Jordan looked up and began to laugh. "My bad, girl, I didn't know how long you were going to be, and with my stressful week, I needed a drink," Jordan said, turning around to give her girl a hug.

Tayese reached over for the warm embrace. As soon as she was released, Tayese sat down in the stool beside Jordan. Once again, the bartender arrived like magic.

"Can I get you something?" she asked.

"I'll take a mojito," Tayese said without hesitation.

The bartender dashed off once again.

"So why you so stressed, miss?" Tayese asked as Jordan took another sip from her glass.

"Just everything, work, home. Just in a funk these days."

"I remember when you didn't even drink like that when we were in law school, and now look at you," Tayese said, laughing at her own observation.

"I still don't drink like that. Just on occasion."

"Well, from the looks of how fast you're sipping on that drink, I might say you are a drinker now."

"Whatever." Jordan laughed. "So how's work?"

"It's good. Of course, they are working me to death over there, but I guess I can't complain."

"I can imagine. I've got to give it to firm lawyers. I don't think I could do it."

"Yes, you could, if you didn't have a family to worry about. Lonely single women like myself have nothing else to do, so we might as well work."

"Don't say that, Ty. You are far from lonely."

"How you figure?" Tayese asked.

"All those men you got beating your door down, how can you get lonely?"

"Yeah, that's until they get to know me better. Then they run off."

"What do you mean?"

"Jordan, I've told you this a million times. You haven't been on the dating scene like that, but men aren't trying to get into serious relationships like that, and especially not with me."

"Why not with you?"

"Because they can't run game on me like they want. I'm controlling and not that easy to please."

"Well, stop being so damn controlling," Jordan said, laughing.

"I can't help it. I need to find a man who can love me for me and accept it. If not, I'm screwed."

"You'll be fine. Our kind is hard to come by; some man is going to be smart enough to realize you're well worth the challenge."

"I hope so. I hope that it's sooner rather than later."

"Change soon come," Jordan said in her fake Jamaican accent.

"Please, I'm trying to get them to realize I'm worth putting away their player card, let alone that I'm worth the challenge that comes after that."

Jordan laughed. "Be positive. We're all in the same boat."

"You have a man, dammit, so I ain't in your boat. You in a yacht; I'm in a raft."

Still tickled by Tayese's humor, Jordan continued, "We are all in the same raft then."

"People with a definite date and consistent dick can't be in my raft. My folks may jump your folks."

"Listen . . . I may have that . . . kind of. Still, trust me when I tell you the grass ain't always greener on the other side."

"Here we go with that patronizing line."

"I'm dead serious. I *had* a man, and now I have somewhat

of a boyfriend. Just to have someone to hold, that title isn't always enough."

"What's that mean?"

"I'm just saying, when I was married, it was different. That was the yacht. It was guaranteed; it was always worth the fight. I said vows, we said vows, I never had to doubt that we both wanted to be there. I never had to second-guess my purpose in the relationship. Now that I'm with Jayon, it's kind of like college all over again. We are allegedly serious and committed to one another, but there's no security. I don't know if he is going to just be done one day, or if I'm going to wake up one morning and not be able to do it anymore. Thing is, unlike when I was married, there is nothing stopping either of us from walking away."

Through all the jokes, Tayese wasn't expecting Jordan to get so deep. She could see in Jordan's eyes those words weren't just in response to why she wasn't on a yacht. This was one of the things that caused Jordan to order her drink before Tayese got there.

"I hear you, J. Thing is, there are never any guarantees."

"You are right, but there's a difference when you just don't know what the future holds and when you don't know what tomorrow holds."

Tayese just lifted her drink and took a sip.

"In some situations, you can love like it's never going to hurt because you know that's all you can do. That person is giving their all, and there's a sense of commitment that gives you a sense of security. Then there are situations that day to day you know something is missing, and you're just trying to get by. Trying to hold on to that life on a yacht because it's all you know, but meanwhile the luxury has been gone for a long time."

Jordan's tone took the conversation in a totally different direction. Tayese was never that friend that Jordan told all of her weaknesses to. Jordan went to law school with her, and although she considered her one of her closest friends, she usually shared her career problems with her and not her personal ones.

Tayese felt for her, though. She wasn't sure if Jordan was on the verge of tears, but she hoped not. She didn't want her silly jokes to turn their happy girls' night out into a sad disaster.

"Well, Jordan, at least you have been married. There are so many of us that just want the opportunity to be loved enough to have a man say 'I do.'"

"I understand that, and I'm thankful for all of my experiences. I loved my ex-husband and I still do. I love Jayon and I always will. It's just that I'm telling you, don't knock your life 'cause you don't have a husband or a steady boyfriend. . . . Things are never perfect, Ty. You got to enjoy your life no matter what is going on with it."

"I feel you, and I do, but I'm not going to stop looking for a man," Tayese said, laughing, bringing the humor back into the "getting way too serious" conversation.

Jordan laughed back.

"You shouldn't. Hell, I'm going to be looking myself," Jordan said with a smile.

"You don't need to be looking. Jayon and you are going to be just fine."

"I guess. Doesn't hurt to have a plan C."

"C?"

"Well, Jayon was plan B, remember? I was married," Jordan said with a chuckle.

"Oh . . . cute. Well, whatever. I'm looking for a plan A, B, and C, 'cause I need all the backups I can get."

Jordan just laughed at her friend's humorous self-pity.

"Girl, ain't nothing wrong with you. You just crazy," Jordan said.

An hour later, the glasses were left with only ice in them and the plates with just the remains from their meals. They had talked and laughed themselves all out about everything from work to their love lives. People had come and gone, and they were still engulfed in their company. Eventually, they remembered they had to wake up in the morning, and the later they stayed and the more they drank the worst their mornings would be. So at about ten thirty, they finally decided to pay the check and head home. Jordan and Tayese both didn't have anyone waiting on them at home, but after dining with their successful friend in a similar boat, they felt better about it this particular evening.

6

"Yes, hon, I'll be there in about an hour," Jayon said into his BlackBerry cell phone.

He hung the phone up and placed it back in the clip on his jeans, then he walked to his dresser and pulled his Armani cologne down. He began to pump sprays of aroma onto his shirt and pants and pulse points. He put the clear bottle back on his dresser top and turned to look in the mirror a few feet away. He picked up the brush that was on the table beside the mirror and started brushing his hair some more, as if he saw a strand or two out of place.

He shook his shirt straight and once satisfied with his reflection began to exit the room. He walked downstairs and went over to the bar. His cell phone, which was sitting on the dining room table, began to vibrate and shake. Jayon reached over and hit the speaker button to answer the call he saw was coming from his close friend, Bill.

"What up, son? Jayon said into the open air as he pulled a bottle of Grey Goose from behind the bar.

"What up?"

"Nothing. What you getting into tonight?" Jayon asked as he began pouring some of the Grey Goose into a plastic cup on top of the bar.

"Nothing. I'm on my way back from Greenwich Village. I'm heading back uptown now."

Jayon walked into the kitchen, removed the orange juice from the refrigerator, and added some to his plastic cup.

"Oh, all right. You going to be in the house for the rest of the night?"

"Yeah, pretty much. You coming by?" Billy asked.

"Yeah, I'll come by a little later tonight. I'm about to run out, and I'll call you when I'm on my way back," Jayon said.

"What you doing right now?"

"Making my drink for the road."

"Where you going?" Bill asked.

"Going to meet up with shorty. I should be back in about two hours."

"Aight, hit me up."

Bill hung up. Jayon pressed the button on his phone to end the call and placed the phone in its clip. He grabbed his keys, grabbed his drink, and headed toward the front door.

Jayon was dressed in a green and blue button-down shirt, dark blue jeans, and white Air Force 1s. His hair cut was clean, his two earrings were shined, and his nails were manicured. On a scale from one to ten, Jayon was at least a nine this evening. At least Jordan would've thought so.

Jayon walked down his driveway. He pushed his alarm to unlock his doors and opened the driver's side door. He sat down in his already reclined driver's seat, placed his drink in the holder, and closed his door. After he adjusted himself, he put his Bluetooth on his ear and began to back out of the driveway. By the time he was at the end of his street, he pressed PLAY on his CD player. Fabolous's latest album instantly began playing, and Jayon began tapping his hand on the steering wheel.

Six songs later, Jayon was parking the car. He looked in the mirror, wiped his hand over his face, and opened his car door.

He stepped out and headed toward the front door. Once there, he rang the bell. Moments later, he heard noise on the other side of the door. He waited a few seconds and the door opened. Jayon looked up, and his memory of Randi didn't do her justice. She was five feet five, brown skinned, thick, slim in the waist and pretty in the face. Jayon's immediate reaction was cool, as if he didn't notice the revealing outfit that she was wearing. What he didn't know was that most women can sense when a man is yearning, and Randi could tell Jayon liked what he saw.

"Hey there," Randi said as she opened the door.

"Hey, sexy," he responded.

As Randi closed the door behind her, she said, "Come on in."

She began to walk into the house, and Jayon followed behind her. As he took a few more steps, he heard the sound of a small bell coming toward him. He looked down and there was a small white dog running by his leg.

"Oh, excuse Diamond. She doesn't bite."

"It's cool."

"You sure? You cool with dogs?"

"It'd be different if it was a pit bull," Jayon said with a laugh.

"No, Diamond is just a seven-pound Maltese."

Randi took a seat on the couch and picked up her remote control. Jayon was still standing.

"Take a seat. Get comfortable," Randi said, patting the couch beside her.

Jayon took a seat. He pulled his shirt from underneath his butt to get more comfortable, and leaned forward with his hands folded together.

Randi turned the television to the ESPN channel, got up, and stepped away for a minute. Jayon tried to get a quick glimpse of her as she walked away. She was wearing red boy shorts with a cutoff wifebeater. Her lean stomach was exposed through the shirt, and her butt cheeks were visible from under the short shorts. Randi's outfit definitely expressed what she had in mind for tonight without having to pull out the Victoria's Secret negligee. She tried to go for that lounging-around-the-house look, but it was evident that it wasn't her typical lounge outfit. Even Jayon knew she couldn't be that sexy all the time.

Randi returned after a few moments with two opened Heinekens, and she placed them both down on coasters on her coffee table.

"Thanks," Jayon said.

"No problem," Randi said.

Jayon took a sip from his beer and watched the news update on football player Michael Vick's legal situation. Randi stretched her legs out and placed one of them slightly on Jayon. Jayon looked down at her leg, then up at her.

"So you called me over here to watch ESPN and drink beer with you?" he said with a smirk.

"Not at all," she said. "I was just letting you unwind from work first before I put you back to work."

"That was considerate of you, but who told you I needed a break?" Jayon said as he put his beer down and headed to her side of the couch.

"No one told me that. I was just making sure you had all your energy."

"Well, don't worry about my energy. You just make sure you have enough," Jayon said.

By now, Jayon was leaning over Randi with his hands up her shirt while kissing on her neck. Randi's initial giggling began to turn into moans as Jayon grabbed her breasts with his masculine hands. He softly kissed her neck, taking various areas of her neck and upper chest into his mouth and massaging it with his lips. She reached around and put her hands up his shirt and began caressing his back. As he groped, she groaned. From the sounds of her moans telling him she wanted more, Jayon began to lower his hands down her stomach and around her waist. He caressed her thighs as he lowered his kisses toward her breasts. As he reached her breasts, he lowered her shirt enough to bare her chest and nipples. He looked at them for a second and began to take them into his mouth. After a few succulent kisses, his excitement grew and his patience withered. Jayon rose up enough to put both hands on her boy shorts, and with one motion he pulled them down to expose a pair of fuchsia-colored thongs. Randi, helping out with the process, pulled her wifebeater from over her head and uncovered her matching fuchsia bra.

Jayon's manhood was at complete attention. He stood up to remove his pants. He began to unbuckle his belt, never taking his eyes off the half-naked woman lying in front of him. Her dog Diamond, as if almost trained to do so, had left the room moments into their kiss. Jayon was giving Randi a look letting her know everything that he was thinking. He wasn't nervous, he wasn't excited, but he was ready. As he began pulling his pants off, he felt his phone vibrating. For a moment he paused, but then he continued. The phone vibrated once more. Jayon tried to maintain an expression that didn't show his distraction.

"You just gonna ignore that?" Randi finally asked.

"I'm busy right now," Jayon replied with a smirk as he put on the condom he pulled out of his back pocket.

The phone call gave Jayon discomfort he didn't want to make obvious. In his mind he was wondering who it was and hoping it wasn't Jordan.

7

With the quick interruption already under the spotlight, Jayon glanced at his phone. The display read "Incoming call from Jordan." Jayon instantly quieted the vibrating and put the phone back. He looked at Randi to see if she was looking, and looking closely she was.

Jayon was now just wearing his underwear and a wifebeater. He knelt back down and came very close to Randi's face before he leaned in for a kiss. The touch of his lips erased the thoughts that were forming from their little interruption. He twirled his tongue around her mouth for a few moments before he started back down to her chest. Jayon slowly took a few moments on each part of her body, kissing and softly sucking as he made his way downward. After passing her belly button, he reached her thong and began to kiss the perimeter of the undergarment. He kissed alongside her inner thigh and began to spread her legs more. He softly kissed the inside of her thighs lower and lower, until he crossed over to the other one and kissed the inside of her thigh going back up. Once he reached her thong again, he took it by its strappy sides and pulled it down.

Randi's toes were curled in anticipation of what her body

was in for. She squirmed some as Jayon removed her thong. Jayon then took her left leg and placed it on top of the back of the couch while the other one was still on the couch. Jayon looked at her va-jay-jay and then looked up at her while biting his bottom lip. Jayon took her other leg and gently pushed it off the couch, to widen the entryway. Jayon then pulled his erect penis out of his boxers and knelt down between her legs. As he aligned himself and entered her, he placed his face in the crook of her neck. Once she felt the initial thrust, Randi arched her back and let out a moan. That was the first of many moans over the next fifteen minutes.

Once Jayon and Randi were both sprawled out on the couch, reveling in the perspiration, they began to return to reality. Randi's reality was that Jayon wouldn't be staying, and that he had to go home and possibly be with his woman. Jayon's reality was that he had to now get his explanation together for his whereabouts and get through Jordan's suspicion and questioning.

Jayon sat up and reached for his phone. He noticed that Jordan left a message and sent an e-mail. He opened the yellow envelope on his phone's screen and read "Missing in action again, huh? Ok. I see you." Jayon knew that wasn't a good sign. That just meant that she was already in investigation mode, with a goal to sift out his lies and expose him. Jayon knew that the sticking-to-your-story trick usually worked, but with Jordan's sometimes out-of-the-box analyses, she surprised him with questions he wasn't always prepared for. This part always got a little tricky. Jayon would tell himself that if he got away with it one more time, he wouldn't risk it again, but he would start to think he could get away with it again and then do it again. This was one of those times. Jayon's mind was racing as to every detail he needed to tell Jordan.

At some point during this down-time, Randi must not have appreciated Jayon's silence and sudden distraction.

"Is there a problem?" Randi said, breaking the silence.

"Nah, babe, not at all," Jayon said as he put his arm around her.

"Jay, I know you have to get out of here soon. It looks like someone is waiting for you. So before we even get comfortable, just go ahead and start getting ready."

"Whoa. What's all the hostility for? I'm not rushing out on you."

"I know, but you might as well. I know you're gonna be worried the longer you're here and the more time you have to come up with something for."

"You think you got my situation all figured out, huh?"

"No, not really trying to figure it out. I just know that you have some lying to do, and that's never easy."

"Well, it would be if she wasn't a trained lie detector," Jayon said with a laugh.

Randi wasn't quite as amused. She had been dealing with Jayon on and off for the past two years, probably having slept together a total of six times. She used to work with him, and throughout his single days and relationships she was kind of just always there. They didn't speak much; they would more so contact each other once in a blue moon, flirt, arrange to meet, have sex, and then fall out of contact for another period of time. Therefore, Randi didn't have any expectations of Jayon. She knew he had a girl and that what they had was nothing more than just sex. Still, sometimes it bothered her to know that even when he was with her his mind still had to be somewhere else. So she'd rather they just leave it at sex, since that was probably the only time she had all his attention.

"Randi, I'm sorry if that bothers you. I really wasn't going to rush out on you."

"Nah, it's cool, Jay. I know your situation."

Jayon reached over, grabbed Randi's stomach, and began to rub it slightly.

"Why don't we plan to hang out sometime next week?" he asked.

"Jayon, you don't have to do this. We do this every time, and then we don't talk for months."

"It don't be months, and you don't be calling me either."

"OK, how about we take it one step at a time. We call each other this week, and then we can make plans to hang out the next. That way, no disappointments," Randi suggested.

"Sounds fair. You'll see, I will be the first to call."

Jayon stood up and began to get dressed. After he placed all his clothes back on, he gestured for Randi to give him a hug. She was still dressed in her bra only and stood to give him his hug. Jayon could read through her happiness that something was on her mind, but he wasn't about to open that can of worms. She walked him to the door and he left.

He sat down in his car, and as soon as he started the engine, Fab's voice came through the speakers. Jayon quickly turned the music down to gather his thoughts before he made a move. He made up his mind that he would call Jordan when he was already home and settled, so he would be less likely to slip up. However, he decided to respond to her text. "I'm still at Bill's house, we are watching this movie, didn't see your call. I will call you soon," Jayon texted. Jayon pulled out of his parking spot and drove down the street.

Two songs later, Jayon heard a beep in his ear. He glanced at his cell phone, saw it was Horatio, lowered the music, and pressed the ANSWER button from his Bluetooth.

"What up? Where you at?" Horatio said as soon as he answered.

"I'm on my way back to the Bronx."

"You still coming by Bill's?"

"Yeah, I'll be there soon."

"Where are you coming from?"

"That shawty Randi's crib."

"Word?"

"Yeah, finally went through there."

"Was it worth the trip?"

Jayon giggled. "Yeah, it was worth it."

"She let you hit again?"

"Yeah, I knew she was, though. That's all she be wanting me to come through for these days."

"Well, you gonna keep giving it to her? Or you done?"

"We'll see. It be aight, so I'm not sure. It is getting a lot more hectic, though."

"Where does Jordan think you are? Let me know in case she texts me," Horatio said, laughing.

"She thinks I'm at Bill's house. Where I'll be in about fifteen minutes, and I'll call her from there with all y'all talking in the background."

"Oh, aight, playboy. You got it all figured out, I see. I'll see you soon, then."

8

"The nerve of him," Jordan said, storming through the living room, dropping her bags on the couch.

"It's about time you brought your butt in here," Dakota said as she watched Jordan whisk by.

Jordan headed straight for the bathroom without looking back. She was wearing her all-black pantsuit with the light pink pinstripes and her light pink button-down bodysuit. It was a lot of clothes to have on when your bladder is about to burst.

Dakota just sat there and turned back to the television. As the humor of Damon Wayans entertained Dakota, Jordan suddenly reappeared in the living room.

"Girl, what is wrong with you?" Dakota said.

"I had to pee," Jordan responded.

"OK, so what was all that 'the nerve of him' stuff?"

"Jayon . . . he has, like, slipped and bumped his head."

"Why, what did he do?" Dakota said, slightly laughing at Jordan's demeanor.

"It's more like what he didn't do. What he didn't do is realize by now that this relationship is falling apart. He comes and goes as he pleases, and he has no regard for what I feel."

"What are you speaking of?" Dakota asked, getting frustrated with the beating around the bush.

"It's just, you would think after I forgave him for the Michelle thing that he would be more appreciative of me and put more effort into our relationship, but he doesn't. To make it worse, he gets mad at me that I have some trust issues now."

"Yeah, men don't get it. I don't know what's taking you so long to get that."

"Do you know he had the nerve to tell me it's not his fault I don't like to do anything but be with him?"

"Wow . . . that's cold."

"Tell me about it. He made me seem like some bum chick that has nothing going for herself. He made it seem like he is paying all my bills and keeping me. I was truly offended by that."

"Well, I told you that you need to do more and stop sitting up under him."

"That's the thing; I'm not sitting up under him. I just don't like clubbing like that. Is that so bad?"

"No, but you see how men get. They get complacent. They take it for granted. You need to get out there to remind them that you can be taken."

"It's so sad, even at thirty-four we still have to play these games."

"Sad, but true," Dakota replied.

Upon finishing her statement, Dakota stood up and walked into the kitchen. She had been babysitting Jason for the past three hours when Omar dropped him off. She had just put him to bed and come back down to get a snack and watch television, but she'd left her snack on the kitchen counter.

Dakota came back into the living room with a plate full of potato chips, some dip, and a glass of cran-grape juice.

"So, all of this stemmed from the other night when he didn't answer his phone when you called?" Dakota asked when she sat back on the couch.

"Basically. When we spoke, I told him he always seems to have some excuse for where he is, and he got all pretend offended and then tried to flip it back on me."

"Why you say pretend offended?"

"Because I know that he sees where I'm coming from. He's late for plans we have all the time; there's way too many times he doesn't answer his phone when I call the first time; he works late a lot. It's just that I don't feel like a priority anymore."

"Well, is he just busier at work and you can't understand that?"

"I don't know, but I know that it's taking my sense of security with him away completely."

Dakota took a gulp from her glass and chewed a couple of potato chips at once.

"You should have never let him move offices. At least if you two still worked together and in the same place, you could know when he is really working late and when he's not."

"I know, but at the time we thought it was best since we weren't together and it was awkward; and the job offer he got was a great opportunity. I wish I would've known it would make things so bad, though," Jordan replied.

"So, think about this question for a second before you answer it," Dakota said.

"What?" Jordan asked.

"Do you trust Jayon?"

Jordan became obviously uneasy. It was a question she didn't want to have dissected. She was well aware that there was no point being with a man you didn't trust, but then at the same time she was well aware trust didn't come accompanied with doubt and suspicion.

"I don't know anymore, Dakota. I can't have you force me to lie to you."

"Well, that's what you need to figure out, because that's what is at the root of all your frustration with him. You don't believe anything he tells you . . . and I'm not saying you should; I'm just saying that you need to be honest with yourself before you can demand that he be honest with you."

It wasn't an easy thing to do, but Dakota shushed Jordan. All Jordan could do was recite that last statement over in her head to resonate the truth to it. They say truth hurts, but this time it stuck. Jordan knew that Dakota made perfect sense, but facing the truth was not an easy thing to do.

9

Tayese was just stepping out of her Lexus when she noticed the gentleman walking up to her. She initially jumped from his unexpected presence, but after recognizing the familiar face, she sighed.

"Did I scare you?" he asked.

"Just a little," she replied.

Tayese continued to get her purse and umbrella out of the backseat. She was meeting with a guy that she had met a couple of weeks ago at a networking event. They had spoken on the phone a few times, and so far things seemed pretty good for the most part. Tonight was the first time they were seeing each other since the event, but she remembered his face and he obviously remembered hers.

They walked inside the restaurant together, and Ryan held the door as she walked through. They walked up to the hostess and asked for a table for two, and she informed them that it would be a five-minute wait. Ryan agreed and guided Tayese over to the waiting area.

"So, what made you choose this restaurant?" Tayese asked.

"I like this place. Me and my ex used to come here a lot, and I always enjoyed the food," Ryan said.

Tayese wasn't quite sure what to say. She wasn't used to hearing ex-girlfriend talk so early on.

"Oh, OK. That's good to know they have good food," she said.

"Yeah, well I thought so. She did too; she used to always order their smoked salmon with rice. Hopefully you'll like it."

"I'm sure I'll find something on the menu to fall in love with," Tayese said.

Tayese was hoping this wasn't the beginning of memory lane at this place, because although she was a confident woman and had no reason to be jealous of this woman she didn't know, she didn't feel like hearing about her all night.

After a little more small talk and some people watching, the hostess came over and notified them that their table was ready. The two of them stood up to follow her to the table. They walked past the rows of tables that filled the dining area, and they ignored the dozens of eyes glancing upon them as they passed. Tayese knew a few of the ladies would sneak a second glance at Ryan, because she knew that he was eye-catching. Ryan stood six feet three and had a muscular build like an athlete; he was brown skinned with a chiseled face and brown eyes. Also, not that the ladies could tell unless he was smiling, he had a deep dimple in his right cheek that was absolutely adorable. He wore a brown paperboy hat, with a tan and brown button-down shirt, jeans, and brown Gucci sneakers. He was a sight to see as he swayed through the restaurant. Tayese knew he was fine, which was one of the only reasons she had agreed to go out with him despite her "no colleague" dating rule. She figured rules were meant to be broken, and with looks like his, what better reason to break one.

They eventually reached their table, which was located toward the back of the restaurant in one of the side booths. Due to the lack of a chair to pull out, Tayese couldn't gauge how much of a gentleman he was just yet. She wasn't looking for Mr. Perfect per se, but she needed some things to put on her pros and cons list when it came down to sizing him up. As soon as they were seated, the waitress came over with menus and began filling their glasses with water. Once they informed her that they didn't want appetizers, the waitress told them she'd give them a few minutes to look at the menu and be back in a few.

"You going to get the smoked salmon?" Ryan asked as soon as the waitress stepped away.

Tayese looked up almost in disbelief and replied, "Not quite sure yet what I'm ordering."

"Oh, OK."

Tayese tried her best to subdue the irritated thoughts she was having, and then she decided she might as well see where this was going sooner rather than later.

"Why?" she asked.

"Why what?"

"Why did you ask if I was getting the smoked salmon?"

"No reason," he replied.

"Oh, OK. I was just making sure you didn't want me to get it or something. Maybe you wanted this to be just like the times you came here with your ex."

Ryan seemed a bit uncomfortable by Tayese's aggressive tone.

"No, not at all. It was just a recommendation."

"OK. Well, once I'm through looking at the menu, I'll let you know what I decide."

They both began scanning the menu without saying another word. Tayese began to feel a little guilty and wondered if she was too harsh. She didn't think that she was being mean or anything, but she wasn't sure if her accusation seemed confrontational or not. Tayese was well aware that she was on the search for her husband, so she couldn't afford to scare off potential prospects. At the same time, she didn't want to waste her time either, so she knew sometimes there was a need to be a bit forward. As she perused the menu, she began to think that maybe she overreacted. It was possible that Ryan was just trying to make conversation or was just trying to make a helpful suggestion.

"I'm going to go with the smoked salmon and rice," Tayese said, putting the menu down.

Ryan looked up at her and after seeing her facial expression, smirked.

"You sure? I don't want any problems."

"I'm sure. I'm going to take your recommendation."

"OK," Ryan said, shrugging his shoulders. "If you want to."

"Nothing else really looks that much better to me anyway, so I'll go with what you know."

Tayese was sure that Ryan was able to tell that there was more to it than her just deciding upon the salmon, but she was hoping he didn't know it was her method to make a truce, because she didn't want him to think she was one of those argumentative sisters that he may or may not have been used to.

Tayese took a few sips of her water before the waitress returned.

"Are you ready to order?" she asked.

"Yes," Ryan replied as he looked at Tayese for approval.

"Yes, I'll have the smoked salmon with white rice and a Coke."

"And I'll have the T-bone steak and potatoes with cranberry juice."

"OK, great. I'll be right back with your beverages," the waitress said as she picked up the menus.

"So, you were able to get out of work on time for once," Ryan said in an attempt to cease the awkwardness at the table.

"Yes, surprisingly; technically I have a ton of work still to do and I should go back to the office tonight, but I figured it's not going to make a huge difference if it gets done tomorrow," she replied.

"You work hard, girl," Ryan said.

"I know," Tayese said as she nibbled on a piece of the bread that was on the table.

"You have to find some time for yourself," he said.

"I do, as much as I can, but it's just me. I don't have any kids or a husband, so I guess I figure better to work hard than do nothing at home."

"Well, how are you going to make time for those things in your life if you are constantly at work?"

"That's a good point, but when I've had more time, it doesn't change my situation for the better. I need my situation to change first, and then I'll make sure to make more time."

"That's understandable."

Tayese was starting to like where this conversation was headed. She was surprised that he was comfortable with such a serious conversation so soon.

"Thanks for the understanding. Believe me, I want to spend fewer hours at work and more at home, but I just need a good reason to do so."

"My ex was a workaholic and it drove me crazy. That's a major part of why we are not together now."

Tayese couldn't believe that his ex was the topic of conversation again just that fast.

"Really? Is that so?" Tayese asked, trying to contain her sarcasm.

"Yeah. I'm not the type that believes a woman's place is in the kitchen; I don't believe that at all. However, I feel that a man can be left to take care of and worry about certain things, and that a woman should have time to be a wife and mother. If a woman is too wrapped up in being independent, then what does she need a man for?"

Tayese knew that there was a lot that she could learn from Ryan if she continued this conversation, but after it was premised with his ex-girlfriend's ambition, Tayese wasn't interested in defending or knocking this stranger's decisions.

"I hear you," Tayese said, trying not to give room for more dialogue about it.

Tayese had liked the progression in their conversation, and just as she was starting to think he was going to propose to her, he brought up his ex-girlfriend again. She was probably more irritated by it than it just being some form of jealousy, but either way, she didn't feel like hearing about his baggage anymore.

At that moment, the waiter approached with their hot plates. Tayese was slightly relieved at the natural ending to their conversation, and she had every intention on changing the topic. At least, if he would let her.

10

Jordan was on the phone, cracking up at Tayese's story from her date the night before. It wasn't that she didn't feel her frustration, but just imagining the scene brought Jordan to tears of laughter.

"Jordan, I wanted to just say so bad, 'She's just not that into you. Let her go!'" Tayese said.

"I can imagine. I can't believe he didn't realize that he was bringing her up like that," Jordan said through her laughter.

"I had to eventually tell him, 'Listen, I really do want to get to know you better, but I feel like all I'm finding out about is you and your ex-girlfriend.'"

"What did he say?"

"Nothing, just that he was sorry and was just having conversation. That was all good, but about fifteen minutes later when we started talking about his job, he said he wanted to get out of the marketing business, but when the timing was good for him, his ex-girlfriend had this artist that she begged him to work with, so he stuck with it longer."

Through the phone, you could hear Jordan's snickers and laughter.

"I was thinking to myself, *You couldn't just say you had a new artist? Must it be your ex this and ex that?* You would think they just broke up a few days ago."

"You said it's been like three months, right?"

"Yes, chile! That's why I didn't understand how he was so oblivious to how open he still was."

"Well, at least you know he isn't a player and he loves with his heart."

"Yeah, but only her," Tayese said, laughing.

"Give him time, girl. He was cool other than that, you said, so just give him some more time or chances. You never know."

"Yeah, yeah. Whatever," Tayese said back.

"Well, I gotta go run into this meeting. I'll call you later," Jordan said.

Jordan didn't have any meeting to run to; she just wanted a quick and simple way to get off the phone so that she could call Jayon. As soon as she hung up, she picked back up and dialed his number.

"Hey, hon," he answered.

"Hey, what are you doing?" she asked.

"I'm just heading back to the office. I had a meeting."

"Oh, how'd it go?"

"How'd what go?"

"The meeting."

"Oh, it went well. May have a new client. We'll see how it goes."

"That's good. Well, I wanted to go eat at Sylvia's tonight."

"Babe . . . we can't do it tonight."

"Why not?" she asked.

"Because I have too much to do. We can go Saturday, though," he said.

"I want to go tonight. Why can't we just go for an hour or so tonight?"

"I just told you that I have a lot to do."

"What do you have to do on a Tuesday night?"

"I'll be at the office late; I have a lot of files to close. Then I have to work out after work."

"Fine, Jayon. Forget I asked."

"What do you want me to do? I have work to do."

"Well, do your work and call me later."

Jayon quickly took the opportunity to hang up the phone before a deep conversation ensued.

Jordan went back to her work, trying not to let herself get upset at the conversation she had with Jayon. She rearranged some papers on her desk and put some Post-it Notes on a few documents. She noticed the frustration from her conversation was still lurking, but she continued organizing her desk. Finally, she tried to distract herself by reading a cease and desist letter that she had just received on behalf of one of her clients from MCA Records. She wrote a small note on the side of the letter, and as soon as she was done, she placed the pen down and picked up the phone receiver. She hit redial and waited while the phone rang.

"Hello," Jayon answered.

"Why does it feel like I am the only one in this relationship?" Jordan asked.

"I don't know why you feel like that," Jayon replied very calmly.

"Do you think maybe because you make me feel that way?"

"I can't make you feel that way."

"See, this is exactly what I'm talking about, your nonchalance about everything."

"Jordan, I have to work. I'm sorry I can't just drop everything so we can go eat together, but that's not me making you feel like you're in this relationship alone."

"If it's not work, it's something. I just know it's very rarely me. Things are changing so drastically between us, and it doesn't seem to bother you."

"We are just going through a downtime for a quick second; we will be fine. We both have a lot of work on our plates, and that's all it is. Our relationship will be just fine."

Although Jordan was relieved to hear Jayon's faith in their relationship, for some reason it only felt like words to her.

"So you think that we can just allow this distance between us to grow, and then we will be just fine once our work schedules slow up?"

"Yes, we don't have to be together 24-7 to have a healthy relationship."

Jordan didn't like the sound of that, because truth be told she would have no problem being around Jayon every minute of the day. However, she couldn't admit that. Especially since he was expressing how he wasn't quite as attached.

"Well, I understand that. I just think that we need to make some time for each other. If you don't have a desire to spend time with me, that's fine, but I can't say I agree that everything will be just fine when you do find time."

"Of course I have a desire to be with you, and I find time all the time. I see you at least a few times a week. So don't make this something that it isn't, J. I'm sorry you feel that way, but I have to go. A client is waiting on me."

Jordan hung up almost wishing she'd never called him back. Of course, Jayon managed to make her feel needy and overly sensitive. Jordan hated coming off as if she was needy of anyone or anything. Still, she had to admit she did feel a bit happier when she was around Jayon. She didn't know if that stemmed from her relationship with Omar, and having been used to always having someone at home with her, but either way, she knew that it wasn't working out so well with Jayon.

As soon as she hung up, her secretary popped her head in

the doorway, as she usually does when she sees the green light disappear on the phone.

"You have a Mr. Darren Williams here for you," she said.

"Oh, okay. Send him in," Jordan said, getting right back in the beat of things.

She began to remove some paperwork from directly in front of her, and before she was done, Mr. Williams was standing in her doorway.

"Hello, Darren," Jordan said as she stood to shake his hand. "Take a seat."

Darren walked over and took a seat in the black plush seats in front of Jordan's desk.

"What brings you to see me today?" she asked.

"I was in the area, and I wanted to come ask you some questions face-to-face, but now that I'm here, I'm thinking I should've called instead."

"Why?" Jordan asked, confused.

"Because I can't have the serious conversation I need to have when I have to look at you. You look stunning."

"Thank you, Darren, but that's a bit insulting. You're saying that I can't do my job."

"Not at all, I'm saying I can't do mine," he said, laughing.

Jordan was trying not to blush and remain professional. The truth was she hated when men made her gender and looks an issue in their business relationship.

"I apologize, Jordan. No disrespect intended," Darren continued.

"I'll try not to be offended. I'm your attorney; you can call, e-mail, or visit whenever you like . . . and your compliments are not going to change your bill," Jordan said, laughing to lift any tension that had settled.

Darren laughed back. "So let me get down to business, since I'm being billed for this time."

"Might as well," Jordan replied.

"Well, I just came from a meeting with the two other owners, and they have some ideas that differ significantly from mine. We discussed separating the company into different areas, and my funds would go solely to the things I agree with. Is that possible?"

Jordan was watching Darren and his mannerisms as he explained his situation. She couldn't help but notice his muscular arms as he moved them and his beautiful teeth as his full lips moved over them. Once he was done, Jordan carried on like she wasn't sizing him up in her mind.

"Well, Darren, it seems complicated but definitely possible. There will just have to be some agreements drafted to clarify the terms of what your partners and you decide upon."

"So, should I arrange a meeting with them and have you present?

"That's fine. I would suggest they have their attorneys there too."

"OK, so I will talk to them and get back to you with a date."

"Sounds perfect. Let me know and I'll have my secretary lock it up in my calendar."

Darren began to stand and walk toward the door.

"Great, so I'll be in touch. Thanks for your time," he said as he made his way toward the door.

"No problem. Speak to you soon," Jordan said as she watched Darren walk out of her office.

She put her head down and began drafting some notes from their discussion to put in their files, as she was trained to do.

"Jordan?" she heard, and she looked up.

Darren was back in the doorway.

"I hope this isn't out of line, but I was wondering if I could take you to lunch one day."

"Darren, I don't date my clients."

"It wouldn't be a date, it would be lunch. Besides, you do a great job as my attorney, so please don't tempt me to find another," Darren said with a smirk.

"I don't take too kindly to threats," Jordan said with a smile.

"Not a threat at all. It's a plea."

"Well, if it's not a date, I'll consider it. Call me tomorrow and we'll set a day."

"Will do," Darren said as he walked away again.

After watching him until he was no longer in sight, she put her pen back in motion. She had to finish her summary of his visit, leaving out the last part.

11

Her arm flung from underneath the covers and plopped down on the nightstand, searching for the alarm clock. The unique laugh of Shaila from the KISS FM morning show was blaring through the speaker. She felt around until she located the oval-shaped alarm clock and instinctively pushed the SNOOZE button. Once silence resumed in the room, Jordan nestled back up under her covers. As she squeezed her eyes shut, trying to make the most of the extra ten minutes she assigned herself, she let out a sneeze. She tried to shake it off and get nestled again, but after a few seconds she decided to get her dreadful wake up over with.

She lifted her feet from under the blankets and dragged her body into a sitting position on the side of her bed. The sunlight danced across her lavender carpet. Jordan just watched the variations of light on her bedroom floor. Her carpet was a daily reminder of all the change in Jordan's life. She had always wanted a purple and lavender bedroom, but had never been able to get one. When she married Omar, he refused to have purple and lavender in his master bedroom, so she put the petty issue aside. However, once the divorce was final and Omar was completely moved out, she hired a designer to come in and make her room over. Years ago, Jordan heard Oprah say that her bedroom was purple, and purple was known to be the color for royalty; so she finally had her royal bedroom. She knew chances were that she wouldn't have Oprah's money in her lifetime, but she could have her bedroom.

Once she was done daydreaming about her lavender carpet, she finally stepped onto it and off her bed. She slowly walked into the bathroom and began to freshen up for the morning. Jordan had been planning for weeks to start running again in the mornings, but she just couldn't seem to find the motivation. This morning, though, she was going to get her lazy butt out there and hit the pavement. Jordan wasn't overweight, but she could definitely use some tightening up, and she wanted to tackle it before it got out of hand.

She put on her black-and-red-striped spandex shorts and sports bra with a wifebeater and headed out her front door and down her street. She tilted from side to side as she started her light run down her street. She was still breathing pretty light by the time she reached her corner, and that's where she made a turn and began to speed it up some. She kept her arms by her side, pulling them in and out as she has seen the professional runners do. She went two blocks at that speed and began to slow down. She could feel her heartbeat racing and her breathing heavy, but she didn't feel that familiar burning sensation in her chest that usually let her know she'd reached her peak.

She turned down Pineville Road and began to walk some. She wanted to pace herself so she could pick it back up at the corner ahead. Jordan's attention was grabbed by a woman holding the hand of a young boy crossing the street. The little boy was about Jason's age, and Jordan couldn't help but feel a wave of guilt that she wasn't there to hold her son's hand every morning. To distract her, she started switching the song on her iPod and stopped at "Lose Control" by Ciara, Missy, and Fatman Scoop, one of her favorite workout songs. She walked and sang along as she passed by all the nice houses in her neighborhood. Up ahead there was a U-Haul truck with the back opened. Jordan thought nothing of it. She noticed the door open to the house it was parked in front of, but it was a few houses ahead, so she turned away to glance at the car passing by. As she went to look back straight ahead, she found herself bumping right into a man stepping from behind some bushes.

"Oo-oops," Jordan said.

"I'm sorry," said the man.

Jordan backed away to put room between them and get a clear view of the man in front of her. He was six feet with a muscular build, brown skinned, with light brown eyes and black wavy hair. He was a good-looking guy for sure, not the manicured magazine type, but something about his piercing eyes was mesmerizing. He was wearing a pair of basketball shorts, a fitted white T-shirt, and some Timberland boots. Sweat was nestled all over his face and neck, and his shirt appeared damp as well.

Jordan pulled her headphones out of her ears.

"That was my fault. I should've been paying attention," she said.

"Well, how about you make it up to me by letting me run with you."

"When? Now?"

"Now, or the next time you go for a sprint."

"That sounds fair, although I don't know how putting you to work is making it up to you, but if that's your wish . . ."

"I like to be put to work, so it's not a problem. Besides, I need to get to know the neighborhood."

"You just moving in?"

"Yeah, as we speak," he said, pointing to the truck behind her.

"Oh, duh . . ." she said, laughing.

"Well, what's your name? It was a pleasure to bump into you."

"Jordan. Yours?"

"Marcus."

"Well, it was nice bumping into you too, Marcus. I guess I'll see you around the neighborhood."

"Well, maybe we should exchange numbers so we can arrange that run."

"OK," Jordan said, sounding more sure about the plan than she actually was.

Jordan wasn't the type to give out her number, especially when she was seeing someone. She knew there was no real harm until there'd been actual phone conversations, but she always felt it was the beginning of trouble. She was standing there, well aware it was too late to chicken out now, and giving the wrong number wasn't an option because she was sure to see him again sooner or later. Besides, with the way Jayon had been acting lately, she had every right to make a new friend; he wasn't being much of one lately. It didn't hurt that Marcus was handsome and had a real nice body; a friend that was nice to look at was always a treat.

Marcus had whipped out his cell phone and began typing her name in his address book. Once he was done, he asked for her number, and she began to read it aloud to him as she typed his name in her cell phone. Once he was done typing in hers, she typed in his, and they began to wrap it up. Just as Jordan was putting her headphones back in her ears, Marcus joked that if she didn't keep her promise within the week, he was going to press charges against her for bumping into him. Jordan just laughed, thinking he didn't know she was an attorney and would eat him alive. As she jogged off, she made sure she had her running form just perfect and cute, so in case he was watching he would be looking forward to running beside her in all her glory.

By the time she turned the corner, she couldn't seem to remove the smirk from her face. Marcus was fine, and although she didn't know much about him just yet, she knew that he was just what she needed to get her focus off Jayon and his crap. A new friend always helped; she knew that firsthand.

12

The office door was open, and Jayon got up to close it. He had just dialed Randi's number and was waiting for her to answer. Randi had called him twice yesterday, and he was starting to feel like she was getting too comfortable and could likely cause some questions by Jordan if she didn't stop. He was trying to get ahold of her so that he could politely remind her of the rules of their arrangement.

Her voice mail came on, and he left her a message asking her to call him back. Once he hung up the phone, he went back to work. He was sitting there when he noticed his BlackBerry light up. He went to look and there was an e-mail from a colleague asking if he had received their e-mail. Jayon thought about it and didn't recall an e-mail from them. He searched their name and found that there was an e-mail from them, sent the day before while he was at Jordan's house. He went back to that time of day, and there were three opened e-mails that Jayon had never seen. He took a few moments to try to understand how that could be, and then it crossed his mind that Jordan could've checked them.

Jayon heard a knock on his office door.

"Come in," he shouted.

His doorknob turned and in walked his colleague, Carl.

"What's up?" Carl said as he went to close the door behind him.

"No, you can leave it open," Jayon said.

"So what's been going on with you? You have been in and out of the office, and when you're here you've been keeping to yourself."

"It's just been crazy these past couple of months, and I have been trying to get some shit together."

"Is everything OK?"

"Yeah, just issues with Jordan, and I had some issues with some of my big accounts, so I had to take a lot of meetings."

"Well, if you need me to help with any of your work or anything, let me know. Unfortunately, I can't help you with Jordan," Carl said with a giggle.

Jayon giggled back, and then began to think a bit.

"Maybe you can," he said.

"How?" Carl said quickly.

"Give me your advice."

"Oh," Carl said, relieved that it wasn't some freaky favor.

"OK, I haven't been faithful these past few months—" Jayon started.

"Aww man, you been stepping out on Jordan? You guys are so good together," Carl interrupted.

"I know. I can't even say why, because it's just been for the sake of doing it, for the fun. Thing is, since I've started I haven't been the same with her, and she can sense it, and we are falling apart. I'm wondering if I should let it go before it gets worse, or come clean with her and try to start all over."

"That's a hard one. The chances of you coming clean and still being able to start over are slim."

Jayon just tapped his pen on his desk. "I know," he said in a low tone.

"I almost cheated on my wife a year ago. I came real close to it, and I didn't go through with it. There was no reason for me to. Me and her was just fine, and I was only doing it because that's what us men are supposed to do, I guess. I chose against it, and I considered telling my wife and telling her how strong I was by walking away from it. Still, even though I didn't do it, I knew I couldn't even tell her I came that close to it without opening the door for mad drama, so I kept it to myself."

"I know. Jordan claims she wants honesty no matter what and then she can forgive me, but I have been such an asshole lately, she may just be through."

"Jayon, you and Jordan have years behind you. If you straighten up and make it up to her, I'm sure you can move past this low point."

"Thanks, man, I'm going to stop messing around and try to make everything up to her."

"You better get it together before you lose your job and then you have no job and no woman," Carl said.

As Jayon was lightening up more each moment that his buddy Carl spent with him, taking his mind off everything, his cell phone started to ring. Jayon picked it up and saw that it was Randi returning his call.

"I'm going to take this call," Jayon said to Carl as he waved the phone for him to see.

"Aight," Carl said as he stood up to exit.

"I'll be right by your office as soon as I'm off."

Jayon answered his phone as he nodded to Carl to go ahead and close the door behind him.

"Hey there. What's up?" Randi asked.

"Nothing, just wanted to talk to you."

"OK, so talk."

"Well, as you know, me and Jordan have been talking about

getting engaged, and even though it won't be this month, I think we should chill out."

"What do you mean?" Randi said, not seeming to like what she was hearing.

"I'm just saying that things have been too hectic, and I think it's best me and you just remain friends."

"Friends . . . OK, Jayon, whatever."

"No, I'm serious. We can even still hang out or whatever, I just don't want us to be physical anymore, because I don't want Jordan to find out."

"Whatever you wish," Randi said.

Jayon could tell that she was being a bit sarcastic, but he couldn't pay that any extra attention. He just had to make his point clear, and since he had done that, nothing else mattered. They continued making small talk for a few more moments, although it was a little awkward at first. They gossiped about Randi's job where Jayon used to work and then wrapped the conversation up after a while.

Jayon felt a lot better knowing that he was doing the right thing. He knew that he had been a different person in his relationship, and he knew that Jordan was trying her best to stick by him. He didn't know exactly why he had been so difficult and uncaring, but he knew that it was a major change in Jordan's eyes, and he did feel guilty on occasion for putting her through all the drama. Jayon also knew that he couldn't fix anything overnight, but he figured if he could at least stop cheating, maybe he could focus more on what mattered and not everything else.

Jayon was going to make his way down to Carl's office when his secretary popped her head in his office and told him Jordan was on the line. *Speaking of the devil*, Jayon thought to himself. He pressed the blinking button on his phone and picked up the receiver.

"Hey, dear," Jayon said.

"Hey," Jordan said, trying not to let his almost upbeat demeanor fool her.

"How's work today? Did you finish that contract?"

"Yes, I finished. The record label is reviewing it now," Jordan replied.

Jayon remembered his earlier discovery with the opened e-mails.

"Babe, question, just asking, have you been checking my e-mails in my BlackBerry?"

"Why you ask me that?" Jordan said, getting a bit defensive.

"I had some e-mails that were open that I didn't read, and I don't see how they were opened."

"Whatever, Jayon," Jordan said.

"Yes or no?"

"I may have had your BlackBerry once or twice when an e-mail came in, and it opened."

Jordan was never good at lying, so although her story was somewhat sensible, her tone said that she wasn't telling the truth.

"It's cool, Jordan; I know you were checking my e-mails. I'm not even going to flip out, but let me just tell you that's not cool."

"Not cool, really?" Jordan said. "Is it cool that you are constantly sneaking around and lying to me?"

"Jordan, you haven't caught me lying to you. That is in your imagination."

"It's not in my imagination. You have girls e-mailing and calling you, and who knows what else is going on."

"See, Jordan, you can't be invading my privacy because you are being insecure."

Jordan hated that word insecure. She never wanted to be labeled that insecure woman. In Jordan's opinion, she had it going on way too much to be insecure, yet Jayon was able to make her behave in some insecure ways.

"Whatever, J, you can make this about me being insecure to avoid the fact that this is about me not being a fool while you disrespect me."

"How am I disrespecting you, Jordan? You have obviously been looking for something and haven't found anything."

"I see stuff, just not worth mentioning just yet, and I am not looking. You have been going out so much; I don't feel like I even know you anymore. Besides, let's not forget that you cheated on me before, so excuse me if I'm trying to protect my heart."

"You can't protect your heart by invading my privacy, and I can't be in a relationship where I have no privacy."

"What does that mean?" Jordan said, hearing his threat loud and clear.

"I'm just saying that it's not cool that you just go into my stuff, and I don't want to be in a relationship where I have no privacy and nothing that I can have to myself."

Jordan knew that she was wrong to read his e-mails and check his voice mails, she really did. Still, when he was missing or acting real funny, her mind couldn't help but wander or assume the worst, and then she would check in hopes to find out something instead of wondering. She never thought it was cool, she just thought it was necessary. Jordan knew there was not much more to say to Jayon. Nothing she had found lately was incriminating enough to throw in his face, so she just decided she would wait until some light was shed on the things done in the dark. Jordan let it go for the moment, and she and Jayon got off the phone soon after.

13

Jordan was mentally drained from all the back and forth with Omar about the arrangement with Jason. It had been a rough week between work and dealing with Jayon, and having Omar tell her that she couldn't have Jason for the two weeks she was taking vacation was not what she wanted to hear right now.

"I don't understand how you think you can just say no."

"Simply, by saying no, Jordan."

"You must be on something," Jordan said, truly surprised by his response.

"I said you can have him either the two weekends or the two weeks, but two entire weeks straight is not gonna happen."

"Why is it not going to happen, might I ask?"

"That's too much adjusting for him. Me and Elisa have a routine with him already, and it will throw everything off."

"Well, how about you and Elisa have a child of your own so you can stop planning your lives around mine? I have plans with my son, I'm taking off work to spend time with him, and you are not telling me I can't have him because you and your fiance want to play house."

"Jordan, I'm not having this argument."

"There's nothing to argue about. This is the second time

you've tried to dictate when I could or couldn't see my child, and I'm not sure what television show you think this is, but if you don't get clear on some things, this whole little arrangement will be switched up quick."

"What does that mean?" Omar asked.

"That means you don't have legal custody of Jason, and if you don't stop this bullshit, I will be in court so fast arranging your visiting times with him you won't even know how or when he moved out."

"Please. You won't get him. You didn't want him, remember?"

Jordan was rendered speechless for a few seconds. That was a low blow, and Omar knew it. She wasn't going to let him paralyze her for the moment.

"I always wanted my son; I was just trying to be a good mother thinking you were right that he needed to be around his father. Obviously I was wrong, and he spends more time with your incompetent fiancée than he does you, so don't tell me I won't get him . . . I will show you just how bad I want him. I'll see your ass in court."

Before Omar could begin his clever comeback, Jordan hung up the phone. She was pissed deep down, even though she knew that she had read him his rights. She always knew that allowing Omar to have Jason wasn't the best reflection of her motherhood, but she knew that her intentions were good. Although most mothers wouldn't agree with her decision, Jordan had to come to terms with it. At this point, it had gone too far, though. Jordan was tired of being told she couldn't have Jason when she wanted him, and she was even more tired of the stories from Jason about things Elisa did to upset him. Omar didn't want Jayon playing father to his son, and Jordan felt no different: she didn't want Elisa playing mother to her son. It was only in her favor that she was the mother and the courts leaned in the mother's favor, so since Omar wanted to get fly, Jordan was all riled up and ready for war.

The office had been pretty calm on this particular day; only a few clients had been in to visit, and the phones hadn't been ringing off the hook. Initially, Jordan had been taking advantage of the calm before the storm to get some briefs and contracts drafted. However, moments after she hung up the phone with Omar, she called her assistant into the office and asked her to bring her the documents from the file room that she needed to start a custody hearing in the court system. Still releasing steam from her ears, and after a few drafts and phone calls to some legal friends that specialized in family and marital law, by 5:00 PM Jordan had the custody paperwork in the outbox to be filed in court and assigned a server to give Omar his papers. She knew Omar would be shocked seeing those papers so fast. He would know next time not to tell her that she wasn't a good mother or that she didn't want her child. Jordan left the office that day feeling great. She'd wanted her child back for some time, but she hadn't wanted to invite the drama into her and her son's life. But since she had finally taken the first step, she felt empowered. It took her mind completely off the fact that it had been three days and Marcus hadn't called yet.

14

"You sure that's what you want to do?" Jayon asked, kind of surprised that Jordan had moved forward so quickly.

"I'm absolutely positive."

"Can you handle it with work and all?"

"Can I handle it? Can I handle taking care of my child that I gave life to? Of course I will handle it."

"I didn't mean it like that. I just meant that you'd have to adjust your work schedule and things."

"I've done it before. Besides, he comes first. So worst-case scenario is I will have to work from home more."

"That's true, and you always have your mother."

"Exactly, Jayon. Don't worry, I won't be expecting anything from you."

"What's that's supposed to mean? Of course I would help out."

"Well, just don't worry yourself thinking that I'm going to be expecting you to fill anybody's shoes. He has a father, and I won't be asking you to take him to a basketball game or anything."

"You tripping right now, Jordan. Nobody said any of that."

"Well, I'm just being clear in case it crossed your mind. Don't want you feeling pressured to see me more than a couple times a week or anything."

"You know what, I gotta go. I'll talk to you later," Jayon said, obviously frustrated.

In no mood to beg or deal with him, Jordan quickly agreed, "OK, talk to you later," and hung up.

Jordan had been in a funk all morning. She had checked Jayon's voice mail, and although she knew she was too grown to be doing that, she felt justified because of his unusual recent behavior. When she heard the messages, most were colleagues and friends, but two were from females that she didn't know. Neither female left a very incriminating message, but from the tones of their voices it definitely could've been something going on. The curiosity was killing Jordan, but she didn't want to play herself and ask about them when for all she knew it was nothing. Then it would only leave her having to explain her invasion of his privacy, and the tables could be turned real fast. So instead, Jordan just kept her anger and questions to herself, the best she could. She was mostly upset with Jayon for behaving in such a way that she had to even feel insecure in their relationship, and she was mad that he didn't see what he was doing.

Jordan had been sprawled out on her bed watching television while she was talking to Jayon, and she hadn't moved since they hung up. She flicked through to some other channels while *I Love New York* went to commercial. She munched on the carrots that she had resting on her nightstand and twirled some strands of her hair around her fingers. This was one of the few times that she hung up the phone mad with Jayon and wasn't still upset after the fact. She had nestled herself back into her comfortable spot in the bed and gone on like she hadn't even spoken to Jayon. Quite honestly, Jordan was getting a little tired of the whole Jayon show and their "dry patch" as Jayon called it.

Jordan had just rolled over to her side when she heard her cell phone vibrating on the nightstand. She reached past the carrots to pick up the phone and noticed before she even picked it up that it read "Marcus" on the display. She immediately sat up and grabbed the phone. She looked at it for a second longer, cleared her throat, and answered.

"Hello," she said, strategically not trying to sound too eager or too relaxed.

"Hello, there. This is Marcus, the guy you bumped into the other day."

"I remember," Jordan said, laughing. "Just trying to throw it in my face, huh?"

"Not at all," he replied. "I'm just sure a lady like yourself meets a lot of guys every day, and I didn't know if you would still remember me."

"Well, it did take you some time to call, but lucky for you I don't give out mine or take numbers often."

"I'm sorry, I have been so busy with the moving in and getting settled and stuff, I barely had the time to do anything. But you're right, I am lucky that I got your number and that you remembered me."

Slightly laughing, Jordan replied, "So are you done unpacking?"

"For the most part," he said. "I still have a lot of boxes to unpack, but I've gotten through most of the hard part."

Jordan was curious as to what Marcus's situation was, moving into such a nice house by himself. She didn't want to take the conversation in a personal direction; she would've been more comfortable with small talk for the entire conversation.

However, she wasn't sure if she would find another smooth segue unless she took advantage.

"So you didn't have anyone to help you move in?"

"No, not really. One of my boys came through and helped me with the furniture, but the rest I did by myself."

"So is it safe to assume you will be living there alone?"

"Yes, that's safe to assume."

"Wow, that's a big house for one person. You won't get lonely?" Jordan asked.

"It's only a three-bedroom house. I needed some space. Besides, I was hoping that you could come keep me company on those lonely nights."

Jordan couldn't dispute that was a perfect opportunity to make a verbal move.

"I guess I set myself up for that one, being nosey," Jordan said with a giggle.

"Yup, now you are obligated, since you are all concerned."

"I'll see what I can do," she said.

"Well, honestly, I'm lonely right now."

"Whatever," Jordan said, laughing.

"I am. I have unpacked, got settled, and now I'm just sitting here all alone."

"Read a book or watch some TV."

"Aw, damn. That's cold," Marcus said with a giggle.

"I'm sorry, not like that. I'm just making suggestions. I'm lonely right now too, and I have my television on."

"Why don't you come over?" he asked.

"Marcus, we barely know each other. You could be an axe murderer for all I know, and you just want me to come over."

"OK, how about I come over there. You can take a picture of me as soon as I get there, e-mail it to everyone you know, and tell them if something happens to you, it was me."

Jordan burst out laughing at his comment. She actually did one of her doofy laughs, one she was kind of embarrassed he got to hear so soon.

"That's not necessary, Marcus, but it's a great idea."

"Whatever makes you feel comfortable."

"Honestly, I'd be comfortable getting to know you better before we visit each other's homes."

"I respect that," Marcus said, brushing off the rejection.

Jordan knew that his offer to come over was probably something she should have accepted being that she couldn't get Jayon to come over because he was busy. Still, she knew that she was only entertaining Marcus because things had been so bad between her and Jayon. More than anything she was hoping that she and Jayon got on course soon. So Jordan wasn't willing to do anything to disrespect her relationship to where it could make things any worse than they were.

By the time Jordan got off the phone with Marcus, she found herself intrigued by his character. He was handsome, single, and living in a big, beautiful house all alone. Jordan didn't ask too many inquisitive questions, because she didn't want to overwhelm him. He already seemed a little surprised when he heard she was an attorney, so she decided to not fit a stereotype. They talked a bit about relationships and their situations, but they were both very vague. That was fine for Jordan, because she didn't know what to say about her relationship anymore and she wasn't too braggadocious about Jayon being the man she gave up on her marriage because of.

Jordan thought about the messages she heard for a little bit, but then she shook it off and went to bed. She was tired of worrying about Jayon and his whereabouts. She had hoped so many times that she was just strong enough to leave him alone. For some reason she loved him too much, and she couldn't look at Jayon any other way than as that guy she could always count on. Even now, when he was constantly letting her down. It was hard to let go.

15

The street was filled with hundreds of people walking about. Halloween decorations were hanging up in all the stores, and the scary day was less than two weeks away. Jordan was trying to hurry back from Columbus Circle at a meeting at ASCAP back down to Madison for a networking event she was meeting Tayese at. She was standing at the corner when she felt her phone vibrate; she reached in her purse before she stepped off the curb to cross the street. She was hoping to hail a cab, but each new corner she tried, she hadn't been successful. It was rush hour in New York City, and sometimes it would be faster to walk than to catch and travel in a cab.

Jordan saw that it was Jason calling her, and she answered quickly.

"Hi, hon," she said, sounding excited.

"Hi, Mommy," the little voice on the other end replied.

"How's Mommy's baby today?" Jordan said.

"I'm fine. . . . I wanted you to come pick me up tonight," he said in one breath.

"Sure I will. You wanted to do something?"

"No, I just wanted to come home and sleep with you."

"OK, you got it. I'll be there as soon as I am done with work," Jordan said.

"OK, I'll see you soon. Can you bring my PSP?"

"I'm not going home first; you'll get it when we get to the house."

"OK," Jason said.

"See you soon, babe. Make sure your father gets you ready to go."

Once Jordan was off the phone, she realized that she had walked a full block and still hadn't retrieved a cab. Then she looked down at her watch and realized that she had left her office close to thirty minutes ago. It was days like this that she hated working in New York City. Just as she had dropped her shoulders in frustration, she saw a yellow cab coming toward her with its yellow light on. Jordan began frantically waving her hand toward the cab. It was three lanes over, and it was looking hopeful that he would be able to cross over the lanes of traffic to pick her up, but the cab slowly passed right by her. Jordan, unaware of her visual tantrum, sucked her teeth and stomped her feet at the possibility passing her by. The sound of a horn blared out, and Jordan quickly turned around to see the cab double parked behind her. She let out a sigh of relief and ran toward the cab.

Relieved to be sitting in a stuffy, slightly smelly bright yellow car, Jordan told the man where she wanted to be and put her belongings down on the seat beside her to take a break for the fifteen-minute ride. She rested her head on the seat and closed her eyes for just a moment to pretend that she was actually done for the day. Her brief dream was interrupted by the vibration from her BlackBerry. She looked down and Omar had texted her. "Why did you tell Jason you'd pick him up without discussing it with me first?" Jordan read across her screen. She was livid. She was so sick of being treated like the stepmother in the situation. *I gave birth to that child; I don't have to discuss shit with anyone if I want to be with my child. Has he really lost his mind?* Jordan began to write back to his text, and tried to remain civil and put her anger aside. "He is in your care at the moment, so if he was able to contact me from a telephone, I would assume you were aware of that. If not, I need to worry about the level of supervision he is getting, don't I? Furthermore, he asked me to pick him up and I told him I would, simple as that. I will see you in a few hours. Please have him ready."

Jordan went back to relax her head some. When Jordan had really bad news, whenever she got angry or upset she could feel her blood pressure rising; her heart would start beating fast and her breath would be at a loss. Although she wasn't quite that upset yet, she could feel her pressure rising and tried her best to put the bold comment her ex-husband had made aside. She opened her eyes and looked out the window a few moments later and noticed she wasn't too far, so she whipped out her makeup bag and began to reapply her lip gloss and eyeliner. She tried to finger comb her hair and make herself crowd ready the best she could.

Moments later, she was pulling up in front of the address she had given to the cab driver. It didn't look that lively from the outside, but that wasn't too surprising since the attendees were mainly businesspeople. Jordan was used to some events having album release signs all over the place and promotional trucks everywhere. At least, that's how most of the music and entertainment events looked on the outside. This was a more upscale and professional event. It was a mixer with one speaker who was addressing business growth and gaining clients. Jayon had told Jordan he would be there as well, but she hadn't heard from him in a few hours and wasn't sure what he decided.

Jordan walked in and immediately spotted one of her colleagues standing with some familiar faces. Jordan went over, said hello, and introduced herself to the others. She stood with the young lady for a while as she scanned the room for Tayese. She dabbled in conversation with them until she noticed Tayese walking through the door. Jordan excused herself and walked over to Tayese before she walked too far off. Jordan caught up to her and tapped her on the back.

"Hey, J," Tayese said as she reached down for a hug. "How long you been here?"

"I just got here a few minutes ago," Jordan said.

"It doesn't look like I'll be staying here too long; these people look dull," Tayese said.

"Well, it's not Diddy's party," Jordan replied.

"Nope, and after this speaker is done giving us his advice on how we can be successful like him, whoever he is, I may just head over to Diddy's party," Tayese said, laughing.

"Yeah, I heard he was having something. I would go, but I promised Jason I'd pick him up tonight."

"At least you have someone that is waiting on you tonight."

"Would you stop with that silly . . . Trust me, you don't want my drama. Why did my baby daddy try to break on me for not discussing with him that I told my son I'd pick him up tonight?" Jordan said, trying to keep her laugh in.

"Your baby daddy?" Tayese said, laughing.

They were both standing by the bar, waiting on the bartender to take their orders. After she came over and started to make their apple martinis, Jordan continued.

"Jason called me and asked me if I could come get him, and I said yes. I would assume Omar knew, being that Jason isn't likely to have just called me on his own. Besides, I don't have to discuss it. I would've hit him when I was on my way."

Tayese was looking at Jordan as she sipped on the drink that she had just been handed from the bartender.

"Trust me, you don't want my problems."

Just as Jordan was finishing her drama to take a sip of her apple martini, a girl came walking up to the bar. As soon as she got close enough, the girl and Tayese reacted to one another.

"Hey," Tayese said as the girl walked up to her.

"Hey," the girl said back as she hugged Tayese.

"What are you doing here?" Tayese asked.

"I was meeting a friend here, but he hasn't gotten here yet. I was told tonight's speaker is really good."

Jordan, having overheard the girl say her friend hadn't made it yet, reminded herself that Jayon said he may be coming and she didn't know if he was there or not, hidden in the crowd. Jordan pulled out her BlackBerry and began to send him an e-mail to see where he was, and she also noticed that Omar hadn't responded yet.

Jordan's movement reminded Tayese of her rudeness, apparently, and she tapped Jordan to introduce her to her friend.

"Jordan, this is Randi; Randi, this is Jordan," Tayese said.

"Hi, nice to meet you," Jordan said as she reached out to shake the girl's hand.

"You as well," Randi said.

"Jordan and me went to law school together, and we both specialize in entertainment law."

"Oh, really," Randi said as she began to become obviously intrigued by Jordan. She kept looking at her, watching her actions, and staring at her face.

"I used to work with Randi when I was in law school, working at that firm. She worked in the finance department, and we became lunch buddies," Tayese said.

"I know how greedy Tayese is, so I know that was bonding time," Jordan said, trying to ignore Randi's looks.

"Yes, she is," Randi said, laughing back.

Jordan had looked down at her BlackBerry and saw that Jayon wrote back that he wasn't there yet and most likely wasn't going to make it. She replied, "That's cool, I have to pick up Jason anyway. Are you coming over?" Randi watched Jordan as she read her BlackBerry and responded. As Jordan looked up, she caught Randi looking at her, and Randi cut her eyes and looked away. Right then, Jordan's Scorpio side came out. She wasn't sure if she was reading things right, but she was almost sure that Randi had just basically rolled her eyes at her. Why, she didn't know, but she wasn't feeling like pretending she didn't notice this chick's looks anymore. Tayese had obviously noticed too, so she was trying to make things more comfortable.

"What time does the speaker come on?" Tayese asked.

"I think he is about to start in a few minutes," Randi answered.

"Oh, OK, because I'm headed out as soon as he is done."

Jordan just sat back, eye mingling with the room. A few times she caught Randi staring at other females, giving off that catty girl vibe. Jordan figured it probably wasn't personal with her; the girl just had an eye problem. When Tayese made her comment, Jordan took a sip from her drink, deciding to no longer partake in their conversation.

"Yeah, I think it's done after that anyway," Randi said.

"So what happened to your friend?" Tayese asked.

"He just hit me and said that he was most likely not going to make it."

"So just chill with us if you want, until the speaker is done, and then we will head out."

"All right," Randi said.

Tayese looked at Jordan to see if she was cool with that, but Jordan had her eyes locked on Randi now. Randi caught Jordan's attention with her choice of words. Those were the same words that Jayon had typed to her, "most likely not going to make it." Her brain was rattling, thoughts moving at one hundred per minute. As she watched Randi for a second, she noticed she seemed to not be awkwardly staring at her anymore. As if she knew that she had just given a hint. Jordan was trained to be suspicious and look for sarcasm, lies, hints, and bullshit, and in this instance she was feeling a detection of something.

Tayese gave up for a moment trying to make the three of them coexist and took some sips from her drink as she listened to the announcer introduce the speaker. Jordan knew that she wanted to maintain the upper hand in this situation if there was one to be had; she had to remain calm and keep her mind clear. So as she tried to see if there were any pieces to put together, she realized that she could just be overanalyzing as she tended to do. Just as Jordan began to pay attention to the speaker, Randi pulled out her BlackBerry and began pressing buttons. Jordan found herself now trying to catch glimpses of her as she read and replied to an e-mail. It made sense: the girl was giving Jordan attitude; Jayon was no longer coming to the event; the girl works in finance, so it was possible she knew Jayon. It wasn't impossible, but it was unlikely. The odds that this girl's male friend was Jordan's man, and it just so happened that they meet at an event that Jayon was supposed to come to . . . The more Jordan realized how random that would be, the more she thought it was unlikely.

"I can't sit through this whole thing," Tayese said in a low voice.

"I don't mind leaving; I have to pick up Jason anyway."

Tayese turned to Randi. "We are going to head out. You ready?"

"Yeah, I'm ready."

The girls started to gather themselves and head toward the exit.

Jordan looked down at her BlackBerry at the incoming e-mail, from Jayon. He replied to her e-mail, "I'll be by. I have to make one quick stop and then I'll be there before Jason goes to bed so I can see him." Trying to make her way through the crowd, Jordan decided she would respond when she got outside and had room.

The girls made it through the exit and stood in the front for a second, checking out the surroundings.

"Let me try to get this cab. My car is parked in the garage by my office," Jordan said as she stepped into the street to flag down the yellow car.

"Where are you headed?" Tayese asked Randi.

"I'm going to meet my friend at 40/40."

"OK, I'm gonna take a cab with J then, because I'm headed her way."

"OK, I'll see you later," she said as she hugged Tayese.

Randi looked over at Jordan and said, "Nice meeting you, Jordan,"

"You as well," Jordan responded as she stepped into the cab.

Jordan scooted to the other side of the cab to make room for Tayese. She told the cab driver where she was going and waited for Tayese to get in. Once Tayese sat down in the cab and closed the door, Jordan went in.

"Hey, what was up with her?"

"I don't know what that was. That's why I had to get out of there. That man was boring me, and then the two of y'all was bugging me out."

"She was normal until you told her we went to law school together, then she just started giving attitude and looking at me all crazy."

"I noticed, but I was confused as hell," Tayese said, laughing.

"I need you to ask some questions about what that was about, because I'm curious and a little mad."

"Why you mad?"

"Because I'm wondering if it has something to do with Jayon."

"How'd you reach to that?"

"Because her friend was supposed to come and changed his mind, Jayon was supposed to come and changed his mind, and I can't imagine what her problem was."

"That would be crazy, but I will surely call or e-mail her tomorrow and see if she tells me, 'cause I can say she was acting strange."

"Where did she work after that firm?"

"I think she went to this financing firm in midtown. She is still there."

"Hmm . . . Jayon worked at a financing firm in midtown."

"You are crazy," Tayese said, laughing at Jordan's Inspector Gadget look.

"Just investigate," Jordan said.

"I'm sure you will too."

"Yup."

16

"Hey," Randi said as she walked up to Jayon.

He was sitting at the bar with another gentleman.

"This is my friend, Randi," he told the guy.

"Hi. Bryce," the guy responded.

"Hello," Randi replied.

"How was that event?" Jayon asked.

"Very interesting," Randi said, making an awkward face at Jayon.

"What?" Jayon asked.

"I spent about thirty minutes or so with my friend, Tayese, and Jordan."

Jayon's face lit up like he just saw a ghost.

"What?" he asked as if he was hoping that he had heard wrong.

"Yeah, Jordan. Your girl."

"How did you know it was my Jordan?"

Jayon knew it was his Jordan, because he knew his Jordan attended the same event. He also knew it was his Jordan because his Jordan was there with her friend Tayese. Although he knew it was his Jordan, he was concerned how Randi knew.

"Well, once I heard she was a lawyer that did entertainment law, I put two and two together. How many black female entertainment attorneys with the name Jordan are there in New York?"

Not really interested in the statistical data or the humor, Jayon ignored her question.

"So, what happened?"

"Don't worry, Jayon, nothing. I didn't say anything to her. We didn't have some girl moment and bash you all night," Randi said with an attitude, fully aware that his concern was the state of his relationship with Jordan.

"I'm just asking. You said it was very interesting."

"Yeah, whatever."

"What's your problem?"

"Nothing. I was tempted to say something slick, but I chose against it."

"I guess I should say thank you."

Bryce, who had been watching the baseball game on the big screens, turned to Jayon when the bartender approached him.

"You want another drink?" Bryce asked Jayon.

"Nah, I'm about to get out of here," Jayon said as he downed the last sip of his drink.

"You leaving?" Randi asked.

"Yeah, I got to get going."

"You made me come all the way here for five minutes."

"I told you I was going to be here; I didn't tell you to come. I never said I would be here late. I had plans."

"It's like that?"

"Nah, I'm not being funny. I didn't plan on staying here long. If you would've told me you was coming through, I would've told you I wouldn't be here that long."

"Whatever, Jayon."

Jayon knew that it was rude to bounce so fast, but he wanted to get to Jordan's house, as he'd promised, as soon as possible. He wanted to ensure that Randi hadn't started any trouble, and he didn't want to make anything worse by getting to Jordan's house after Jason fell asleep. So although Bryce didn't seem ready to go and Randi was clearly upset, Jayon scooted off his chair, gave Bryce a pound good-bye and Randi a kiss on the cheek, and was out.

Once Jayon walked in the house, he could hear Jason's laughter. He was relieved that he had made it in time. He hadn't seen Jason in two weeks, and he knew that if he missed out on this opportunity to spend a little time with him, it would look like he didn't care. Jayon had been around since Jason was born; people had spread rumors that Jordan named him after Jayon. It was important to Jayon that he didn't treat Jason different because he was with his mother; he still wanted to have that uncle relationship with him.

When he got upstairs, he found Jason sitting in front of his television, watching the Disney Channel. Jordan was in her bedroom changing clothes, and she heard Jayon coming up the stairs and poked her head out the door before he went into Jason's bedroom. She signaled with her pointer finger for him to come here. Jayon walked past Jason's room as he glanced in at him, then went straight into Jordan's room.

"What's up?" he said in a casual tone as he gave her a kiss hello.

"What happened to you tonight?" she asked.

"Bryce stopped by my office. He needed some help with something he was working on, and we stopped by 40/40 real quick after, and now I'm home," he said.

Jayon had no idea the hot seat he was in. *40/40 huh*, Jordan told herself. That's where Randi had said she was going when she left them. Jordan's blood pressure began to rise again, because she knew drama was on the rise. She was trying to be strategic and not jump the gun breaking on him so she didn't lose ground.

"So, you were at 40/40 before you came here?"

"Yeah, just for a little while. I had one drink."

"Who were you there with?"

"Bryce," Jayon said, trying to remain calm through her line of questioning, completely unaware of what she knew and didn't know.

"That's it?" she asked.

Jayon didn't know what to do with this question. He hadn't gotten a chance to feel her out yet, but Jordan appeared calm and regular.

"Yeah, me and him left from my office."

"Oh, OK. I should've stopped by, but I had to pick up Jason."

Using that as a perfect opportunity, Jayon stood up.

"Let me go check on my lil man," he said as he headed out of the room.

Jordan continued to slip into her night clothes and brush her hair into a ponytail as she talked to herself about the situation. She knew that there were more than enough coincidences with the situation, and she also knew that she wasn't bugging that the girl was acting real strange, because Tayese noticed it too. More than anything, her gut was telling her that it wasn't to be ignored.

Jordan finished up and decided that she would remain calm until she got a report from Tayese, even if it was the next day. Jordan headed over to Jason's bedroom to hang with her fellas. When she walked in the room, she saw Jason sitting with his PlayStation controller in his hand.

"Where did he go?" Jordan asked.

"In the bathroom."

Jordan looked and noticed the other controller on the floor along with Jayon's sneakers and BlackBerry. Jordan walked toward the bathroom and knocked.

"I'll be right there. Give me a few minutes," Jayon said through the door.

"You taking your daily doo-doo?" she asked, laughing.

"Yup," he replied.

Jordan headed straight back to the room where Jason was waiting.

"He'll be right back," Jordan assured Jason.

Jason continued to select the options on the screen and prepare the football challenge that he and Jayon were about to have in Madden's virtual world. Jordan sat on the beanbag beside Jason, picked up the BlackBerry and controller and put them on her lap. A few seconds later, she selected the outbox on Jayon's phone, scrolled to the time she was looking for, and there it was. An e-mail to Randi Hertz that said "I'm most likely not going to make it." Jordan's heartbeat was racing a million times a minute as she continued to scroll and saw another e-mail to Randi Hertz that said "I had to help my friend with something, and now we are headed to get a drink at 40/40." Just as Jordan was looking for more, she heard a noise from the hallway. She quickly hit the HOME SCREEN button and put the phone back on her lap along with the game controller. Although she was pissed, she needed time to assess her game plan. She wasn't ready for him to know what she knew yet.

17

Jordan had only been in the office for fifteen minutes when she picked up her office phone to call Tayese. She had gotten through the night the best she could. She went to sleep before Jayon came to bed so she could avoid any conversation with him. He and Jason had spent hours playing Madden, and Jordan told Jayon not to let Jason go to bed too late, and that was that.

She had decided that she knew that Jayon knew this young lady, and he purposely didn't mention that she met them at 40/40. Although it could've been innocent or just a colleague, because this woman was giving a nasty attitude, she still had a strong belief that there was more. She didn't want to flip out or say anything until she had all her facts straight, and she was banking on Tayese to come through for her.

"I haven't hit her yet," Tayese said as soon as she answered.

No hello, no nothing. Straight to the point to let Jordan know she knew exactly why she was calling. They both started laughing.

"You not funny, heifer, now call her."

"You are a mess."

"No, I know he knows her. I also know that when she went to 40/40 after she left us, she met Jayon there. I need to know what the extent of their relationship is."

With no more laughter in her tone, Tayese said, "How you know all that?"

"He told me he was at 40/40, and I looked in his phone and saw that he and her were e-mailing each other. Her last name is Hertz, right?"

"Wow, yeah it is. What a small world."

"Yeah, yeah. Call that chick and find out what I need to know."

"Now I don't know if I want to get involved in this."

"Tayese, stop playing. You are my friend. If Jayon is up to no good, I need to know."

"Aight, girl, I'll hit her as soon as I hang up with you."

Jordan hung up the phone an emotional mess. She didn't know what she even wanted to happen. A piece of her wanted to get the information that she needed, that she was expecting, because it would answer so much. His behavior and lack of enthusiasm, his lack of interest in sex, and his attitude a lot of the time. She wanted to be able to curse him out and say everything that had been in the back of her mind for weeks. Yet on the other hand, she wasn't ready to face the painful truth that he had betrayed her trust and once again broken her heart. She couldn't really imagine how it would feel to hear that he was creeping around behind her back.

Jackie came up and broke her trance.

"Darren Williams is on line one," Jackie said.

"Thanks," Jordan said as she reached for the phone.

"Hello, Mr. Williams," Jordan said when she answered.

"Hello, Ms. Moore," he responded.

"How may I help you today?"

"By accompanying me to lunch," Darren responded.

"You just won't quit, will you?" Jordan replied with a giggle.

"No. You're not the type of woman you just give up on."

Jordan had to admit to herself that she could use the flattery right about now. A reminder that she was one in a million was exactly the cure to replace her backbone. The past ten hours or so, she had been trying to figure out how Jayon could be so stupid over some short, half-cute support staff and risk losing all that she was.

"You want to go to lunch when?" she asked.

"Today would be nice," he responded.

"How about tomorrow?" she replied.

Jordan knew she was in for a dramatic day; she couldn't bother with anything additional.

"OK, tomorrow at one. I'll be by the office."

"See you then," Jordan replied as she hung up.

Jordan was dying to call Tayese back, but she figured she wouldn't rush it. When she left the house that morning to drop Jason off at school, Jayon was almost ready to walk out too. When Jason was home, Jayon would get up before Jason and lay on the couch. Jordan didn't want her son seeing another man sleeping in the same bed with his mother, so she requested Jayon respect that, and he did. When Jordan was leaving, Jayon pulled her aside and whispered to her that he missed her last night. Jordan was surprised at his sudden sweetness, and although she wanted to embrace him so badly, she knew there was a good chance she would be finding out something dreadful, and she didn't want to open her heart up any more than it already was.

An hour had gone by and Jordan still hadn't heard anything from Tayese. Jordan hadn't gotten any work done; she had been completely distracted. She had called Chrasey and told her what happened, and Chrasey told her it was probably nothing. Jordan knew she probably didn't want to agree that it was pretty suspect, just being a friend. Tayese probably was hesitating to call back for that same reason—she didn't want to be the bearer of bad news. Jordan was sitting at her desk, attempting to read over a contract that her thoughts wouldn't let her comprehend. Jordan picked up the phone and began dialing Jayon's number.

"Hey, dear," he answered.

"Hey, Jayon," she said.

"What's up?"

"I have a question to ask you, and I need you to be completely honest with me."

"What's up?"

"What is the relationship between you and Randi Hertz?"

Jayon took a second.

"What do you mean?"

"Jayon. You know exactly what I mean."

"We used to work together."

"And?"

"And, we are still cool. We kind of stay in touch."

"Has there been anything between you two, then or now?"

"Where is this coming from?"

At first his hesitancy was giving it away, but that question said it all.

"What do you mean, 'where is this coming from,' Jayon? It's a damn question."

"But I tell you she was my coworker and we kept in touch, and you jump to asking me has there been something between us."

"Since you want to act dumb, why don't you put two and two together? Me and her were both at that event last night that you conveniently avoided; you don't think I am asking for a reason? If you want to see what I know before you answer, not a chance."

"Jordan, I just don't know where this is coming from. Randi is just someone I'm cool with, and we used to work together."

"And that's it? You never fucked her?" Jordan blurted out, pissed off.

"This is crazy," Jayon said.

"I bet it is. Crazy to you or me. Crazy that you have been walking around here pretending, and making me seem like I was bugging when I said you were acting strange, and all along you were playing games again."

Jayon didn't say anything.

"Jayon, I'm going to ask you one more time. Is there anything you want to tell me about you and Randi?"

"I'm sorry, J!"

Jordan's heart dropped. She called his bluff, but really she was the one who lost after all. Those three words were enough; she knew what was to follow. Overwhelmed with all of her emotions, she hung up, jumped up, and closed her office door. Jordan didn't even make it back to her desk before she collapsed on the floor in tears. She could feel her heart in her stomach. All she could think about was this skank staring at her like she was a fool, knowing that she had been with her man who knows how many times, and that she was on her way to see him right then. The chick was watching while Jordan stood there so confident and so together, but in this chick's eyes it was all false because she knew what Jordan didn't. Jordan was so angry and so hurt all at once, she couldn't think straight.

She heard her phone vibrate, and she heard her secretary tell her over the intercom that Jayon was on line one. Jackie knew not to knock when Jordan had the door closed and was ignoring the intercom; she knew that probably meant that she wasn't to be interrupted. Jordan lay there bawling, until she heard Jackie say over the intercom that Tayese was on line one. Jordan quickly stood up and went over to the desk. She wasn't sure why, but she wanted to hear everything. She was definitely embarrassed, but Tayese was a good enough friend that she could be vulnerable in front of her.

"Hey, girl," Tayese said as soon as Jordan got off the line.

"Hey," Jordan said.

"You sound like you been crying."

"I have. Let's just say my instincts are always on point."

"Yeah, I figured. But don't let it get you down, J. It's not the end of the world."

"What did you find out?" Jordan said, cutting to the chase.

"Nothing really. She just said they started messing around when they used to work together, and it has been kind of an on and off thing. Of course I had to promise I wouldn't tell you, but I'm sure she knew it was a possibility."

Jordan wasn't paying a bit of attention to the agreement they made, and she was trying to dissect everything in her mind.

"On and off, continuing through now?"

"I think so."

As Jordan listened to her friend, she dug the courage back up to face Jayon with it. The pain subdued for a minute, and the anger was taking over.

"Tayese, let me call you right back," Jordan said suddenly.

"OK."

Jordan hung up and dialed Jayon's number.

"You're sorry?" Jordan said with a very curt tone when he answered.

"Yes, Jordan, I am. It's not how you think."

"You've been fucking that bitch on and off for over a year, the entire time you were supposed to be only with me. What's not how I think?"

"Jordan, it wasn't like that."

"I really wish you would grow up and stop making excuses for yourself. Admit that you have insecurity problems that lead you to need acceptance and ass from any woman that is willing to give it to you."

Typically, Jayon remained silent while Jordan vented. She tried to fight her tears back; this was not a moment to be vulnerable. This was strictly to let him know that he was a piece of dirt.

"If you want a whore like Randi that doesn't even respect herself enough to at least expect to be acknowledged, have that. She is cool with being the secret, because she isn't worth being spoken for, and that's why she plays her position so well. So, have that, because it's obvious that you are not worth having me."

Jayon still didn't say anything back. Jordan sat there for a few seconds awaiting some sort of response, and once she realized that there was nothing for him to say, she hung up again.

18

Jordan had canceled all of her appointments for the day, including her lunch with Darren, and then spent the day at home. She had slept pretty late, woke up with puffy eyes from crying the night before, and was just getting around to making herself some coffee in the kitchen.

"I can't believe you e-mailed her," Chrasey said.

"Yes, I did. It was easy to remember. It was her name at Jayon's old company. I e-mailed her and told her it was home-wrecking no-class bitches like her that ruined the essence of sisterhood."

"You didn't say essence of sisterhood, did you?" Chrasey said with a giggle.

"Yes, I did too. I proceeded to tell her that she could have him, although the truth was he didn't want her. I said Jayon doesn't respect sluts, and being that all you were was ass to him for all this time, you will never be anything more. Maybe if you had enough respect for yourself, to where you didn't sleep with him while he was in a relationship and knew you had to be quiet when I was on the phone, or couldn't call him after a certain time, maybe he or I would've thought you had some self-respect. But since you played your position so well, that has become your permanent position: side ho. Enjoy it."

"Damn, Jordan, you said all of that?"

"Oh, the e-mail was long. When I finished writing it, I cc'd Jayon."

Chrasey burst out laughing. "You playing, right?"

"Nope, and I called her a slore."

"I wonder if she'll figure out that means slut whore."

"I'm sure she's familiar with the term."

Jordan had been in her kitchen telling Chrasey the story as she finished making herself some coffee and an English muffin. She was still in her robe and Victoria's Secret bootie slippers. She had decided hours ago she wasn't going in to the office. She needed a day off to just clear her mind and do whatever healing she could in twenty-four hours. She was numb on the inside, and she didn't really have the desire to share her embarrassment with too many people. She wasn't planning on telling Chrasey either, but when she called to see why she wasn't in the office, Jordan went ahead and shared the drama with her.

"So, you aren't considering forgiving him?" Chrasey asked.

Jordan didn't know what to say. Her instinct was to say hell no, but she knew there was a piece of her that would always remember the Jayon she once knew. That piece of her would always find it hard to hate him.

"Forgive Jayon, my boyfriend? No, I don't think I can do that this time. Try to forgive Jayon, my friend? I'm hoping I will one day."

As Jordan tried to answer the question, her emotions got the best of her and a tear fell from her eye.

"I understand," Chrasey said.

"Maybe we were trying to make something that wasn't there. We were great friends, but maybe that's all he was capable of. Maybe I wasn't more than his homegirl, and the relationship thing wasn't for us."

"But y'all were really good together. You can't say that. It's not like y'all were forcing it."

"Well, obviously he felt forced to do something. He wasn't obliging with monogamy."

"That was him feeling forced to be faithful, and that's just a man issue. Nothing to do with the two of you."

"I guess," Jordan said as she wiped away the tears that had fallen.

As Jordan placed the tissue down, she heard a noise coming from the front of her house. She tried to peek out the kitchen door, but she couldn't see anything from where she stood.

"Hold on," Jordan whispered as she got up from the stool. She walked more toward the kitchen door and could hear the noise was coming from the front door. She put the phone back to her ear.

"Someone is at my front door, and it better not be Jayon."

"You didn't get your keys back yet?"

"Chrasey, when? I haven't seen him."

As Jordan watched the front of her house, she saw Jayon appear in the front entryway, looking a bit nervous.

"It's Jayon. Let me call you back," Jordan said as she hung up the phone.

Before Jayon even took another step, Jordan walked toward him.

"What do you want, Jayon?"

"Jordan . . ."

"What do you want, Jayon?"

"I want to just talk to you."

"Oh, now you want to talk? When I wanted to talk for the

past few months, you didn't have time. You told me that it was nothing to talk about because we were fine. Now . . . now you want to talk."

"Jordan, just hear me out."

"Jayon, there's nothing to talk about. We are fine."

Jayon let out a sigh. He realized at that moment that this wasn't going to be easy. He knew that already, but he had let the fact that he had made it through the door and she hadn't thrown something at him fool him into thinking that there was a chance they could be civilized. As far as Jordan was concerned, he was a day late and a dollar short.

"Jordan, I know you are mad at me and you have every right to hate me. Still, we are both adults. Can we just talk about it?"

Jayon sat on the couch after he finished his statement. Jordan cut her eyes over at him as if he had just said something bad about her mama.

"We are adults? *We* are adults? Are we really? *I* am an adult. You are a damn child. You lie like a child, you're sneaky like a child, and you manipulate like a child. Don't feed me your mature talk, because there's not shit your childish ass can say to me."

"The name calling is necessary, Jordan?"

Once again, Jordan looked at Jayon with fury. He just didn't get it. He had no room to judge or ask questions.

"Get the hell out of my house," Jordan said, fed up with Jayon's presence.

Jayon went to say something, but Jordan didn't even give him a chance.

"Get the hell out of my house, Jayon. I have absolutely nothing to say to you. You go be an adult with Randi."

Jayon just dropped his head.

"And give me my keys," Jordan added.

Jayon didn't move.

"Jordan, I'm not leaving here without at least saying what I have to say."

"What, Jayon? What do you have to say?"

Jordan's heart was beating ridiculously fast. She had gotten herself all wound up, and as usual, Jayon was cool as a fan. She wanted to jump over the couch and strangle him.

"Jordan, you are never going to forgive me for this, I know. I know this because we have been here before, and I promised you this wouldn't be an issue again. I wish I could take it back, but I can't. I wish I could tell you a good enough reason for it, but I can't. I have to deal with my stupidity for being so selfish, and I know that."

"I know all this already, Jayon. So what is it you feel the need to add?"

"That it's not your fault."

Jayon looked up at Jordan and stared her dead in her face. Prior to hearing that sentence, she was ready to break and continue her verbal lashing, but when she looked in his eyes and heard his words, she knew that he was trying to convey something that he had thought about. Jordan just dropped her eyes, trying to fight back the tears.

"I didn't deserve you. I never did. I knew that, and I always wondered if you knew that. I'm not sure if it was my fear that one day you would wake up and not want to do this anymore, but I couldn't let myself be hurt again."

Jordan shrugged her shoulders and did a "yeah, OK" sound when he said that, but before she could get defensive, Jayon hurried to continue.

"I'm not blaming Dawn for breaking off the engagement; I'm just saying that it was my fault. Not that Randi was a solution, but she was just someone that seemed easier to be with."

"Oh, so she was easier . . . You want it easy. . . ."

"No, I just knew she wasn't better than me, and I mean . . ."

"Jayon!"

"What? I'm serious, and I just felt that you were."

"Who told you to feed me this bullshit? Was this Horatio's idea, 'cause it's good."

"Jordan, I know it sounds crazy, but it's true. I've been thinking about this all night. I couldn't sleep."

"Well, neither could I, Jayon, and although I appreciate you coming by here to assure me I'm worthy of a man, I never doubted that it was you. I have been nothing but good to you, and if you couldn't appreciate that, then that's on you. Easy gets you just that . . . easy. So you and Randi enjoy your life on your level."

"I don't want her, Jordan."

"I really don't care what you want, Jayon. Truth is, you don't know what you want."

Jayon didn't argue with that point. He knew that he had to agree that he was confusing himself. Here he had a woman he had known for almost two decades, who loved him with all her heart, and he decided to push her away. He knew it was foolish. The truth was that he didn't think he would get caught; he thought he would have his cake and eat it too. As far as Jordan was concerned, it was that simple.

Jordan had had enough of his lame-excuse party, and she couldn't stand the sight of his face anymore. She just made a sharp U-turn and headed out of the living room. She knew as well as he did that things would never be the same. She couldn't move on from this, not again. Jordan had been through one too many sad and tear-filled nights, and she couldn't keep putting herself through it. Jayon had sent his message loud and clear with this one. Dead smack in the middle of their relationship, one where they had "planned" to get married, he was screwing some slore behind her back. She was through. Sick and tired of being sick and tired.

19

Jordan wasn't trying to be laying around the house sulking. She had taken two days off of work already, and had been on the phone for numerous hours of venting. She was actually tired of telling the story and saying the same old "I'm not the one" lines. It was Thursday, and she had just finished getting dressed to go running. She threw on her black sweater over her black sports bra and some leggings. Once her sneakers were tied, she headed out the front door with her iPod and cell phone.

Jordan turned onto the sidewalk past her lawn and began a brisk run. She was refreshed to feel the chilly wind on her face. She hadn't been running in over a week, and she needed this. She needed the time to clear her mind and embrace her fresh start. She had contemplated for the past forty-eight hours if there was any room to possibly forgive Jayon and make up. She realized when it wasn't just about what a fool people would think she was, and what a fool he would think she was that she couldn't do it. More important than what people or Jayon would think, she knew what she would think. She couldn't respect herself if she was one of those women who just allow their man to cheat on them over and over again, and with no more than a simple sorry move their way right back into their hearts. Jordan knew that she could never trust Jayon again, and like her and Jayon always agreed, without the trust, there is nothing.

Once she made her way around the corner, she picked up a little more speed, trying to burn more calories. The last two days of lying in bed eating wasn't going to get her any closer to getting a new man. She came to the corner of Marcus's block and slowed down to a light jog toward the next corner. She passed by some homes and noticed the landscaping, trying to get an idea of what she wanted to do with hers. She smiled at the one old lady who was in her garden planting seeds, then kept going. Finally, she reached the house that she met Marcus in front of, and she glanced in the yard. She looked around at the windows and surrounding areas and saw no sign of Marcus or anything interesting, so she kept going.

She reached the corner and slowed down to catch her breath. She looked down to switch her iPod to a slow song that she could do a cooldown to, and as she looked for an India Arie favorite, she noticed the shadow of someone. She looked up and saw Marcus running toward her with his headphones in his ear and his sweats on. Jordan gave a smirk upon his sight.

"Are you cheating?" Marcus said as he walked up.

He pulled the headphones out of his ear as he came to a halt in front of Jordan.

"What are you talking about?"

"Why are you walking?" he said.

"I was cooling down. I ran almost two miles so far."

"Two miles? Where did you start?"

"From my house . . . and wait, don't judge me," she said, laughing slightly.

"I'm not."

"Question should be what are you doing running?"

"I run four days a week."

"Oh, well let me let you get back to your run," Jordan said as she began fiddling for that song she had been looking for.

"Don't you owe me a run?" Marcus asked.

"I thought you forgot," Jordan said, laughing.

"Not at all. I would never forget that you owe me."

"Well, I'm finishing my run for today. We should schedule for Saturday morning."

"How about you come around the corner with me. I'll fix you a smoothie and we will chat some, and then we can call it even."

Jordan knew it sounded crazy. *You want me, Jordan Moore, to come to your house, Marcus . . . I don't even know your last name, and chat,* Jordan thought to herself as she tried to think of an adult excuse to make.

"Come on, stop thinking of an excuse to chicken out," Marcus said as he began to step toward the corner.

Jordan laughed at how he read her mind.

Jordan began to turn around and head toward the corner too. Something inside of her was still holding her back, but there was another voice whispering inside her head, telling her to live a little. She didn't know what she was afraid of. It was just a friendly visit with her neighbor in the early morning time.

"You taking the day off?" Marcus asked.

"I'm not sure yet. I haven't been in the office for a couple days. I need to bring my butt in."

"Oooh, I'm telling," Marcus said.

Jordan laughed as they continued around the corner. She was trying to concentrate on all the confusion in her brain, trying to decide if she should go through with it. She finally started walking with authority; she decided it was no big deal. She knew that she was capable of making a big deal out of nothing.

Once she stepped inside his house, her gaze began to wander over the things in his living room. He had a large and very creatively decorated living room. The color scheme was earth tones, and he had several paintings hanging on the wall over the fireplace. There were about six boxes stacked up in the corner, and two suitcases beside them. Jordan was impressed with the house—it was gorgeous—but then again, so were most of the houses in her neighborhood. Marcus had been in the kitchen, which was right over the island that separated the living room from the kitchen.

"So you want a fruit smoothie or something else?" Marcus asked as he placed some fruit on the countertop.

"I'll take a fruit smoothie with just strawberries and bananas."

Marcus began to cut up the bananas, then turned on the kitchen sink faucet. He reached in and began to rinse the strawberries off.

"I didn't take you for a smoothie man," Jordan added as she watched him prepare the beverage.

"Actually, I'm not. It was a housewarming gift, and I'm finally getting a chance to use it."

"Oh," Jordan said, a bit humored.

Marcus reached over and picked up the remote that was sitting on the countertop. He pointed it at the huge flat screen hanging in his living room and turned the television on.

"What do you want to watch, the Oxygen network?" Marcus asked, flashing his beautiful white smile.

"How about Court TV?" she answered.

"Excuse me, big shot," he said as he began flicking through the channels.

"Channel Forty," she informed him.

They both exchanged a slight smirk as Marcus hit 4-0 and placed the remote down. Jordan sat down on one of the wooden stools at the island and swiveled around toward the television. For some odd reason, Jordan felt comfortable. The little voice in her head had quieted down, and she was no longer fearful of being in this strange man's house. It wasn't even about Jayon. She knew that him and her were so over, this wasn't even to spite him. It was just her making a step toward letting go.

Marcus finished the smoothies and went over to the couches with them.

"Come sit over here and make yourself comfortable," he said as he placed the glasses down on top of the coasters on the glass-and-gold coffee table.

Jordan got up and made her way over to the oversized, plush auburn couch.

"This couch is both cozy and beautiful," Jordan blurted out.

She was nervous and looking to make conversation. Marcus sat down beside her before thanking her. He sat down and put one of his legs up on the couch, making himself real comfortable. Once he was sitting, Jordan for some reason scooted back in the couch and made herself comfortable as well.

"So why did you miss work this week?"

"I needed some time to clear my thoughts," Jordan replied.

"Everything OK? If you don't mind me asking."

"Well, let's just say I had a rough week," Jordan said, trying to use her words carefully.

"OK . . ." Marcus said, catching the hint.

"No, I found out my ex was cheating on me this week."

"Sorry to hear that," Marcus said.

Jordan laughed a bit. "You said it like there was a death in my family."

Marcus giggled.

"No, but he was my good friend for years, so the whole thing has really been taking a toll on me."

"I understand. Well, not to sound cliché, but he was definitely a fool to give up such a good thing."

"Thanks, but that does sound like a typical line," Jordan said after letting out a laugh.

"No, I know. That's why I didn't even want to say it," Marcus said with a smirk. "But it's really true. You are truly what they consider brains and beauty."

"How do you know that I don't suck at being a girlfriend, though? Maybe I'm too strong-minded; maybe I don't let my man be a man; maybe I'm too jealous. Maybe I'm controlling. How do you know that it wasn't me and not him?"

"I don't know if it was you and not him, but I do know that no one is perfect and you must learn to take the good with the bad."

"That's insightful," Jordan said.

Over an hour had gone by, the smoothies were gone, Court TV had broadcast two television shows, and Jordan and Marcus were still engulfed in their conversation. Jordan had received a lot of answers to the things she had been wondering about. She was curious as to what kind of business Marcus was in that he was able to afford such a beautiful home, the CLK in his driveway, and still afford the luxury of spending a Thursday afternoon with her. Marcus explained to her that he made investments in companies, bought and sold real estate, and had a few small businesses on the East Coast. Jordan was impressed by his drive and ambition. She immediately compared him to her complacent ex, Jayon, who never took the steps to follow any of his dreams, like going back to school. He didn't have any children and had never been married. Too busy with his career, he claimed.

The more Jordan sat on his couch laughing and talking with him, the more at ease she felt. His smile was one of the most amazing that she had ever seen. His teeth were perfect and white, and the way his lips curved over them just lit up his face completely. Jordan knew that she was in no condition to even think about starting a relationship with anyone, but she had to admit that Marcus was a nice man. He was still in his sweatpants and cutoff T-shirt from his morning run, and his muscular arms were flexing as he moved them during his conversation. Jordan was definitely wondering how no woman had snatched his fine behind up.

Somehow Marcus had made his way closer to Jordan during the course of their chat, and before Jordan knew it, he was slightly leaning on her leg, coming in for a kiss. Her initial reaction was to jump back. She didn't know how she didn't see that coming. She hadn't been intimate with another man since she had started seeing Jayon, and before that not since Omar. Two men in the last two decades left her feeling very awkward with the feel of a new man's lip on hers. Marcus jumped back with a look of embarrassment.

"I'm sorry. No disrespect," he said. "You're just so beautiful, I couldn't help myself."

Jordan had her head low, embarrassed that she couldn't handle the sudden attempt at affection. She tried to rationalize with herself that she wasn't overreacting. She tried to search for the right thing to say or do, and then suddenly she decided that was just the opposite of what she wanted. Jordan looked up and into Marcus's brown eyes. She leaned in and began to kiss him. He immediately grabbed the back of her head and began to kiss her back, a little over the top with passion for a Thursday morning. Jordan's juices must have begun flowing at the thought of having spontaneous sex with this sexy man that she would've never thought about sleeping with a week ago, at least not this fast. Something about the thought was turning her on, because as they kissed she could feel herself getting horny.

Marcus took his hand and began to slowly rub down her arm to her thigh and back up. After the second stroke, he slowed down by her thigh and began to rub the outside of her thigh toward the inner thigh. Jordan slowly opened her legs, inviting Marcus farther over, so he would know that her initial jump was not an indication of her interest in him. She allowed him to caress her legs, and the feel of his big, strong hands made her moist. She was loving it, and although Jordan rarely even showed Jayon her aggressive freak Scorpio side, she couldn't tame herself. Jordan took her free hand and slipped it down Marcus's sweatpants to begin massaging his penis. It was already hard as a rock and felt like it was a pleasingly nice size. She massaged it some and then slowly began to get up. Marcus was looking up at her as though he couldn't believe she was becoming such a different person.

Jordan removed her leggings and slowly began to push Marcus back so that he would be lying farther back on the couch.

"You have a condom?" she asked.

Marcus reached into his pocket and pulled a condom out of his wallet. He placed the condom on as Jordan began to pull his sweatpants down. Once he was done putting on the condom and Jordan had fully removed his pants, she pulled the crotch area of her panties to the side and slowly lowered over Marcus. The look on his face as he enjoyed the feeling of being inside her excited her more. Jordan began to ride Marcus up and down. She was throwing her head back while enjoying the feeling of his shaft filling her walls. Although Jordan's body was in ecstasy while enjoying every minute of Marcus's thick, curved penis, she didn't expect this ride to last too long. After several minutes had passed, she realized Marcus wasn't the average—he was going long and strong.

Just when Jordan was trying to give her best, Marcus placed both of his arms around her waist, stood up with her wrapped around him, and turned around to place her on the couch. Once she was safe and lying on the couch, Marcus inserted himself inside of her and took control of the action. With his immediate long strokes, Jordan could do nothing but throw her head back and moan. She had no idea that Marcus would be so well worth this sudden experience. She glanced up at the sweat that was glistening on his forehead and watched how he bit his lower lip, and it turned her on even more. Jordan wasn't expecting to orgasm, but it became obvious that Marcus was expecting her to. Before Jordan could even realize what hit her, her body was quivering and she was breathing heavily. She laid there, enjoying the last few strokes, before Marcus too came to a halt as his body clenched tight.

Wow was all Jordan could think to herself. Marcus's body wasn't just false advertisement. That sexy, muscular, chiseled body was a fair representation of the man behind the image.

"I'm going to get us some water," Marcus said as he walked to the kitchen.

Jordan lay there, not sure what to do next. She had never been in this situation where she'd had sex with someone she barely knew. Jordan had only had sex in her last couple of relationships; she didn't know how to engage in casual sex. She didn't want that to be too obvious so Marcus couldn't tell what a big deal the sex they just had was to her. Jordan knew she couldn't figure it out there, so she began to get dressed.

"I'm going to get going, Marcus," Jordan said as she straightened herself out.

"Are you sure? You are welcome to stay," Marcus said.

"Thanks, but I have to go handle some stuff. I guess I am taking another day off, but I have to get some work done," Jordan said, laughing.

Jordan was hoping that Marcus couldn't sense her discomfort. She didn't want to appear that she had just been used or anything. She wanted to seem like the women that do stuff like that all the time, like it was nothing to her and she was capable of just brushing it off and going home. Jordan couldn't tell what was being conveyed, because her conscience was starting to set in, and she could feel the regret taking over. Inside she wanted to cry at how stupid she had been to go against everything she had ever known in the past hour. However, on the outside she seemed confident and looked beautiful. Maybe Marcus had been in the situation before, but he was able to sense that Jordan wasn't leaving with as much confidence as she came with.

"Jordan, I had a great time with you today," he said.

"Me too, Marcus."

"I really hope that what we did doesn't change anything."

"Not at all," Jordan replied quickly.

"Jordan, I know you're wondering if I'm going to think less of you or some 1950s thoughts like that, but I don't. You're grown and I'm grown. You're sexy and I'm sexy," Marcus said with a giggle. "There was no need to play games, in my opinion. I would still love to spend time with you, getting to know you better."

"That's fine with me," Jordan replied.

Jordan knew that Marcus wouldn't understand exactly what was going through her mind, so she just decided to leave it at that. She made her way out the door and down his block toward her home, remaining calm. Jordan was feeling strange. She had very mixed feelings about what just happened. One thing was for sure: That was exactly what she needed physically. Mentally, that was another story.

20

"I'm just a little too old to hate being home alone," Jordan said aloud.

She was looking in the mirror, facing someone she hadn't faced in a long time: herself. Jordan had spent so many years chasing her dreams, she hadn't slowed down to get to know herself. Since she was in high school, Jordan was the "relationship type." She only had three childlike relationships before she got married to Omar, whom she had been with since college, and now Jayon made five. At the age of thirty-four, Jordan had spent all of her adult life working on a relationship and not herself.

As Jordan stared back at herself in the mirror, she realized she was finally facing her biggest fear: being alone. She knew it was kind of pathetic, and she didn't want to admit it, but regardless of how much she denied it, she hated being alone. Who would think such a young, beautiful, successful, independent woman like herself would have this flaw? Regardless of what those around her saw, Jordan had several insecurities and fears that she tried to hide. Most of them stemmed from the relationships Jordan saw in her own family: her parents, aunts and uncles, cousins and siblings. Jordan was no stranger to infidelity and the sight of someone growing old alone, and although Jordan was still fairly young, she knew she didn't want to live that life. Still, as Jordan stared into her light brown eyes in the mirror, she was saddened by the sight of the life she was living. She was living a life of not only fear but destruction; she couldn't expect to possibly be a good mate when she was in it for the wrong reason. She never realized it before, but that wrong reason was comfort and security from the world of dating, from the possibility of growing old alone.

Jordan took her lavender washcloth and rinsed her face. She wiped the tears away along with all the day's dirt. The scent from the fresh linen-scented candle burning above her toilet was beginning to reach her nostrils, and she inhaled and exhaled slowly. Jordan looked back at herself in the mirror and stared into her own eyes dead on. She just stared for several seconds, blinking.

"It's time for a fresh start, Jordan Moore," she said to herself. "It's time for a new Jordan."

Jordan looked back at herself to see if she was serious. The longer she looked into her own eyes, the more she liked what she was hearing.

"It's time to stop being afraid of what may happen, and what people think; it's time to live in the moment and step outside your box."

The sight looking back at Jordan began to look stronger and more serious.

"You have spent all your life playing by the rules, putting your heart on the line, and it's time to make your own rule book."

Jordan wiped her hand over her face and looked back at herself once again.

"That's it, starting today. I'm going to love me and take the world by storm."

She remembered the guy Alan she just met the other day while she was at lunch with the girls, and she decided to make a phone call to someone new. Jordan flicked off the light beside the mirror and walked out of the bathroom. She headed into her bedroom toward her nightstand. She grabbed her BlackBerry and began looking through her address book for the number of that lawyer she'd just met. She scrolled down through the Ts looking for Timothy, and after a few pushes, she found it. She got ready to dial it when she paused to think about what she should say. "Hi. When you first tried to talk to me I gave you the wrong number, but now me and my boyfriend that I left my husband for broke up, and I'm available." She wasn't quite sure that would come across right. As she tried to think of a better opening line, she asked herself what she was doing.

Calling some new guy, adding another guy to the equation, was only going to confuse things. This was her problem now, always needing a man's companionship to get by. What Jordan needed was some time to herself, to enjoy herself. She just didn't know why that was so difficult for her. Hell, she should love herself as hard as she worked on herself. For some reason, though, Jordan always desired a man's love to feel complete. Maybe it was because it was all she had ever known. Jordan knew when it came to her self-esteem she was as confident as they come, which was the reason she never settled for less in life or with her career. Jordan chose to be in a relationship rather than just be out there. She was more content settled down with one person, enjoying them. She wished she could change that about herself after she spent an entire day crying her eyes out over Jayon, and she wished she could change how her anger toward him allowed her to sleep with Marcus, who she barely knew. At that very moment, she wished that she was built for it.

Jordan made her way downstairs to make a cup of hot chocolate to soothe herself. She hadn't spoken to Marcus since yesterday after she left, although he did call her a few hours after. She just wasn't quite ready to talk to him and have the uncomfortable conversation that she was expecting. She and Jayon hadn't spoken either in a few days. He too called once or twice, but Jordan didn't even bother to answer, because she knew that he didn't have anything to say to her that would really make a difference. At the end of the day, it was time for Jordan to move on; she was too old to subject herself to a relationship that she knew wasn't going anywhere. It was one thing that they probably weren't getting married, but she couldn't bear the cheating. Not from Jayon, not from someone she gave so much credit.

Jordan sat on her couch with her hot chocolate and kicked her feet up. Jordan had officially taken the week off. She hadn't been to the office all week, although she spent a few hours responding to e-mails and phone calls. Jordan needed this time off anyway, but this week more than ever, she didn't need to be in the office, distracted and cranky.

She heard the phone ring the first time, but she didn't budge; she didn't feel like it. Then, after the third ring, she leaned over and grabbed the cordless off the cradle. She expected it may be a telemarketer, but when she looked at the caller ID it was Tayese.

"Hey, missy," Jordan said.

"Hey, stranger," Tayese replied.

"I know, I been out all week, I've been such a loser," Jordan said and laughed.

"I know you ain't been sulking at home like a high school girl."

"Yes and no. I had some crying nights, but I have also been clearing my head, relaxing, and catching up on some work."

"You stayed home every day this week?"

"Except the one day I went to visit my new neighbor."

"Visit?"

"Yeah, visit."

"What new neighbor?" Tayese said in the "spill it" tone.

"Marcus . . . he moved in about a month ago. We met one day while I was running."

"OK . . . sooky sooky now," Tayese said. "And here I was worried about you getting over Jayon."

"Marcus is not solving any of my problems; he just helped me get through this week."

"How did he help you?" Tayese said, trying to tease Jordan.

"Chile, don't ask."

"Jordan! You didn't!"

"Tayese, I did!" Jordan said with a snicker.

"Wow, you are really trying to get over Jayon, huh?"

"Yes, I am, but I wasn't expecting that to happen, in all honesty. We were there just talking, and next thing you know, I said f—it."

"Wow. I'm still in shock. You are the last person I would expect to do something like that."

"I know. I am still shocked myself. I'm a little regretful of the decision, but he is so fine and he gave it to me so good."

"What are you regretting it for? You are grown and single, and you needed a quick reminder that Jayon is not the world. What in the world are you regretting? Especially when you said it was good. Girl, you bugging."

Jordan and Tayese laughed for a few seconds before they redirected their conversation. Twenty minutes later, they were off the phone and Jordan was watching television. Jason was supposed to be coming by later, so she was relaxing for the couple of hours she had before she had to get ready to take him to Dave & Buster's. It seemed that the more time that went by, the more Jordan became comfortable with what she had done with Marcus. The reality was there was no taking it back, so she had no choice but to get used to it.

21

Relieved to finally have found a parking spot, Jordan hurriedly grabbed her purse from off the passenger seat, and hopped out of the car. She reached in her black clutch and pulled out her Oh Baby Mac lip gloss to refresh her gloss. The cool air whisked the hair on her head slightly out of place, and as Jordan quickly walked down the street, she tried to finger comb her hairstyle back into place. The noise and chatter from all the people walking down Twenty-third Street in midtown, along with the sounds of horns and mufflers, was just a reminder to Jordan that she was in for a night of chaos.

As Jordan got closer to the front of the club, she pulled her BlackBerry out and began to send her girlfriend Tayese a text. She was supposed to be meeting her there, but she hadn't spoken to her since they both alerted one another that they had reached the city. Once Jordan completed her text asking Tayese for her expected time of arrival, she looked up and noticed she was only a few doors away from the club. Not wanting to appear too startled, Jordan tried to ignore the man and woman standing beside her in front of a closed clothing boutique, engrossed in a passionate kiss. As if the sight wasn't enough, Jordan could hear the spit swapping and moaning coming from the two. She didn't know if they were two strangers that just walked out of the club or they were a happily married couple, but she knew they needed to get a room. Jordan just passed them by without trying to look too hard and ended up standing in front of the club. Jordan glanced down at her phone and noticed that she had missed a call from Tayese. She hit the CALL button and began calling Tayese back, hoping that she was close by.

"Hey, I just called you," Tayese said the instant she answered her phone.

"I know, I must not have felt my phone vibrate. Where are you?"

"I'm a few doors away from the club."

"Where?" Jordan said as she turned around to look behind her.

"Ill," Tayese said through the phone just as Jordan spotted her walking down the street in her navy blue dress and pumps.

"I know, get a room, right?" Jordan said, laughing as she saw Tayese scurry past the horny couple toward her.

As Tayese came within feet of Jordan, they both hung up their cell phones. The gentleman standing beside Jordan moved aside so that Tayese and Jordan could have a bit of personal space.

After Tayese noticed the guy, she mouthed to Jordan, "You can stay, cutie."

Jordan laughed at Tayese's silly comment as she too tried to get a glance of him. From Jordan's facial expression, Tayese could tell that she agreed with her offer. The gentleman was about six feet two with a well-built frame, brown skinned with thick shaped eyebrows, plump lips, and almond-shaped brown eyes. He wore khaki pants with a white and tan button-down and some tan sneakers, but it was the tan front-snap hat that added that extra flavor to him.

Jordan had turned her eyes away from the guy and looked back at Tayese. Once their eyes met, they both giggled at their similar thoughts.

"So you ready to go in?" Jordan asked.

"Yup, let's go," Tayese said.

Jordan walked up to the front, gave her name, and informed the bouncer that she was on the guest list. The bouncer spoke with a short Latin man regarding Jordan's comments, then the bouncer let Tayese and Jordan in.

They began to walk by the bouncer when he said, "Is he with you?"

Jordan looked back, and the fine brother in tan was standing behind Tayese. Jordan looked at him and told the bouncer, "Yes, he is with us."

The three of them walked by the bouncer without saying a word to each other. Once on the other side of the door, the short Latin man approached all three of them and gave them silver bands to put on their wrists to identify their special guest status with the security throughout the club. The short Latin man walked them by the cashier and toward the area where the other silver-banded guests were.

"Thanks," Jordan said to the man.

Tayese and the gentleman had been following behind Jordan. Neither of them appeared to have sparked a conversation yet; they were probably waiting until they settled. Jordan spotted a love seat and immediately headed toward it. Tayese and the stranger in tan followed along, and they all sat in the chosen area.

"So . . . nice to have you join us," Tayese was the first one to comment.

"Thanks for having me," the young man responded with a giggle. "My name is Donovan. Yours?"

Tayese and Jordan both gave their real names and shook hands with Donovan.

"So were you planning to party alone tonight?" Jordan asked. "We don't want to cramp your style."

Donovan chuckled. "Not at all. My friends went to the wrong club and are on their way here."

"Oh, OK. So for the time being we are just fillers so you don't look lonely in the club?" Tayese asked with a smile.

"No, you both are just a pleasant treat to start the evening off."

"Well, we are glad to be of service, Donovan," Tayese said.

Jordan minimized the smile that had been on her face during the cute banter between them, and she stood up.

"Can I excuse myself for two seconds? I just want to say hello to a few people," Jordan said.

"Sure, but hurry back. I know how you can do," Tayese said.

"I'll be right back."

Jordan walked away toward a crowd of people chatting by the bar. She made her way through a couple of people dancing to the blaring music and past a security guard. Jordan approached the men and women by the bar and random chatter ensued. After giving hugs and kisses to everyone, Jordan and the group began laughing and chatting about the club and other business gossip. After a few moments went by, Jordan looked over her shoulder at Tayese and Donovan, who seemed to be engulfed in their conversation. Jordan remembered that Tayese warned her not to take too long, and she told the folks by the bar she would be back shortly, then headed back to her seat.

Once she sat back down beside Tayese and across from Donovan, the two of them shifted their attention toward her.

"Was that quick enough?" Jordan asked.

"Yeah, wasn't that bad," Donovan answered.

Not expecting Donovan to have answered, Jordan looked at Tayese for her approval.

"That was better than usual," Tayese said to Jordan. Then she looked toward Donovan and said, "I hate going out with her sometimes, because she bumps into so many folks and they start holding these long conversations, and I just feel like grabbing her by her hand and pulling her away."

"It's not like that, Donovan. She is exaggerating some," Jordan said, defending herself.

Donovan just laughed at his displacement in the debate. "I wouldn't have a problem going out with you," he added.

Jordan's eyebrows crinkled, showing her confusion. She wasn't sure if Donovan was flirting or just making a general comment. So instead of playing herself and commenting back, she just giggled it off.

"Who was that over there anyway?" Tayese asked to ease the awkward moment.

"That's Tony and some other people from Bad Boy. One of their artists performed here earlier," Jordan answered.

"Oh, that's cool," Tayese replied.

"What do you ladies do, if you don't mind me asking?" Donovan interjected.

"We are both attorneys," Tayese answered. "Jordan and I specialize in entertainment and corporate law, and I also dabble in matrimonial and labor."

"Wow," Donovan replied. "You are both attorneys; that is impressive."

"Thanks," both ladies replied.

"So if I'm trying to start a business, you could be of service to me?" Donovan asked Jordan.

"I should be able to be of help," Jordan replied.

"Can I get your business card?"

Jordan reached in her clutch, pulled out her business card, and handed it to Donovan.

"This is a very interesting business card," Donovan said while still studying it.

The business card was made of a matte grayish black card stock with pink raised writing.

"Yeah, I hear that a lot. I wanted them to be personalized to me, and I like black and pink. Plus, I'm interesting."

"I hear that; I guess when you head your practice you can have whatever type of card you want," Donovan said after noticing the firm's name included Jordan's.

"Pretty much," Jordan responded.

By this time, the club was getting more and more crowded, including the area that Jordan, Tayese, and Donovan were sitting in.

Donovan looked down at his phone and said aloud, "Oh, they called me like ten minutes ago and been texting me."

"Oooh, they going to get you," Tayese responded.

Donovan began to text his friends back. "I know, I was so consumed by our conversation that I didn't notice," he said as he continued typing in his text message.

"You're going to let them know where you are, or you're going to go meet them?" Tayese asked.

"I'll have them join us if you don't mind," Donovan said.

"That's fine," Tayese answered.

For a few moments, they all just sat back in silence while Donovan typed on his phone and Tayese sipped on the drink that the waitress had brought her while Jordan stepped away. As they sat there enjoying the sounds of DJ Bobby Trends, Jordan's eyes followed all the scantily dressed girls walking by. It seemed that as the years went by people wore less and less to the clubs. Jordan had on a purple and black spaghetti strap minidress with some purple pumps, and she felt dressed for winter compared to what some of the other girls were wearing. Jordan realized fast that if that's what the guys were looking for and that's what she was up against, she didn't stand a chance.

Moments later, two guys were approaching the love seat

where they were sitting. Jordan looked at the two gentlemen, and neither one of them were hard on the eyes at all. She looked over to see if Tayese had noticed them, and sure enough she had. One was a light-skinned guy, maybe five feet eleven, medium build with a low ceasar haircut and hazel eyes. He was dressed in jeans and a black and gray rugby shirt with black Prada sneakers. His friend was dark skinned with brown eyes and a smile to die for. He was about six feet tall with a muscular build; he had a nicely trimmed mustache and beard that bordered his full lips.

As they came closer, Jordan noticed a few nearby women checking them out as well. As Jordan scooted back to let them walk by, she noticed them slowing down. They stopped in front of Donovan and smiled at Jordan and Tayese.

Donovan and the two gentlemen exchanged words and pounds. The ladies realized at this point these were the friends that Donovan had been waiting for.

Tayese looked over at Jordan and said, "I thought only bad things come in three."

They both laughed and tried not to seem so obvious that they liked what they saw. Being that Tayese strutted her single status, having never been married and having no children, her radar was always on high alert. Jordan, on the other hand, had been there and done all that, but as a newly single woman, she knew what she was missing and was just as open to finding good company.

By the time the fellas had finished their chatter, Tayese and Jordan had started a conversation of their own. Donovan apologized for interrupting before he introduced his two old friends to his two new friends. The light-skinned one was Eddie, and the brown-skinned one was Tremaine. Pleased to meet them both, Tayese and Jordan shook their hands.

For the next few minutes, the girls were engaged in the

conversation they were having before they were interrupted, and the guys seemed to be laughing at how Tremaine and Eddie ended up at some other club. Out of nowhere, this guy came and knelt down in front of Tayese and Jordan and started a conversation.

"I'm trying to figure out why both of you two gorgeous ladies are sitting down," the guy said.

"Just enjoying the music," Jordan responded.

"What about you?" the guy said to Tayese.

"Same. Haven't been here that long."

"Well, can I have the pleasure of a dance with you?" the guy asked.

From the look on Tayese's face and her discreet glance in Donovan and his friends' direction, it seemed as if Tayese didn't want to necessarily dance just yet, and not with him per se. However, she didn't want to be rude. The guy wasn't half bad-looking, either, and for all she knew Tremaine, Eddie, and Donovan could have been gay, so she wasn't ruling anyone out. Tayese handed Jordan her purse and made her way to the dance floor with the guy.

"Your girl left you," Donovan said as soon as Tayese was beginning her two-step.

"Yeah, it's okay. I'm a big girl; I can handle myself," Jordan replied.

"I can see that. I didn't notice you telling her to hurry back."

Jordan giggled at his sarcasm.

"Let's dance?" Eddie interjected.

Jordan looked at Donovan, and he gave a look of unsure approval, as if to say "don't let me stop you."

Jordan figured she could sit there and use her purse babysitting as a sure-fire excuse, but instead she figured she might as well. She did get dressed and go out to have a good time, not to sit down all night. Jordan stood up and headed toward the dance floor with Eddie in pursuit. Once she reached where Tayese was, she handed her her bag and turned back to face Eddie. Tayese gave a smirk and continued on with her two-step with a twist.

Bobby Trends was playing the remix of R. Kelly's "I'm a Flirt," and everyone in the club was singing along. Eddie was dancing pretty close to Jordan, but with no hands. Jordan despised, so she was happy he hadn't messed up with that. Jordan enjoyed a dance just like the next person, but when guys in the club put their strange hands on her body or poked their privates anywhere near her, it put an end to the dance. Jordan's thing was "they don't know me like that." So, prude or not, Jordan always kept some distance between her and her club dance partners. Eddie was following along just fine. He was bopping and two-stepping in accordance with Jordan, and Jordan was staying aligned with Tayese as well. Tayese's guy wasn't being too aggressive, either. He was dancing a bit closer, but nothing that was unacceptable. It was obvious that he was enjoying the vision of Tayese as he smiled most of the song away.

Tayese was very attractive. She was five feet six, 140 pounds, dark brown eyes, tan skinned, with thin lips and long black hair. She was shapely, a 34C with a rump to go with it, minus the excess waist and thighs. Tayese was single for the same reason a lot of attractive and successful women were single: Men were intimidated by her. At least that's what most people concluded, because she didn't have many flaws. Once the song ended, Tayese and Jordan headed back to the seats that were being held by Donovan and Tremaine. As they excused themselves past some folks, the guy Tayese was dancing with tapped her on the shoulder.

"I was hoping we can keep in touch and get to know each other better," the guy said, looking a bit nervous.

Tayese reached in her bag and gave him a business card. "Here you go. Call me when you get the chance. I don't mean to run off, but I'm here with some friends."

"No problem, I'll be in touch" the guy said, seeming excited to have gotten the digits.

Once back at their seats, Donovan and Tremaine made some jokes about how fast they all returned. Tayese blamed it on her heels, and Jordan and Eddie didn't comment back. The five of them pretty much remained in those seats until they decided to go. There was a lot of conversation, several flirtatious comments, and a lot of grown-up talk, but it was unclear who was interested in whom. By the time the night ended, they all said they would try to get together again. Tayese and Jordan had given all three guys their business cards, and Donovan and Tremaine had given Tayese and Jordan theirs. Eddie didn't have business cards, so he just gave hugs and kisses. Although they had all just met, they seemed pretty comfortable with one another. A few months ago, Jordan wouldn't have spent her entire night with some random guys at a nightclub, but tonight she figured what the hell, life is short.

22

Omar had called and said he wanted to talk when he came to pick up Jason. At first Jordan was hesitant, but then she knew that she too hoped that she and Omar could get along better.

When he walked in, Jordan had to admit Omar was looking quite handsome. It looked as if he had a fresh cut, and he was dressed pretty sharp. He was wearing new cologne that smelled real good, and he walked in with a sense of confidence. Jordan tried not to stare or show her recognition of what he was working with. Jason was upstairs in his bedroom, playing his PlayStation. Jordan had just finished doing his homework with him, so she told him he could play for an hour because she knew she would need the time alone with his father anyway.

Once Omar and Jordan were settled on the couch, Omar started right up.

"So listen, Jordan, me and you have to work at this a little better. Jason's getting older, and we have put him through enough."

"I couldn't agree with you more," Jordan replied.

"Well, since we agree on that, I'm assuming we will agree that going to court over him is also not a good idea."

"Omar, it's like you forgot I birthed and raised that boy just because I tried to be fair when we split."

"Fair?"

"Yes, not selfish . . . You said you wanted him to stay with you and that he needed his father, and I was feeling guilty enough, so I convinced myself that it was the best situation for Jason."

"I think it was, but I can't say that you weren't selfish."

"I was selfish in regard to our marriage, I admit, but with Jason that decision was the most unselfish thing I ever did. You can keep thinking I did it so Jayon and I could be alone, and you will continue to be ignorant to believe that. Just shows you don't really know me."

"Nah, I know you love your son and you weren't putting Jayon before him, but the whole situation was just crazy."

"I know, Omar, and I think thus far we have been pretty good with everything, except Jason."

"You want him all the time, and it's disruptive to his lifestyle," Omar said.

"Omar, his life has already been disrupted. I want my child, Omar. I miss him, and I'm tired of beating myself up. He doesn't like Elisa, and he needs to be here with his real mother."

"All the time? You really want me to give him to you for good?"

"Omar, it's not giving him to me. He is mine."

Omar just sighed and dropped his head in frustration.

Jordan continued: "I will let you have him as much as you would like. You can come over here when you like. I wouldn't keep you away from him, but you know it's best, Omar. I am his mother. He needs me, O, and I need him."

"Jordan, it will be really hard for me to let Jason go just like that, but maybe we can take it slow."

"We can do it gradually, but by this time next month he

will be living with me, Omar. You can take these next few weeks to get used to the idea."

Omar didn't seem like he was completely with it, but he seemed to be coming to terms with the fact that he couldn't just have it his way.

"Jordan, I don't want to be back and forth with you in court, and I definitely don't want to put Jason through any more drama, so I will compromise and work this out."

Jordan wasn't sure what Omar meant, but she wasn't trying to keep going back and forth. She figured to herself as long as he understood the end result, he could rationalize it any way he wanted.

23

Jordan had stepped inside her office and began to unpack her briefcase. She settled at her desk and turned her computer on. From her desk she could see the staff walking back and forth, trying to get the day started. Jordan glanced up a few times to see who was getting work done and who was just killing time.

Jordan was checking some e-mails on her computer that she hadn't pulled off her BlackBerry yet when her assistant popped her head in the office door. Jordan looked up in her direction.

"Hey, hun," Jordan said.

"Hi, Ms. Moore. I just wanted to remind you that Darren is coming in at noon today."

"Oh, OK. Thanks. Can you pull his file for me?"

"Sure."

Jackie headed back to her desk, and Jordan went back to responding to e-mails. She was e-mailing legal documents to clients, answering legal questions, and responding to Dakota and Chrasey's e-mails. The girls had an ongoing e-mail session during business hours where the three of them sent and replied to e-mails to keep abreast of their life updates and work drama.

Jordan was caught up in the humor of one message from Chrasey about how Keith was driving himself crazy trying to see if she was cheating. She was so caught up she didn't even glance at the phone when it was ringing. After two or three rings, Jackie answered. Moments later, Jackie popped her head in the door.

"There's a Donovan Shields on line one," she said.

Jordan took a second to think, and then it dawned on her that it was the guy from the club the other night.

"I'll take it," Jordan said.

Jordan hit SEND on her response to Chrasey, and then went ahead and picked up her phone.

"Jordan Moore speaking," she said.

"Oh, OK. This is the professional side I'm speaking to. I met the booty-shaking side the other night," Donovan started.

Jordan began laughing at his introduction.

"Ha ha ha, aren't we funny?" Jordan asked.

"I'm joking. How are you, Ms. Moore?"

"Can't complain. How are you?"

"I'm good. Just trying to get to Friday so I can enjoy my weekend."

"You have a special weekend planned?" Jordan asked.

"No, just running to the Poconos with some friends."

"That sounds nice. I could use some quiet Pocono time."

"You are welcome to come," Donovan said.

Jordan didn't even realize how she had set that right up.

"No, I'm OK. I wish I could, but I have a ton of work."

"Well, you can't give me that all-work-and-no-play bit, because I saw you shaking your butt at the club."

Jordan laughed. "OK, you are on a roll here, I see."

"Well, I was calling because I was hoping we could go to lunch to discuss my business venture."

"That's fine. I'll have my secretary set a time with you and put it in my appointment book."

"Oh, it's like that?"

"No . . . stop picking on me," Jordan said with a light laugh. "She has my calendar, that's all. She knows which days I'm in the office and when I don't have a conflict."

"So who do I set it up with if I want to meet after business hours?"

Jordan wasn't sure how to take it, being that she was under the impression that Donovan was interested in Tayese. One thing she knew for sure was that he was making a pass at her. Jordan made it clear that she was taken aback by the delay in her response.

"Well, I think I oversee my evening hours," Jordan said.

"So can I schedule something with you for next week, Ms. Moore?" he replied.

"Sure, but let me check with Tayese and see when she can make it."

"Well, if Tayese is coming, let me invite Eddie as well."

Jordan didn't want to sound conceited and jump the gun, but she was unsure at this point if Donovan was just trying to conduct business with her or something more. Eddie was the one she had danced with, so maybe he was saying since Tayese was coming he would invite Eddie for her. Jordan didn't want to play herself, so she figured that she would have to clear up her confusion through conversation and not by asking a blunt question.

"Well, that's fine. Let's shoot for Friday, at 8:00 PM at the Olive Garden on Forty-second Street."

"You like to take control, huh?"

"I must admit I do, Donovan," Jordan said.

"Well, there's nothing wrong with that. Friday at 8:00 PM at the Olive Garden it is."

"Okay, I'll let you know if we have to reschedule after I hear from Tayese."

"All right, sounds good."

"Talk to you later," she replied, taking advantage of the perfect opportunity to wrap up the conversation.

Jordan hung up the phone and went back to what she was doing before the call. She couldn't help but be distracted by the conversation, because she wasn't sure what exactly she should do. She definitely thought Donovan was fine, she'd been interested in him from when she first saw him. That night just went so strangely, she couldn't tell if he was feeling her or Tayese. She assumed his call clarified where his interest laid, but she still wanted to make sure Tayese wouldn't feel a certain way. All Tayese said about him after they left that night was that he was fine, and Jordan agreed, nothing more, nothing less. Jordan figured she would tell Tayese he called and see what she had to say.

After coming to her conclusion as to how she was going to handle the situation, Jordan began to send Tayese a message to her BlackBerry to tell her and invite her along on Friday. Jordan sent the e-mail and then went back to her computer. She began some legal research and put the phone call behind her. Four of her clients were coming in for meetings today, and she was trying to get some work done before they began arriving. Jordan was taking notes from a case she pulled up when she heard her BlackBerry vibrate. Jordan reached up and saw that it was an e-mail from Jayon. Jordan immediately dropped the pen she was writing with and picked up the BlackBerry to read it.

"Hey there, Jordan, I was thinking about you. I miss talking to you. Hope all is well."

Jordan could immediately feel her emotions rising. She hadn't spoken to Jayon in weeks. She had purposely tried to erase him from her life and thoughts. He had been out of touch ever since she asked him to please leave her be, so this sudden contact surprised her. She knew that she shouldn't respond; she knew he didn't deserve a response. Still, the thought of Jayon brought on so many emotions. He was a lost friend and lover, and she still hadn't finished grieving over either.

Jordan put her BlackBerry down, not ready to respond to him just yet. She didn't want to respond filled with emotions; she preferred to wait until she could think rationally. Truth was, Jordan's feelings felt more like anger than sadness. She had allowed her pain to turn into disappointment and then anger. When Jayon asked Jordan to please forgive him, she told him "the feeling of betrayal from someone you trust and love is an indescribable feeling." Jayon couldn't respond to that statement, because he knew what he had done would scar her emotionally. Not because he was some special gift or anything, but simply because he was so special to her.

24

It was about time to go home, and Jordan was just finishing up some last-minute projects that she was working on while waiting on a client. She had spoken to her son for about an hour, and was in a pretty good mood hearing how excited he was to come back home with her. After receiving the e-mail from Jayon the day before, Jordan had found herself reliving all the emotions that stemmed from their breakup. It felt like every time she got stronger, something would make her weak, whether it was Jayon or the thought of him, a feeling of loneliness at night, or just the harsh realities of what her life had become. She had ignored his e-mail then spent the whole night debating if she should reply and what she would say to him. After a few hours, she found herself dwelling on her problems. They lingered and followed her through the morning and her day at work, but she was fighting the feeling.

Jackie showed up in her doorway, dressed in her coat and carrying her bag.

"Darren is here to see you," she said.

"OK, send him in."

"OK, I'm going to head out afterward," Jackie replied.

Jordan sifted through her inbox and pulled out Darren's

file. She sat back in her office chair and waited for him to enter. Seconds later he appeared in the doorway dressed and a black and gray suit under a trench coat. As soon as he walked in the office he smiled at Jordan, quickly reminding her of their blurred line between business and personal. Jordan gestured toward the seat in front of her desk, letting Darren know he was welcome to sit down, and he accepted the invitation. Jordan hadn't held late appointments like this in quite some time, but with the chaos in her life, she had to catch up.

"Technically you owe me lunch, you know?" Darren said as he sat down.

"I know, please forgive me. Some things came up."

"Its OK, you can always make it up to me."

Jordan smirked. "I will," she replied.

"I'm looking forward to it."

It was obvious the meeting was taking a left turn rather quickly, so Jordan tried to regain control before it went too far.

"So how did the meeting go between you and your partners?"

"It went pretty well actually, but there are still several outstanding issues that we have to tend to."

"Do you have any of the contracts or notes from the meeting with you?"

"Actually, I don't. I left them at my office."

"How do you expect to make any progress when I can't see any of the documents?" Jordan asked.

Darren stood up and began to walk toward Jordan's chair. Jordan's eyes remained locked on him the entire time.

"We can make a lot of progress without the documents," Darren said.

Jordan remained speechless as Darren made his way toward her. It was as if the fire inside of her was all dampened out, because there was no question that Jordan's instincts would've normally kicked in by now and kept him at bay. Instead, she allowed him to get closer and eventually place himself on her desk before her chair and lean over her.

"Darren," Jordan said. "I don't think—"

"Don't think," Darren interrupted. "Just let me do."

Darren was caressing Jordan's shoulder, and although she pretended not to notice, she did. One thing that she decided made the most sense was his advice not to think. That's all Jordan ever did was overthink. Before she could get out her delayed response, Darren was leaned over, kissing on her neck. Thoughts were running through Jordan's head, one of them being Jayon. The little guy on her shoulder that was telling her to stop him and pull herself together was being out-screamed by the guy on the other shoulder telling her "Go ahead, why not? What are you saving it for? Another husband or best friend?" The more her thoughts of anger and pain resurfaced, the more into it she got. Before she realized it, his hands were caressing her breasts and his tongue was in her mouth. Seconds later, all within one motion, he had picked her up and placed her on the desk.

At this point, Jordan didn't need to convince herself anymore. She had decided to just go with the flow and enjoy the ride. He had begun to remove her shirt while simultaneously kissing on her. It seemed he didn't want to take any breaks in the foreplay so that she couldn't change her mind. He had scooted up her skirt, licked his lips, and headed downtown. For a split second, Jordan couldn't believe what was happening. After only seconds of being down there, Jordan leaned back on her desk in ecstasy, erasing her prior thoughts. Darren knew what he was doing, and it quickly became apparent where all of his confidence and boldness came from. Jordan was overwhelmed with pleasure as she squirmed and moaned on her desk. She could tell that she was going to have one of her Top

10 fastest orgasms. Sure enough, moments later, Jordan's body was tightening up with joy.

Once Darren was done, he stood up with a smile and began to back away from the desk. Jordan could tell that what he had in mind was to leave her with that gem, but Jordan couldn't let it go like that. She quickly placed her hand on his side and guided him to sit in the seat behind him. When Jordan placed her hand in front of his face and requested protection, Darren didn't hesitate to reach in his back pocket and oblige. After he placed on a condom he was carrying in his wallet, Jordan began to straddle him. She carefully placed her legs around the chair and over his lap to allow easy entry. Jordan slowly lowered herself onto him, and they both made a quiet noise as he snuggled inside of her. Jordan then slowly rose a few inches and lowered again. She repeated this motion continuously as they both reveled in the sensation.

"You wanted it. Now you got it," Jordan whispered in his ear as she lowered onto his penis for another stroke.

"Yes, and it's more than I ever expected," Darren said back.

Jordan slowly lifted up until the tip of his penis was barely inside of her, and she held herself there for a moment.

"You sure you can handle it? You want to give up?" Jordan asked.

Darren smirked, but his facial expression told her that it was too good for him to give up.

"Stop playing," Darren said as he placed his hands on Jordan's waist and lowered her back down.

His aggression and horniness was turning Jordan on even more, and she began to slightly wind her hips as she moved up and down on top of him. Jordan was enjoying the ride just as much as he was enjoying being ridden. Jordan never expected she would do something like this, but she had to admit that she was taking the attorney-client privilege to the next level.

25

It was as if the girl had studied long and hard as to what she was going to say back to Jordan. Four weeks had gone by since Jordan sent Randi that e-mail cursing her out for being a home wrecker, and Randi was just now writing back. She probably asked every friend she had what their opinion was on strategically choosing every word in the e-mail. One thing was for sure: she didn't know much about Jordan, because if she did, she would know that she would never win the battle.

When Jordan signed on to her computer that morning, she saw a familiar e-mail in her inbox, and it took only seconds for her to recognize the address. The e-mail read:

Dear Jordan,

Although you chose to resort to name calling I'm going to rise above your immaturity. You can blame me all that you want, but I am not the one who was committed to you. I do not even know you; Jayon on the other hand broke interest, not I. I won't deny that I knew about you, but you are not my problem or concern. I knew Jayon, we became acqaintances, we got to know each other better, I wanted something, and I took it. If he respected you and cared enough about you, maybe I wouldn't have got what I wanted, but I did and it was always great. As for him not respecting me, I guess that makes two of us because he didn't respect you either. Many nights he left my house having been inside of me, and came to your house and was then inside of you, and you call me nasty. For your sake, you better hope I'm not. You say I can have Jayon, but I don't think I needed your permission, but I will take him and continue to enjoy him. You take care of yourself now, and maybe I'll see you soon.

Razzy Randi

"Dumb bitch, can't even spell acquaintances right," Jordan said aloud to herself as soon as she finished reading it. Jordan was fuming mad. She wanted to punch a hole in the wall, she was so mad. She felt like the punk rock-and-roll kids who damaged their rooms and threw stuff everywhere when they got mad. How dare this ho write her and have the nerve to have no shame in her game. Jordan knew that she couldn't respond under these conditions. Not only would she just flip out and curse her out, only showing that she had gotten to her, but she knew that she wouldn't get her point across. So instead, Jordan called Jayon to curse him out until she could calm down enough to respond to that trifling tramp.

Jayon answered on the third ring. He sound surprised yet excited to see Jordan's name appear on his phone. Jordan's tongue rolled off the second he said hello.

"You tell your bitches don't let my law degree fool them. I will meet that bitch in her driveway and beat her ass, you understand me?"

"What are you talking about?" Jayon said, sounding confused and nervous.

"You used to come to my house and have sex with me after you had sex with her? You fucking asshole!"

"No, I never did that. What happened?"

"Jayon, don't act innocent. I am tired of your act. Enough. You don't have to pretend anymore. I am not your girl no more. You can put on that charade for your new girlfriend. I just want the fucking truth."

"I am telling you the truth. I never left her house and came to yours, ever. And I don't have a new girlfriend."

"Well, according to Randi, y'all are together now, and you used to bring your dirty dick to me after you were done screwing her and put it inside of me, and Jayon I swear I will cut your fucking balls off if I find out that's true. You better change your fucking locks," Jordan said, and she hung up the phone.

Luckily, Jordan's office door was closed, because in her rage of fury she didn't stop to think if anybody could hear her. She sat in her office chair, buried her face in her hands, and let out a scream. She shook her head back and forth until the inevitable tears rolled out of her eyes. It didn't matter how strong she tried to be, she was hurting so much inside. She missed the hell out of Jayon and hated him to death all at the same time. She didn't understand how he could do this to her, how he could tell so many lies and ruin so many plans. One thing that bitch Randi said that was right was Jayon had just as little respect for her as he did Randi, if not less. At least Randi wasn't lied to; at least Randi wasn't full of love for a man that would end up causing her such heartache. She may not respect herself, but at least she didn't have to worry about anyone else hurting her. Dumb bitch.

Jordan had finally pulled herself together; she went into her office bathroom and washed her face. She couldn't let this chick and Jayon, who wasn't worth it, get her down anymore. Jayon had tried calling her back twice already, but Jordan had nothing else to say to him. Jordan went about her workday as if her terrible morning never happened. If Jordan was in the mood, she would've forwarded the e-mail to Dakota and Chrasey and got them all riled up so she could have a battery in her back when she replied. Thing was, Jordan wasn't in the mood. She had decided that if she responded, it wasn't going to be now. Besides, she knew Randi was waiting for her response, and Jordan figured she could wait. By the time Jordan wrote back, it was going to be all that she had to say.

It was the end of the day, and Jordan had calmed down over what Randi had written to her. When it crossed her mind throughout the day, she felt her blood boiling up again, but she just kept trying to ignore it. After a while, Jordan knew that she wasn't going to be able to forget it until she replied and gave Randi a piece of her mind. So just before Jordan closed up her office and headed home, she sat down and responded to Razzy Randi's e-mail.

I resorted to name calling, because ho that's what you are. You pride yourself on going after what you wanted, but if that's all you wanted was some sex from somebody else's man that's pretty damn pathetic, and just in case you haven't heard that's what makes you a ho. I will rise above my own immaturity and even apologize for the name calling, because there's no need for that. You look at yourself in the mirror everyday, you know you got issues. Every woman knows, misery loves company. You're single, grown and alone and you're miserable. So you figure flirting with and trying to take another woman's man means something. Randi, every man chases pussy that's dangled in their face, get serious and then gain some respect for yourself and people's relationships. Not for me, but for yourself; because if by chance one day you do FINALLY get your own man you will want some respect given to you.

The usual thing is to tell you you're ugly and I don't see what he see's in you, but that's not necessary. You aren't ugly, you're a decent-looking chick, and problem is that's all you got. You think cause you have a decent career, I say decent because—let's face it—you're not balling, and you have somewhat of a cute face and body that you are the shit; but it's apparent you don't have shit else. It's apparent because to be the shit, you have to know your worth and obviously you don't if you are willing to settle to be the side chick. You see how you said he left your house several nights to come to mine—he LEFT YOU to COME to ME, that should tell you something. Even worse you knew that he left you for me and you allowed him to do it to me, which sums it up right there. Sure he is to blame, because he is the one that betrayed my trust, but it's women with no respect like yourself that allow him and men to do that kind of dirt. Let me guarantee you one thing, I will NEVER be that woman getting left. My men come home to me; my place is not the pit stop on the way to their wifey. So as long as you're good with being that pit stop, you will still remain the nasty slore I informed you were two weeks ago. We clear?

Now you take care of yourself, and hope to see you around.

Jordan Moore, Esq.

P.S. You did need my permission, because if I didn't say so he would still be coming home to me. I unlike you respect myself, I don't share. So enjoy.

(Although according to him, you are still just the meager pit stop so I guess you're still enjoying what little he gives you. So sad.)

Jordan didn't look the e-mail over; she didn't even do a spell check. She just finished her last sentence and hit SEND. She said what she had to say, and she was done. She had a couple more things to say to Jayon as well, but she figured it could wait, and if she still wanted to tell him later, then she would let him know another time.

Jordan packed her things up, turned off all the lights, locked her office door behind her, and headed home.

The entire ride home she was still thinking about what she had said to Randi in her e-mail; she analyzed what else she should have said and what she shouldn't have said. It was too late to retract the e-mail, but she was hoping that Randi felt as low and slutty as she wanted her to feel. Jordan hated girls that would just settle for anything and had no self-respect, and Randi was just that type of chick. Jordan's car swerved through traffic on the LIE as she rushed home to just change her clothes and try to get some peace of mind.

As Jordan pulled up in front of her house, she saw the UPS man standing at her front door. Jordan pulled into her driveway trying to remember if she was expecting anything. As she pulled into her driveway, the five feet eleven, brown-skinned delivery guy turned and faced Jordan. Sitting on the floor beside him was a huge brown box.

"Are you Jordan Moore?" he said to her as she stepped out of the car.

"Yes," she said.

"This is for you," he replied.

Jordan stepped out of the car, grabbed her briefcase and walked toward the young man. He extended the electronic machine for her to sign, and Jordan took the pen with her free hand and signed for the package.

"Do you mind bringing it inside my porch, please?" Jordan asked him.

"Sure," he said as he lifted the box to bring it inside.

Jordan keyed into her house and held the door open for him to place the box down inside the house. He placed the huge box down on the floor by the living room entryway, and headed back toward the front door.

"Thanks," Jordan said.

"You're welcome, have a good day," he said as he headed toward the truck parked in front.

Jordan closed the door behind him, walked into the living

room and kicked off her navy blue pumps and removed her suit jacket. She sat there for only a few seconds before she jumped up to see what was in the box.

She walked over to the box and began to pull at the flaps. She couldn't break through at first so she used her nails to poke the tape. After she pulled the first flap she saw another white box inside with a piece of paper on top. She ripped the paper off the box and opened it. After looking at the slip, Jordan noticed the box held a fifty-inch flat-screen television. Jordan immediately looked over the paper to see where the television came from, and she saw Marcus Shields. Jordan couldn't understand why he sent her a television, so she instantly went to her cell phone and called him.

He answered the phone on the third ring.

"Hello," he said.

"I have a fifty-inch flat-screen television sitting in my living room. Do you happen to know anything about this?" Jordan said with a hint of sarcasm.

Marcus giggled. "My bad, babe, I meant to tell you. I ordered it for my bedroom but I was out of town for a few days so I put your address down."

"That would have been nice to know," Jordan replied.

"I'm sorry. I meant to tell you, but it slipped my mind."

"That's fine, it will be here when you get home," she said.

"The next package will be a gift from me to you, for being such a sweetheart," he replied.

26

Jordan had no intention of making evenings with Marcus a habit, but this wasn't the first time she was home alone and looking forward to his company. Earlier he had called and said he was going to stop by on his way home from a meeting. The last time he came by, they didn't do anything but watch television, so Jordan didn't interpret his visit as a booty call. Still, when she got out of the shower, she prepared to do the do just in case. She put on, of course, a matching bra and panty set, Victoria's Secret, and she lotioned up to everywhere, including her nooks and crannies with her smell-good stuff. Then, to disguise the effort, she put on a white and pink T-shirt with some pink boy shorts.

It was a Wednesday night and Jordan had only been home for about two hours herself, but she had some time to kill before bedtime and she didn't mind the company. She contemplated making dinner but quickly decided against it. She wasn't doing anything special for no man, because it wasn't worth it. She didn't want to take her anger toward Jayon out on Marcus, but she couldn't help the way she felt. Jordan was lying on the couch cuddled up with a throw pillow, watching the late episode of *Oprah*. She thought Marcus would be there by now, but he never did give an exact time, and she damn sure wasn't calling him to see where he was. He was not her man and she was not his girl. Where he was was none of her business, and she wanted to keep it that way. It was a lot less stressful not having to worry about somebody and what they were doing and if they were being faithful. At least this way she just assumed the worst.

It was about nine thirty when the bell finally rang. Jordan got up and walked toward the door, then shouted "Who is it?" as she got closer. Without waiting for a response, she pulled the door open. Jordan's mouth instantly went dry, and her eyes opened wide at the sight of Jayon standing on her front steps. The left part of her brain said slam the door, but she was still frozen from the shock and was speechless. Before she could finally react, Jayon walked past her and started talking.

"Jordan, I know you are mad at me, and I don't blame you," Jayon began.

"Get the hell out of my house," Jordan said as soon as she heard him start his speech. She was still standing with the door open and her hand on the knob. It didn't take much to snap her out of her shock and bring her back to reality. Not only did she have absolutely nothing to say to Jayon, she was expecting Marcus at any minute. Not that either one of them meant a great deal to her, but she didn't feel like the awkward moment or having to spend any time with Marcus answering questions about Jayon.

"No, Jordan, hear me out. I'm not leaving until you at least listen to me."

"You don't call the shots, Jayon. You're leaving now. I don't want to hear shit you have to say," Jordan said as she pointed through her open doorway.

"No, I'm not. This is getting ridiculous. We at least owe

each other to sit down and talk this through. Even if you don't forgive me, we need to talk."

Jordan started laughing. "Owe each other? Are you kidding me?"

From the look on Jayon's face, you could tell he knew he used the wrong choice of words.

"I don't owe you shit," Jordan said.

"Listen, I get your point. I know that I fucked up."

"Jayon, what do you want?"

"I just want us to sit down and talk about this, clear some stuff up and just . . . just . . . talk for two seconds."

Jayon's stuttering let Jordan know that he had a lot on his mind and it was taking a lot for him to come over and make this bold move. Jordan felt herself getting slightly weak and tempted to hear what he actually had to say, but before she could respond, a noise from behind startled her. When she looked back, it was Marcus coming up to the doorway.

"Damn," Jordan said aloud, even though she meant to keep that to herself.

"Is everything OK?" Marcus asked.

Before Jordan could respond, Marcus had stepped through the doorway and seen Jayon standing a few feet away.

"Everything is fine," Jordan responded. "Jayon was just leaving," she said.

It killed Jordan inside to make Jayon feel the way he must have felt at that very moment, but she knew that he deserved it. Besides, it didn't compare to how she felt when she found out about Randi or when she read that damn e-mail she wrote her. Jordan expected prideful Jayon to just walk out on that note and give up before things got any more discouraging, but it seemed Jayon felt he'd come too far to leave now.

"How you doing?" Jayon said to Marcus as he reached out to shake his hand.

As they shook hands, Jayon introduced himself by giving his name.

"Marcus," Marcus replied.

"Listen, Marcus, I'm sorry to interrupt y'all evening, and I mean no disrespect by being here, but I really need to talk to Jordan, and it technically can't wait."

"No problem, brother, I can respect that."

"Nuh-uh: What the hell do you think this is?" Jordan said, looking at Jayon in disbelief that he was really trying to dismiss her company.

Then she looked at Marcus with the same disbelief for gracefully bowing out so easily.

"Marcus, pay this no mind. Like I said, Jayon was just leaving."

Marcus looked like he didn't want to get involved with what was going on. He could tell that Jordan was not in any danger, but that there was something pretty deep or emotional at hand, and he didn't want to get in the middle of it.

"Jordan, I need to talk to you."

"There is nothing to talk—" Jordan started before she was interrupted by Marcus.

"How about I will just wait in the living room until you guys are through?" Marcus suggested.

"That's cool," Jayon said, answering before Jordan could.

Marcus began heading toward the living room, and Jayon waited for him to be out of hearing range. Jordan was fuming mad at this point. She didn't want Marcus all up in the mix of this drama, and she didn't want to talk to Jayon, especially not with Marcus in the next room. She couldn't expect Marcus to kick Jayon's butt or anything—besides she wouldn't let it get to that anyway—but she still wasn't feeling how he was respecting Jayon's feelings more than hers.

"Jayon, I'm going to ask you one more time to please leave my house," Jordan said in a calm manner.

"Jordan, I'm going to ask you one more time to please listen to me."

Jordan closed the door and stepped back inside and sat on the chaise on her porch. She didn't know what else to do. She knew that she could make a scene and yell and scream and kick Jayon out, but she really didn't want Marcus to see all of that.

"Jordan, I know you are justified to be mad at me and never want to speak to me again, but there is a lot that you have mistaken and a lot that you don't understand."

At first, Jordan was subdued and was just listening to what he said. He was talking in a low tone, to keep from being heard by the man in the living room.

"It is killing me right now to see another man in your living room, and I am doing everything inside of me to try to overlook that."

Why did Jayon say that? Why did he remind Jordan that she had yet another man in her living room that wasn't her husband? Why did he remind her that it was supposed to be him in her living room, but he ruined all that? Why did he have to act as if he had a right to be upset about Marcus being in her living room? Why did he ruin his shot at talking to her, because now she no longer wanted to hear it?

"It is killing you?" Jordan asked. "Let me share with you my slow death, then," Jordan continued without an answer. Her voice got louder as she continued on. "Imagine how I felt going out with a friend one night to a work event and meeting a young lady who kept giving me dirty looks, and then slowly gave me hints that we had something in common. Then I come home and find out that you, who was supposed to be my man and best friend, had just spent the evening hanging out with her. Then later come to find out that you had been fucking her behind my back for who knows how long. Imagine that. Then imagine having the bold bitch send me an e-mail weeks later telling me how easy you were to take from me, and how eager you were to disrespect me. Killing you? You don't know how that shit feels, so please."

Jordan stood up, walked straight through the living room, passed Marcus, who made it quite obvious he heard every word of what she said, and headed upstairs. She couldn't take it anymore, and she didn't want Jayon or Marcus to see her breakdown. As soon as she reached the top of the stairs, she burst out in tears as she rushed to her bathroom.

Jayon stepped inside the living room, unsure if Marcus was going to go up to console her, and he knew he didn't want that, but he was hesitant to go himself. It was as if Jayon was just realizing how real this whole thing really was. He just assumed that some time and talking would mend things back, but he was realizing that he had done some permanent damage to Jordan. Damage that he didn't seem to have the touch to repair—not anymore at least.

Jayon looked at Marcus; he just looked at him and shrugged his shoulders. Marcus wasn't going to leave, at least not yet, not without making sure Jordan wanted him to. Jayon didn't know what to do. All he wanted was to have Jordan hear him out, but it seemed no matter what he said he dragged up some feelings inside her and he couldn't get a word in edgewise.

"We were real good friends before we started messing around," Jayon said.

Marcus looked up at him, shocked that he was actually talking to him.

"For like fifteen years or something like that. She is real good peoples."

"Yeah," Marcus said, not knowing what to say back.

"Shit happens sometimes, things get messed up, and it all happens so fast," Jayon said.

"Yeah, life happens. Ya know?" Marcus said as he stood up. He wasn't about to sit there and be this dude's counselor.

"Let me go check on her," Marcus said as he was about to head toward the staircase.

"Nah, let me. I got to handle this," Jayon said as he walked toward the staircase, which he was already closer to.

Marcus was tempted to put an end to this charade. He was way more muscular than Jayon and knew that he could help Jordan gain control of this situation, but he didn't want any problems up in Jordan's house, and he figured if they had fifteen years of friendship, Jordan would prefer that he not do anything to him. So Marcus sat back down.

Jayon walked up the stairs slowly. He really didn't want to face it, but he damn sure couldn't sit downstairs while some dude he didn't know was upstairs consoling Jordan in her bedroom. He glanced in Jason's bedroom as he passed by and walked through Jordan's doorway across the hall. The bathroom door was locked inside her bedroom, and he knew she was in there. Jayon thought to call her name, but he didn't. Instead, he just sat on the bed outside the bathroom door. He saw her lotion on the nightstand with the cap on and her towel thrown on the seat by the bathroom door. He figured she had just taken a shower and gotten ready for her guest that was downstairs. He knew because that's what she usually left behind when she was getting ready for him to come by at night. The sight of it and the thought of what they may have been doing if he wasn't there just made him feel even worse inside. He knew that Jordan didn't take sex lightly, and if she was sleeping with this dude, either she really liked him or she was really trying to forget about him. Either way, Jayon wished that he could change the way things were. The sight of Jordan's face when she saw him sitting on the bed let him know that wasn't possible.

She had come out of the bathroom with a tissue in her hand, drying her face, and seen Jayon sitting on her bed. She immediately rolled her eyes and went to turn back around.

"Jordan," Jayon said as he jumped up before she could lock herself back in the bathroom.

"Did I come over and sit on your bed when you were spending time with Randi?" Jordan said as she turned back around to head through her bedroom.

"Can you please stop this, Jordan? Your stabs aren't getting us anywhere."

Jordan stopped. "You talking to me isn't getting us anywhere, either. Where we were going you messed up a long time ago. Technically, you messed it up the first time you cheated on me, but according to you, we weren't officially a couple then. So this time, you nailed it. It's done, Jayon, and there's nothing to talk about."

When she was done, she turned around to get some lounge pants from her drawer. She didn't feel comfortable in her short shorts in front of both her ex-boyfriend and her new friend downstairs. Before she could pull her pink-and-white-striped Victoria's Secret pants out of the drawer, Jayon walked up behind her and put his arms around her. She tried to wiggle free, but he was holding on tight.

"I'm so sorry, Jordan. I am truly so sorry."

Jordan stopped moving. She just sat there, remembering what it felt like for him to hold her. She closed her eyes and felt the moment, felt him, felt his apology, felt her love for him all over again. She dropped her head in disgust that this was even happening.

"Jayon, I hear you. I hear and accept your apology, but I am not ready to forgive you," she said as she began to break free from his hug. She walked toward her bedroom door, heading back downstairs to apologize to and sit with Marcus. Before she walked down the hallway, she turned to see if he was following, because she wanted him to leave.

He just looked at her. He had given all he had, it looked like. Then again, so had Jordan. They were finally in the same place, realizing that it was over for good.

27

Jayon had walked by Jordan and Marcus sitting on the couch as he headed to the front door. In an attempt to save face, he gave a head nod to Marcus as he walked by. He walked past Marcus's CLK that was parked directly in front of Jordan's house and opened the door to his Audi across the street. He wasn't happy with the way things happened, but he was quite clear that Jordan was in a different place from where he thought she was. He hadn't seen her like that in all the years he knew her; he guessed it was as she used to say "when a woman's fed up." He never thought she would choose another man over him, but when he walked out the door and that handsome muscular dude was still sitting on the couch, it was obvious who she wanted to be there with her, or at least who she had chosen.

Truth was, deep down inside, Jordan wanted Jayon there. She wanted him to lie beside her and tell her everything would be OK, and she wanted to believe him; but she knew that wouldn't be possible. She didn't want to allow some man she had only known a couple of months come before a man she knew damn near half her life, but she had been the good girl long enough.

Jayon hadn't made it two blocks before he called his boy Bill to tell him how terrible things had just gone. Billy was the one who told him he needed to put his pride aside, go talk to Jordan, and at any cost let her know how he felt. Billy didn't tell him what to do in case there was another man on the way over. Billy didn't pick up the phone, and Jayon left a voice mail. With the silence in the car, Jayon got to thinking about all that Jordan said, and he remembered the part when she said Randi had been hinting at stuff when she saw her, and the crazy stuff she said in the e-mail. Jayon got mad that he'd risked his relationship with such a dumb chick, but then he got even madder thinking about how she was trying to mess things up between him and Jordan by doing that. She knew he had a girl. *Why all of a sudden was she acting like a woman scorned,* he thought to himself. She knew the deal.

Jayon had been keeping his distance from Randi these past few weeks. Suddenly, she was a huge turnoff to him; she wasn't as exciting now that he didn't have his main girl. He had slept with her one time since him and Jordan broke up, like a few days after. He was still all messed up over it, and Randi had called saying all these things he needed and wanted to hear, and somehow he ended up staying the night with her. That was the last time, though. Since then, he'd barely even spent twenty minutes on the phone with her. He had things on his mind other than going back and forth to check on her. That was before, though. Now he had a whole lot of stuff to say to her.

Randi answered on the third ring.

"Hey, hun," she said.

"Randi, why did you say all that to Jordan?" Jayon started out immediately.

"Say all what?" Randi replied, losing her initial sweet tone.

"All that stuff you put in an e-mail."

"She wrote me first, calling me a home wrecker and shit,

so all I said was it wasn't much of a strong foundation because it wasn't hard to wreck."

"Randi, I don't need you making the situation worse for me. You know things ain't good right now, and you saying stuff and adding stuff that ain't true isn't making it any easier on me."

"Seriously, do you think I care about you and Jordan's relationship?"

"I know you don't, or you would have never got with me, but that's between me and you, so don't go saying nothing to her."

"She says something to me, I'm going to respond. Besides, what did I lie to her about?"

"She said you said we were together now or something like that," Jayon said.

"I didn't tell her that. If you don't want us speaking, then you tell her to leave me the hell alone. She's the one that hit me up, like I owed her something. I didn't. You did."

Hearing those words that he owed Jordan reminded him of what Jordan had just said at her house, that she didn't owe him anything. It reminded him again that she was at her house with some dude, and all he wanted to do was go back there and kick him out of there. He knew he didn't have any place to do that, but he was wishing he hadn't known that Marcus was there with her. It was just making the whole thing worse.

"I gotta go," Jayon said before he hung up the phone. He couldn't talk to her anymore; she was a part of the reason he was in this mess. She would tell him that he had never had anything like her before and say all this perverted stuff in texts to get him to give in to the temptation. He knew that there was no excuse that he went ahead and went through with it, but she enticed him for at least a month before he gave in. She would tell him she wasn't trying to come in between him and his girl; she just wanted them to have some good sex. When he tried to resist when they worked together she would lean over in front of him and say all this slick stuff. She knew what she was doing. Now, all of a sudden, she was this coldhearted chick that was just out for hers and talking like she could care less what happens to his relationship.

Jayon hung up and drove back toward Jordan's house; he wanted to see if Marcus's car was still parked outside. As he was turning down the street that led to her block, he began to slow down, unsure if he should go through with it in case they were outside. Then he figured it was unlikely, so he turned down the block anyway. From the corner he could tell that Marcus's car was still parked outside, and when he drove by the house he could see that the lights were still on. As he reached her corner, trying to peek back in his rearview mirror, his cell phone rang. It was Billy calling back.

"Hey, man, you're not going to believe how the whole thing went down," Jayon said.

"What happened?"

"First I get there, she ain't trying to hear me. Then when I almost get her to hear me out a little bit, some dude comes walking up to the door."

"What? Some dude? Who's the dude?"

"Some dude Marcus; I still don't know what's going on with that or where he came from."

"Damn, son, so what happened?"

"Nothing. She asked me to leave. I asked him to leave."

"You asked him to leave?" Billy said, laughing.

"In so many words, but Jordan wasn't having that. So he went in the living room to wait. It was crazy. Then as I'm trying to tell her that this whole thing is getting to me, I must've said the wrong words, because she got all upset talking about how bad I hurt her and how this bitch Randi e-mailed her telling her all kinds of stuff."

"Stop playing," Billy said.

"I'm serious. Just spoke to Randi. She's bugging. Talking about she don't care about me and Jordan's relationship, not that that is a surprise. It don't even matter, though."

"So what happened with Jordan?"

Jayon had no intention of telling him that he just rode down her block like a stalker, at least not yet. He wasn't sure if he was going to be driving through looking for that car again, so he left that out for now.

"She went upstairs crying. I was so stressed I start to talking to homeboy on the couch for a second, and then he gets ready to go upstairs behind Jordan. I can't stomach that, so I go up there, and when I get up there I can tell she was getting all sexy for this dude downstairs. It was tearing me up, being the outsider like that. When she came out of the bathroom, I just held her, and I told her I was sorry. She finally let me hold her for a second, but she's through. She told me she can't forgive me. She gave me this look when she walked out of the bedroom, and I can tell in her eyes she don't see me the same no more."

Billy could hear the pain in Jayon's voice, and he really didn't know what to say. "Damn, man," Billy said.

Billy was usually one with many words of advice, but even he was at a loss for words. What could he do? If she was done, he was done. Billy knew that just a little over a month ago, Jordan was happily in love with Jayon while he was creeping and crawling, trying to keep Jordan happy and sneak in time with Randi. At the time it was just an interesting and exciting game; neither of them looked forward to this day, when the game was over.

28

Jordan was happy that Marcus had handled her little situation the other night so well. Once Jayon left, he pretended like it didn't happen. He told her there was no need to apologize and settled down to a television program with her like it was nothing. Jordan wasn't really in the mood for sex after Jayon left, and Marcus didn't try anything because he probably figured the groove was ruined.

It was Friday, and Jordan was getting ready to head out to meet Donovan, Eddie, and Tayese. She was wrapping things up around the office, closing programs on her computer, and straightening up her desk. Jordan had worn something she could transition out of easy, so she could have a professional look by day and with a twirl be fit for a night on the town. She changed out of her gray skirt suit with the white-collared bodysuit and gray pumps, into a more dressed down in the city look, and she released the bobby pin from holding her hair up. Once she was done shutting down her computer, she headed to the bathroom to freshen up and reapply her makeup.

As she was heading out, her office phone rang and she glanced at the caller ID and saw it was Marcus. Jordan felt a slight flutter and answered the phone.

"Hey, how did you know I was still here?" she answered.

"I didn't know. I just figured I'd try."

"Why didn't you just call my cell phone?" she asked.

"I don't know, I just dialed the first number that popped up in my address book. Why, is there a problem?"

"No, not at all."

"So when am I going to see you again?" Marcus asked.

"I guess whenever, you tell me," Jordan said. "I live right around the corner, so I'm only a hop, skip, and a jump."

"Well, I'll hop, skip, and jump over there tomorrow night when you get home."

"OK, I'll call you when I get home later," Jordan replied.

She wasn't sure if she was 100 percent comfortable with that, but she knew she could always make up an excuse to get out of it if she wanted to.

"OK, see you later," he responded.

It was seven thirty when Jordan headed out of her Manhattan office and into the street to wave down a taxi. She walked toward the corner as she waited for the banana-colored car to come into sight. Jordan hated when a cab didn't come quick and easy. She made it to the corner, and when she spotted a taxi coming in the other direction, she frantically waved her hand. She leaned into the street slightly so the driver would definitely see her, and just as it looked like it was too late, the driver pulled over. Thankful, Jordan walked across the street toward the taxi. Just as she was heading there, a man was walking up to the car door as well. Jordan gave him a look to let him know that she was getting in the cab.

"Oh, this was for you?" he asked.

"Yes, I waved him down."

"Actually, I waved him down," the man said, pointing a few feet away.

The taxi driver was just looking without saying anything.

"He was way past you when he stopped, which means he didn't see you."

The man looked back to where he was and looked quite annoyed at the ordeal.

Jordan ducked her head into the cab. "Which passenger did you stop for?" she asked.

"I saw both of you," the older gentleman replied with an accent.

"How about we just share the cab. Where are you going?" the man said.

"I'm going to Times Square," Jordan said.

"That's fine; I'm going uptown as well."

The gentleman took his seat and scooted over. Jordan wasn't in love with the idea of strange company for the ride, but she wasn't in the mood to give up the cab or fight any longer. Jordan sat beside him and gave her destination to the driver as she whipped out her BlackBerry. She began typing to Tayese that she was on her way, and the funny story that she was sitting in a cab feeling real uncomfortable with this strange man.

Midway through her text, the strange man said, "I'm sorry about this, by the way. I would've been a gentleman and let you have it alone, but I am running so late for a business dinner, and I have been waiting twenty minutes for a cab."

"Sorry to hear that, but it's OK. I would've let you have it as well, but I'm on my way to a business dinner too, and these heels are not the most comfortable."

The guy began to laugh. Just then, Jordan noticed how attractive he was. His smile brought his face to life.

"I understand," he said. "The ride will be short and painless."

The sound of a phone ringing came from the guy's pants. He pulled out his BlackBerry and silenced it.

"I won't bother you with conversation that you don't want

to hear. That's the least I can do," the guy said as he put his phone away.

"You can take the call," Jordan said.

"It's too late," he said as he put the phone back in his pocket.

"My name is Jordan," She said as she put her hand out for a handshake.

"Shakai," the gentleman said back as he shook her hand in return.

For a moment, Jordan didn't know what else to say. She didn't want to bother him with small talk, but she was interested in the strange man beside her now. She finished her text to Tayese and then sat there a few moments looking out the window. She looked back toward the front and was trying not to look too much at him. Shakai was about six feet, two hundred pounds. He had a very lean body build and broad shoulders. He was dressed in black slacks with a green collared shirt. His cuff links read "S." on them, and his black loafers were intact. He wore a black cap with gray and green stripes through it. His green shirt went well with his medium brown complexion and light brown eyes. Jordan was eager to look back at him and take in more of his physical features, but she didn't want to look as though she was interested.

"So, where uptown are you headed?" Jordan finally asked.

"The Shark Bar," he responded.

"Oh, wow. I haven't been there in a long time. Great food."

"Yes, their food is some of the best in the city. I have most of my business meetings there," he replied.

"That's nice. I'd weigh three hundred pounds if I ate there that often."

Shakai must have found that funny, because he began to laugh a real laugh.

"So what do you do, if you don't mind me asking?" Jordan asked.

"I'm an accountant," he responded.

Jordan immediately thought of how Jayon was an accountant, and that was one strike against him.

"That's interesting. How do you like it?" she asked.

"I've always liked numbers, so I love it."

"That's great."

"What do you do?" he asked.

"I am an attorney," she said.

"Oh, OK," he said, not showing his opinion.

"Where is your business dinner tonight?" he asked.

"Just meeting some colleagues at Olive Garden in Times Square."

"Oh, that's nice."

They were close to Forty-second Street; the streets began to get wider and more crowded with people and cars. The hustle and bustle of New York City close to the holidays was like no other. Jordan glanced up at the meter and began to reach in her bag to get her wallet.

"Please, let me handle it," Shakai said.

Jordan looked at him, expressed a look of hesitation, and then put her wallet away.

"OK, thanks, but you really don't have to."

"It's the least I can do for being so rude," he said.

Jordan reached into her wallet anyway, but she pulled out her business card and handed it to him.

"Well, keep in touch," she said.

Shakai reached in his back pocket and pulled his business card out as well.

"You do the same," he said.

The cab had pulled to the side of the road, and Jordan opened the door to step out. She waved good-bye to her new friend and walked toward the Olive Garden. She walked in and went straight upstairs to look for Tayese, who had said she was already there. She spotted her sitting in the back with both

Donovan and Eddie at a booth. Jordan made her way through the tables and toward them.

Once she reached the booth, Donovan scooted over to make room for Jordan. She looked around the table, and noticed that on Donovan's other side was Tayese, and beside her was Eddie. Jordan sat down in the room that was made for her and wondered if this gesture from Donovan was once again a hint as to who he was interested in. She assumed if he was thinking that Eddie was there for her, he would've waited for or told Eddie to move down, or better yet scooted away from Tayese so she could move down, leaving room for Eddie to scoot down and make space. Regardless of what could've happened, Donovan made room for Jordan and was now sandwiched between her and Tayese.

"We ordered appetizers already, but if you want to add something, it's not too late," Donovan said.

"I'll just pick at what's coming," Jordan said.

"Oh, and I ordered you a piña colada," Tayese said.

"Thanks," Jordan replied.

For a second she felt her heart skip a beat. Piña coladas were her and Jayon's thing. He used to make her one all the time when they were having movie night or just relaxing at home. He made a mean piña colada, and she knew she would miss them just as much as she missed him.

"I did want to talk to Jordan here about my business ventures, but she didn't feel safe unless her best friend Tayese was here," Donovan oh-so-boldly added.

Tayese and Eddie laughed as Jordan dropped her mouth open in disbelief.

"Oh, it's like that? You trying to blow me up?"

"Nah, I'm just kidding," Donovan added.

"I wasn't afraid in the least bit. You obviously don't know me," Jordan said, trying to sound tough.

"Well, I know her," Tayese interjected, "and that is something she would do."

"What?" Jordan said, humored by the sudden attack.

"I mean, you just met him a little while ago, at a club at that. You don't play those games," Tayese added.

"True, but if it was business, I can handle my business."

"That's true," Tayese said, backing off.

"Well, I guess she just wanted to make sure it was business first," Donovan said.

Jordan was all confused. She was now feeling conceited, like she didn't want to seem. Then she realized that it was in her head. She was tempted to blow him up as to the things he was saying to make her question his intent, but she still didn't know what was said before she got there between him and Tayese.

"All you had to say is you wanted to discuss business and you would've preferred that I didn't invite her, but instead you said you would invite Eddie—so don't even try it," Jordan said.

Donovan laughed. "That's true. Get out of here, guys," he said, laughing.

They all laughed. Jordan didn't realize that Donovan had such a feisty and humorous side about him. She couldn't say she didn't like that in a guy, but at this point she didn't know what to think. She didn't know if he was trying to let her know he was only interested in a business relationship, and wanted Tayese to know it too, or if he was just being funny to break the ice again.

By the time the waiters finished taking all of their orders and brought their drinks out, the four of them had broken all the ice there was to break and were laughing at and discussing the night they met at the club. Right after they finished laughing at Eddie and Tremaine, their other friend, for going to the wrong club, most of them began to pick at the appetizers.

"We are not getting any business done," Donovan said out of nowhere.

Jordan was taking a sip of her drink, and she looked up. She looked at him, trying to read what the feelings were behind his words.

"How about this, Donovan," Jordan said as she placed her drink down. "We will deem tonight as business in the sense that we got to know each other and make a decision if we want to do business together, and if we choose to do so, we will have a meeting at my office."

Donovan seemed unprepared for that comment.

"OK, that sounds fair," he replied.

"So don't worry, my time tonight will be free of charge."

Tayese started laughing, and so did Eddie.

Donovan couldn't help but drop his head in defeat. "OK, you got that one," he replied.

"I'm just saying, in case that's what you're worried about, getting a bill for three hours and all we did was talk and eat."

"Yeah, 'cause I'm sure your time ain't cheap," Eddie interjected.

"Not at all," Jordan said, looking straight into Donovan's eyes.

"Understandably so," Donovan said, looking directly back.

Tayese and Eddie continued picking at their appetizers, as if they didn't notice the unspoken words being said at the moment.

Jordan felt her BlackBerry vibrate and removed it from the clip to check it. It was a text from Tayese that read, "Isn't he cute?" Jordan looked up at Tayese and smirked as she tried to play off her confirming response. Jordan quickly typed back, "Which one?" Jordan took another sip from her drink as Eddie and Donovan exchanged a few words about something. Jordan felt her BlackBerry vibrate, and when she looked at it, Tayese had replied, "Donovan." Jordan just smirked, trying to also disguise her confusion. "Yeah, he is," she typed back.

The waitress approached the table with a large tray with plates of food. Their eyes locked on their food, and their mouths began to water. The waitress placed the four plates down in front of them as she called out the names of the dishes. The steam from Eddie's stir-fry filled the table and his nose.

"Mmm, this smells good," Eddie said.

"It looks good," Donovan said, looking at Eddie's meal and not at the lemon chicken with linguini that was placed in front of him.

"Get out of my plate," Eddie said, picking up his fork and getting ready to dig in.

Forks were picked up and mouths began to fill. Within seconds there was silence at the table. Everyone was enjoying their meal and too focused to incite a conversation. As Jordan took forkfuls of her fettucciné Alfredo, she was realizing that she still didn't know exactly what was going on at this table. There weren't any flirtatious or implicative comments made, no one was sitting too close to anyone else, there was nothing to draw from to say what was going on one way or the other. Jordan wasn't sure if Tayese's comment about Donovan meant she had her eye on him or she was encouraging Jordan to go for hers. Jordan didn't know if this was a date, a business dinner, a casual dinner, or just four young black folks getting to know each other better in New York City.

29

Jordan was driving home with a full stomach and feeling beat for the night. She'd had a long day at work and had just left a three hour dinner with Tayese, Donovan, and Eddie. By the time the cab dropped her off by her car and she was en route to home, it was already midnight. She had her radio tuned to 98.7 KISS FM as usual, and she was listening to Bugsy's reports on the weather, news, and celebrity drama in between her songs. Bugsy was filling in for Lenny Green, and he kept her laughing and entertained while she drove.

She was driving down the street, heading toward the midtown tunnel, when her cell phone rang. She pressed the button on her steering wheel that turned on her Bluetooth connection.

"Hello," she said.

"Hey there, miss," the voice on the other end said. "It's me, Donovan."

"Oh," Jordan said with a giggle.

"Where are you?" he asked.

"Heading home, are you?" Jordan said.

"Come meet me. I'm at the W on Seventeenth Street."

"What?" Jordan said, not expecting that request.

"Come meet me. I'll be here for a while."

"I just left you," Jordan said.

"Well, that was fun, but this will be just the two of us," Donovan said.

Jordan was surprised to hear him make such a leading comment. Still, she felt like she had been misled before by his statements.

"Why do we now need to spend time just the two of us?" Jordan asked.

"Because now we can really have fun and really get to know each other better," Donovan said.

Jordan knew that Donovan had a couple of drinks at the restaurant, and he seemed a little touched when he was getting in the cab afterward, but now she could tell that he must have been feeling really free.

"So that we can see if we want to do business together?" Jordan asked, trying to regain control of the conversation.

"Yeah, that's why," Donovan said in a sarcastic tone.

"I'm right by the tunnel," Jordan blurted out, realizing how tired she was and how she really didn't feel like hanging out any longer.

"Oh, come on. You live once. The night is still young and so are we. See you soon?"

Jordan let out a loud sigh and slowed her car down.

"See you soon, Donovan, but I'm not staying long," she said.

"OK, that's fair. See you soon."

The black BMW truck made a slow, cautious U-turn on the wide city street and headed away from the tunnel. All the lights were green or were just turning green as Jordan approached, so the drive was going quite quickly. There were no moments for her to sit still and think about her decision and change her mind. The farther away from the tunnel she got, the more she felt that there was no turning back. In theory she wanted a good reason to turn back around and go home. The problem was there wasn't any really good reason. There was nobody waiting at home for her. No one waiting on her, period, other than maybe her mother who would prefer a call from Jordan to let her know that she got in safe. The closer Jordan got to the W, the more depressed it made her that her life had become one with no "reason to turn around."

She stepped out of the car once she found parking and then reapplied her Covergirl wetslicks lip gloss as she headed toward the dimly lit lobby of the W Hotel. Once she stepped inside, the variety of faces reminded Jordan she was out of her realm. She was there to meet a guy that she barely knew, and she didn't know where he was, either. She thought to pick up her phone and call him, but she knew with the loud music that wouldn't help. She was going to text him, but she figured she would look around for him for a bit first.

All the swanky New Yorkers were chatting it up with the friends and colleagues that they had decided to spend their Friday evening with. Most of the ladies and gentlemen had drinks in their hands, some also typing into their BlackBerrys. Jordan knew the look of "being important" with the usage of one's BlackBerry a mile away. It was a look that she mirrored quite often, not intentionally but essentially. Jordan excused herself past several people, trying to make her way to the back where there seemed to be more available space than there was in the front. One woman looked as if she didn't want to move for Jordan. She was dressed in a gray and black sweater dress, that must have been hot to death, if Jordan had to say so herself. She was rocking the new Gucci bag with the gray mink all over it, and some black Gucci stilettos. Something about this woman's attire and attitude told Jordan that she thought she was something extra special. Jordan wasn't impressed by much, though, so she pushed her way past the lady when she didn't move after Jordan's second request.

"Did she just push me?" the lady said to someone she was standing with, once Jordan made her way past.

Jordan overheard her and was very tempted to turn around, but she figured if the lady wanted her attention she would have directed the question at her. Jordan kept heading toward the area in the back, by the second bar. As she looked over some people, she recognized Donovan sitting by the bar talking to a young lady. Jordan walked in his direction without him having noticed her just yet.

Once she got within his eyesight, he looked up and appeared quite surprised to see her before him.

"Hey, Jordan," he said.

"Hey there. Why do you look so surprised to see me, like you weren't expecting me or something?"

Donovan giggled at Jordan's blunt comment and dismissal of any games he may have been trying to play in front of his little female company. Jordan didn't come all this way to be bothered with any nonsense, and she was making that very clear.

"Not at all," Donovan replied. "I was expecting you, I just didn't know that you had made it here so fast," he continued.

"I wasn't that far away," she replied.

The young lady sitting at the bar beside Donovan pretended to not be paying attention as she sipped her drink and looked at her phone.

"Come take a seat," Donovan said as he patted the stool beside him.

As Jordan walked toward the stool that was waiting to relieve her feet from the pressure of the three-and-half-inch elevation in her shoes, Donovan gestured toward the young lady.

"Jordan, this is Nicole: Nicole, this is Jordan," Donovan said to the two of them.

Jordan extended her hand to shake Nicole's. "Nice to meet you," Jordan said as the girl shook her hand. Jordan then sat on the stool, still curious as to who this Nicole was, but she knew she didn't care enough to be so curious. Whoever she was, this was Donovan's web that he had woven, and all she knew was that he better find a way to fix it without putting her in any drama.

"Can I get a Malibu pineapple, please?" Jordan asked the bartender the second he came over to Jordan's area.

"Not wasting any time," Donovan said to Jordan in a joking manner.

"Well, I see you are, so no, I'm not."

"What is that supposed to mean?" he asked.

"You had company, so why did you call me to come join you?"

"Do I sense jealousy?" Donovan asked.

"No, you sense irritation."

"Jordan? What's wrong?" he asked.

Jordan realized that she was being quite nasty. It was a mixture of the crowd that annoyed her on the way in, her anger from not having anyone waiting at home for her, and a variety of other personal issues—none which had to do with him.

"Nothing. Just a rough day."

The bartender sat her yellow-colored drink down in front of her, and Jordan began to sip on it.

"You were fine a little while ago at dinner," he said.

"Yeah, I know. Just been going through a lot of stuff. It keeps me a little bit moody."

"I understand. Well, let's try to work you back into a good mood tonight," Donovan said.

Jordan just looked up at him, letting him know that she had her eye on him. She didn't bother looking past him to where his friend was sitting, and for a moment she forgot she was sitting there. Nicole must have felt she was forgotten as well, because as soon as Jordan turned back to her drink, she noticed Nicole rising up from her seat in her peripheral vision. Still unaware of who exactly she was, Jordan watched as she gave Donovan a not-so-sincere good night.

Once she was out of sight, Jordan looked back over at Donovan and cracked a smile.

"Oooh, you are in trouble," she said through her slight smirk.

"Oh, you think you're funny, don't you?" he said.

"Me? No one told you to try to be a player and have a double date with two women."

"I wasn't trying to be a player," he said in defense of himself. "And who said that either of you were a date?"

Jordan cut her eyes over at him to catch his expression and determine whether he was being funny or trying to play her. Before she could reach a conclusion, he continued.

"I was on a phone call and she just sat down beside me. When I was done with my call, she was still sitting there and the bartender had brought me over a drink and said it was ordered by her. I began to have light conversation with her, but by no means was it a date or me trying to be a player. It was just conversation."

Feeling a little silly about her accusation and his explanation, Jordan replied, "You don't have to explain anything to me."

"Whatever," Donovan said.

Jordan didn't even really care if he was bothered by her comments. A large part of her didn't want to be there in the first place, and she definitely wasn't in the mood to be treated like some jealous crazy chick. He invited her back; she didn't ask to be there. Still, she didn't take the time to come back just to have a miserable time with Donovan, so she decided to change her tune and make the best of it.

"So you come here often?" she began. The attitude-imprinted

expression she had been wearing for the past ten minutes was erased.

Donovan looked at her; it was obvious he was curious where this change of heart was coming from. He didn't ask any questions, though, or provoke her anymore.

"From time to time, it's real chill on Friday nights."

"Is it? I have been here a couple times, but the crowd has never been the same, so I couldn't tell."

"Yeah, I usually enjoy the crowd and the music. It's a cool after-work spot."

"It's your own little Cheers?"

Donovan chuckled. He seemed to be enjoying the lighter side of Jordan much more. Jordan was reaching in her purse looking for her BlackBerry when she felt a nudge. Jordan's eyes scanned the room in the direction the nudge had come from. She caught Donovan's eye as she scanned, and he was looking to the left of Jordan. Jordan looked to her left and noticed the woman in the gray and black dress from earlier stepping on the stool beside Jordan, trying to get the bartender's attention. Jordan could only assume that this was the person who accidentally nudged her, and although she knew it could've been innocent, she figured it was childish, intentional retaliation. Jordan knew that she was just as noticeable as this chick in gray, and the girl was probably threatened by that, as ridiculous as it may have been. Jordan was rocking her black high-waist pants with the suspenders over a white ruffled button-down shirt and her black Gucci stilettos with the Swarovski crystal heels. She was looking quite sassy and chic herself, so she wasn't thinking about that lady once she passed by her.

"Did she just push me?" Jordan asked Donovan, pointing behind her with her thumb and imitating the scene from earlier.

Donovan laughed and didn't respond.

"People got issues," Jordan said as she went back into her purse and pulled her phone out.

"Are you talking to me?" the lady in gray asked Jordan.

Jordan looked up and stared the lady dead in her eyes.

"Did I say your name? Did I look in your direction? If I was talking to you, trust me, you'd be the first one to know it."

Donovan stood up to get ready to stand in between the two ladies if need be. He could tell from the looks on their faces that their interaction wasn't going in a productive direction.

"Oh, it just appeared that you were speaking about me," the girl said back with an attitude.

"About you, yes. To you, no. Like I said, if I was speaking to you, you'd be the first one to know."

"Oh, about me, yeah?"

"Listen, I don't stutter. If you have a problem or want to ask me a more direct question, get to it. Otherwise, I'm not interested in getting to know you better."

Jordan wasn't sure why she was so short-tempered this evening, but she knew that she wasn't hesitant in any way to let this woman know that she wasn't in the mood for her antics. Donovan finally stood in between the ladies, as he realized more people were noticing their unfriendly contact.

"Come on, ladies, let's be nice."

"Whatever," Jordan said as she dropped her eyes to check her BlackBerry.

Next thing, out of nowhere, Jordan's head was jerking backward. The lady in gray had grabbed a handful of Jordan's hair and pulled her head backward. The sudden move startled Donovan and surprised Jordan. Jordan quickly wiggled and turned her body around and off the chair, while both ladies began shouting obscenities. As Donovan tried to pry the woman's hands off Jordan's hair, Jordan reached her long fingers around Donovan, grabbed the chick by the neck, yanked her backward, and began swinging with the other arm. Donovan was trying to create room between the two, but with their grips on one another, it wasn't working. Both women were trying to swing for the other, making a few light connections here and there. By this point, another gentleman stepped in and helped Donovan separate the two ladies. He was trying to take a hold of Jordan's arms and loosen her grip, but Jordan's fists were swinging so rapidly he was struggling to get a hold of her. The two of them were both infuriated and cursing at one another, swinging for each other, and creating a very unladylike scene. The second guy that was helping out finally managed to get Jordan's grip from around the girl's neck, moments after Jordan's hair was freed.

The lounge's patrons that were sitting nearby had moved out of the way and were watching in disbelief as these two grown women, who appeared to be quite classy, were acting like ghetto-class teenagers. Jordan finger combed her hair as she tried to regain her composure. She was still in defense mode and pissed off that this woman had the nerve to not only start trouble with her but put her hands on her. Jordan hadn't fought in ages, and never would she think as a grown professional she would be engaging in a bar fight. She was both pissed at the woman and herself, but she was still too angry to stop her madness.

"What a punk ass, grabbing my hair from behind," Jordan said as she fixed her clothing.

"Whatever, bitch, you said people have issues. I was giving you an issue."

"I don't have the issue. I'm good. You just better be glad I was too busy whopping your face up and didn't grab that weave from out of your head, you bootleg bitch," Jordan said.

"Whatever," the lady said, repeating herself over Jordan numerous times.

The security guard from the front door came walking up to where the ladies were as if he was actually making a record-breaking reaction time. Overhearing the ladies' exchange of words and seeing the looks on their faces and their displacement, he could tell that their was tension. The onlookers gave it away even more with the stares that were waiting for round two of the thirtysomething-year-old tackle.

"I'm going to have to ask you ladies to leave," the security officer said.

"We have a room here," Donovan interjected as he stepped beside Jordan.

Jordan looked up at him. He looked back at her to confirm his statement visually.

"Well, ma'am, I'm going to have to ask you to go," the security officer said, speaking to the lady in gray.

"Whatever. She's probably a high-class prostitute, and because she has a room she can stay. Whatever," the lady said as she gathered the things that had fallen out of her purse.

"Prostitute?" Jordan laughed. "I'm an attorney, bitch, and you better be happy that I don't press charges. You're wearing all you're worth, anyway, so I won't bother . . . but you got one part right: high class. As long as you know."

"Whatever. I know you ain't talking. That Gucci bag is so last season."

Jordan burst out laughing.

"Actually, this one just came out two months ago, but of course you are going by what the bootleggers are selling you," Jordan said, laughing at her own joke.

The woman repeated her safe response of "whatever."

"The simple fact that you analyzed my entire wardrobe and broke it down into seasons just explains why you came over here in the first place. Hate is an ugly color on you. Sad thing is when you get escorted out of the hotel, I will still always look this good. What a waste of hate," Jordan added.

Donovan looked amused at Jordan's slick comebacks, but he seemed more annoyed with the delay of removing this woman. The security guard inched closer to the woman every time she stood up from picking up one of her belongings. Finally, she was done and began to walk away, mumbling more junk as she went.

"Let's go upstairs and get you cooled off," Donovan said.

"Oh, you really do have a room?" Jordan asked.

"Yes, I do," he replied as he placed his hand behind her arm and walked her toward the elevator.

Jordan was so eager to get away from the scene and get all the eyes off of her that she was easily convinced to change locations. They stepped inside the elevator and there was no one in it but the two of them.

"I'm so sorry about that," Donovan said.

"You? I'm sorry about my behavior and temper getting the best of me like that. I'm supposed to be a professional. I'm actually quite embarrassed."

"You did kind of take it to the street, Jordan. I was surprised."

Trying to release a laugh, Jordan just dropped her head.

"What are you sorry for?" Jordan asked.

"For causing such a terrible night for you. I called you back; you had to deal with my uninvited company at first and then the psycho chick. I just feel bad. You would've been in your bed already if it wasn't for me."

Jordan laughed at him taking the blame.

"You are right. You did put me in this situation," Jordan said, laughing his comment off. "But how do you assume I would have been in the bed by now? You just assume that I have no life at home."

Donovan made a face. He realized Jordan was right, that was an assumption. The elevator door opened, and ahead of them was the view of the shiny marble floors. The two of them stepped off the elevator and headed down the hall. They stopped in front of room 7614, and Donovan pulled out his key card. Jordan looked down the hall to see if anyone else was on the floor or could see her entering a hotel room with this man, but she didn't see anyone.

She stepped inside the room and the scent of vanilla-cinnamon filled her nose. She walked in and turned the corner that separated the bed area from the corridor. Across the way was the bathroom, and she looked at Donovan and gestured to him that she was going to use the bathroom. He nodded his head in approval. The awkward feeling of being in the hotel room together must have caused the suddenly silent form of communication. Jordan went in the bathroom and witnessed the scratch above her eye and her frazzled hair. First things first, she couldn't stand to see her hair like that. She pulled the comb out of her purse and began fixing her hair back into place. Once she was done, she reapplied her Lancôme juicy lip gloss and used a cotton swab from the countertop to tend to her scratch. After some time had gone by, she realized that she had been in the bathroom for a bit and was leaving ample time for Donovan to get comfortable and make a plan of action. So she finished up and headed toward the bathroom door.

Donovan was resting on the side of the bed with the television turned to a football game. He instantly turned to Jordan when she walked into the room.

"You OK?" he asked.

"Yeah, I'm fine," Jordan said with a smirk.

"You ready to go back down, or do you want to chill for a bit?" he asked.

Jordan paused for a moment to think. She wasn't sure if spending time in his hotel room was the classiest thing she could do, but at the same time she didn't feel like seeing all the people who had witnessed the brawl looking at her again.

"We can chill for a little bit and then go back down," she said, thinking to herself that was the best choice for a happy medium.

"OK, relax," Donovan said as he kicked off his shoes.

Jordan placed her purse on the desk and sat on the bed on the opposite side of Donovan. She removed her BlackBerry from her clip and began to send a text out informing Dakota and Chrasey of what had happened. She hesitated to tell Tayese just yet, because she wasn't quite sure how she was going to explain her being at a hotel with unclaimed Donovan. Once Jordan finished typing and sending her text, she placed her BlackBerry on the nightstand to await their reaction to her story. Once she placed it down, Donovan turned over and looked her right in the eyes.

"You know, I'm not just telling you now because we are in my hotel room, I was hoping you caught on from the first night I met you, but I am really feeling you."

Jordan froze momentarily. She was thinking to herself, *Yeah, what an inopportune time to tell me*. She was trying to take a millisecond to figure out what to say back.

"Honestly, I wasn't sure. I didn't know if it was strictly business or if you were feeling Tayese or what. I was just going with the flow."

"Tayese? Nah, Eddie is feeling her though. I had my eye on you. I did want to do business with you, but if I had to choose one, my heart says no."

Jordan giggled at his cute game.

"Your heart says no?" she asked. "You got that from some Jodeci song or something?

"No, I'm serious. I really like you, so I would prefer that we get to know each other better and see where things might lead," he said, shrugging off her innocent insult.

"I'm not against that," Jordan replied.

Donovan scooted over a bit closer to Jordan, and Jordan instinctly backed up some.

"I'm sorry. I didn't mean to invade your personal space."

Jordan realized how her reaction came off, and although that was what she meant to do and how she normally would respond, she remembered that she was supposed to be a new Jordan. She had to ask herself what she was running from, why she was moving away from this fine black man that could possibly give her some great loving right here in this nice plush hotel room where no one could hear her scream.

"No, not at all. I'm sorry. I was just caught off guard," Jordan said as she eased back into her original position.

As soon as she was done, Donovan leaned in to kiss her. When their lips and tongues met, Jordan could feel her body's uneasiness and tried to mentally calm herself down. She chanted in her mind, *Relax, you're an adult. Live a little,* or combinations of it. Moments later, Jordan had eased herself into his arms, while his tongue eased its way around her mouth. Jordan had no complaints; Donovan surely knew what he was doing with his tongue, lips, and fingertips as he caressed her lower back. Jordan resisted as long as she could before her body gave in to the attention.

30

There wasn't much on Jordan's mind the past twenty-four hours other than her rendezvous last night with Mr. Donovan. By the time she got home, she knew there was no way she was getting to work on time. Sure enough, Jordan awoke at 10:30 AM, and by the time she showered, got ready, and drove in to the city, she walked into her office at 12:30 PM. Lucky for her, she didn't have any clients scheduled to come in. However, she did have a client coming in at three that she still hadn't prepped for. Jordan knew she was being irresponsible, and she couldn't afford to lose money in her practice because she was handling a lot of bills on her own. Jordan knew she had to get back on track, and soon.

Once she got to work, her mind kept wandering back to the details of their yummy time together the night before. It didn't help that her two silly, high school–minded friends kept sending her random e-mails making jokes and asking intimate details about the episode. Jordan couldn't help but laugh at their questions and comments, but on the inside she was feeling a little solemn about the whole thing. She had to remember both Dakota and Chrasey had someone at home to keep them "honest," so to say, and she couldn't help but feel in a way that she'd become the damsel of the group.

Jordan opened one e-mail that was sent from Chrasey: "What is going on with you? You're fighting in clubs, having sex with random men, you have the complete 360." Before Jordan had opened it, Dakota had already responded, since all three of them were cc'd on the e-mails. Dakota's e-mail read "I told you, Jordan is the younger version of *Stella Got Her Groove Back* lately." Jordan laughed to herself when she read what they wrote, but at the same time she knew she had to laugh to keep from crying.

Jordan headed toward her office door to go inform her assistant that the last few files she went through were not updated. As she made her way closer to the door, she heard her assistant announce over the intercom that she had a Shakai on line one. Jordan stopped in her tracks and paused; she slowly turned back around and headed for her desk as she tried to fully recall the person known as Shakai. It only took a second to remember that Shakai was the young man from the cab ride the day before.

"Hello, Ms. Moore speaking," Jordan said as she answered the phone.

"Hello, Jordan?" he replied.

"Yes, this is she," Jordan responded, pretending as if she was still assuming she was on a business call.

"Hi, it's Shakai, the guy from the taxi ride the other day."

"Yeah, I remember you. I'm glad you called."

"It was nice meeting you the other day."

"Yes, it was nice meeting you too."

"Did you think I would call this soon?"

"Actually, no, but I was hoping you would."

"Well, are you free any time this week? Maybe we can meet up."

"Tomorrow night I can do dinner."

"How is eight?"

"I have a seven o'clock meeting. Let's shoot for nine."

"OK, see you at nine."

Jordan was about to hang up the phone when she realized that they didn't make a definite plan.

"Wait!" Jordan said. "Where are we going to meet?" she added.

He laughed, realizing how silly that was.

"Do you have any place in mind?"

"I haven't been to Mr. Chow's in a while."

"OK, so let's go there."

"OK, I'll see you at nine."

Jordan hung up the phone and quickly entered the date in her BlackBerry. She then got up and headed back toward her office door. She initially forgot what she was going out there for, but then she remembered she had to talk to her assistant. When she got to the hallway, Jackie wasn't in sight. Their intern, Hewan, was sitting nearby, looking over some documents. Jordan asked if she had seen Jackie, and Hewan told her that she had stepped out for lunch. Jordan was a bit annoyed because she had told Jackie time and time again to notify her when she left for lunch. However, instead of making a big deal, Jordan just left a message with Hewan about updating the documents.

Jordan went back into her office and took a moment to reflect on her plans with Shakai and again on last night. She tried to think to herself how many guys she'd be dating at one time if she continued on this path. It would only take a few guys more before it became a roster. It would be different if she had not become sexually involved with more than one of them at once. She told herself that with Shakai she would try to keep it from getting physical for as long as possible. Marcus had been in Jordan's mind numerous times, but she tried extremely hard to keep her feelings from getting involved. Marcus was beginning to call more frequently and send more intimate texts, and although Jordan tried to deny it, she liked Marcus. Still, Jordan refused to allow herself to get hurt again, so she wasn't willing to not see Donovan and Shakai, or anybody else she met for that matter. Besides, Jordan was confident that Marcus probably had some friends of his own, just like Jayon did.

31

Jordan took the night just to spend some time alone and do nothing. She had come a long way from the girl who hated going to clubs, wasn't big on partying, and was against casual sex. Lately, these things felt like they were more important than her career and family, and at one time that's all that mattered. When Jordan was home alone, she couldn't pretend that her newfound way of life was making her happy. She felt empty inside, and she knew that she was doing all these things to fill the void. Of course, she knew that these guys could not fill the void of her child, husband, and best friend. Although she hadn't given up on her child, she had given up on her husband and best friend and all men that pretended to be honest. There was a point when the thought of her son ending up with a girlfriend and treating her wrong made her feel a certain way about him even, but she had every intention of teaching him how to be a better man.

Jordan had run a bubble bath and placed her iPod in her Bose speakers; she went to her R&B playlist and headed into the bedroom to get undressed. Jordan had a television in her bathroom, but she wanted some time to just relax. No television, no stressful thoughts, nothing. Just some candles, some soft music, some hot water, bubbles, and Jordan time. The thing was, most of the time Jordan didn't like being alone, because she had to reflect on all the wrong she was doing and all the wrong that had been done to her. It was just easier to keep busy and try to distract herself. Well, rather, it had been easier.

Jordan had sunk into the hot tub and begun skimming through a magazine. Usher's latest album was playing, and Jordan was actually feeling at peace with herself. Just as she started to hum along to one of her favorite songs, her doorbell rang. Jordan glanced up at her BlackBerry and noticed she had no missed calls and couldn't figure out who could be at the door. She wasn't expecting anyone, so she decided to ignore it. The bell rang again, and after a few more seconds the curiosity got the best of her. Jordan stood up, grabbed her towel, and dried off. She put her robe on and headed downstairs.

"Who is it?" she yelled.

"Marcus," she heard from the other side of the door.

Jordan wasn't sure what to do. She was standing there in her robe and didn't know if she should answer the door or make him wait. She figured it would be rude to make him wait, and since he had seen all she had anyway, it didn't make a real big deal either way. Jordan walked up to the door and opened it; Marcus was standing there dressed in all brown.

"Sorry to show up unannounced," he said as soon as Jordan opened the door. "I hope you didn't forget I was stopping by."

"I didn't hear from you, so I wasn't sure if you were still coming by," she said.

"I would've called first, but I was walking by your house and thought I'd just stop by now," he added.

Jordan giggled. "You sure you weren't trying to run into my ex again?" she joked.

"You got jokes. I'll come back later if you want."

"It's OK; I was just taking a bath."

"Oh, I'm sorry. I didn't mean to interrupt."

"No, not a problem at all. Come and sit down."

"Are you sure?"

"Yeah, if you don't mind waiting for a bit."

"Sure, take your time."

Jordan headed back upstairs to the bathroom. She was tempted to continue her bath and just make him wait, but she knew that was rude. Still, she wanted to at least rinse off since she had rushed out of the bathtub. Jordan went into the bathroom to let the water out of the tub and then walked into her bedroom to get some clothes out of her drawer. By the time she was done, the water was pretty much out of the tub, and Jordan turned on the shower. She hopped in and began to lather up with soap. A couple of moments went by and she heard footsteps. She peeked her head around the shower curtain and noticed Marcus walking toward her. At first she was extremely startled, realizing that this man could murder her right here in her own home and nobody would know.

"Marcus," she said in a high-pitched voiced.

"I'm so sorry to scare you. I just got excited sitting downstairs thinking about you up here naked."

Jordan tried to laugh, but that didn't completely ease her nerves. Marcus began to remove his shirt, and it was then that Jordan realized what he had in mind. She was feeling a little nervous but liked his idea. Showering with a man was a bit personal, Jordan felt, and having to be mindful of her hair getting wet wasn't the sexiest love scene, but Jordan couldn't object to spontaneity. She had sex with Jayon and Omar in the shower before, but that was it and it was not often. Still, the sight of Marcus, with his built upper body, made her willing to try it again. Within seconds, Marcus was fully undressed and stepping into the shower with her. As soon as he stepped in, he wasted no time at all and began to kiss her and let his hands wander all over her body. It didn't take long before Marcus had Jordan bent over like a scene in a porno. It wasn't the shower that Jordan had in mind, but after a few strokes she wasn't complaining.

32

"I've never had sex with two guys in one week. I need to see a counselor," Jordan said in a low, crackly tone.

"Yes, you do. I don't know what has gotten into you," Chrasey replied quickly.

"Calm down. It's not that serious. You just need to get over this Jayon thing quick before you hurt yourself," Dakota said.

"It is serious. Jordan has been bugging out since she caught Jayon cheating," Chrasey replied.

"That's what I mean. She is not built for this and needs to knock it off," Dakota said.

"Hello? I'm right here. I can hear you two," Jordan interjected.

The ladies laughed.

"I know that I'm not built for it and that this has just been my way of forgetting Jayon," Jordan added.

For a moment, Jordan's honesty kept the women silent. They all knew how it felt to be her; they had all experienced the pain of betrayal. Better yet, they had all wanted to throw caution to the wind and live in a place where no pain could hurt them. Hell, it was Dakota's creed at one point, for years to be exact, until David came along. For Jordan, it was the exact opposite. She always had her heart on the line. She always believed that if you gave your all, good things would come your way. She also believed if you were honest and loved wholeheartedly, that love would conquer all, but on two different occasions with the two men she trusted most, she was proven wrong.

"Trust me, Jordan, we know what you are going through. We have all been there at one time or another," Chrasey said.

For real, Chrasey was just there not that long ago when she was infatuated with Trevor.

They all giggled, but Jordan quickly got serious again.

"I know, ladies, but I think I'm losing myself. When Marcus left here last night, I felt so cheap and so outside of my body. I have to admit I was ashamed," Jordan said.

"Why? You said you like him," Dakota asked.

"Yeah, I do. I guess that means I like Donovan too, who I just had sex with two nights ago, and Darren, who I was with last week."

"Yeah, girl. You are on a roll," Dakota said, laughing. "I think you got me beat."

"You better be using protection, that's all I know. You are too grown to be out there carrying on like some high school floozy," Chrasey said.

"Thanks, Chrasey," Jordan said. "Not only am I a floozy and a ho, but I'm dumb too."

"Nobody said all that, but you seem all caught up in the moment, and I can't tell if you're using all of your senses."

"Yes, I am. Of course I am using protection. You think I'm trying to be on the *Maury* show, trying to find out who the baby's father is or something?"

Dakota had been there before and she knew there wasn't anything fun about that.

"For real, it is not cute not knowing who the father of

your baby is. There is nothing more that reads whore across your forehead," Dakota laughed, trying to make fun of the situation.

"Well, thank you, ladies, very much for your comforting advice and kind words," Jordan said in a sarcastic tone.

"Stop it, J, we are just messing with you," Dakota said. "You have to understand this seems unreal, us having to lecture you. The tables are so turned we don't even know how to handle it."

"Shut up," Jordan said with a giggle. "I gotta go; I will call you guys later." The girls didn't put up a fight to keep talking; they had been on the phone long enough.

Jordan hung up the phone and went back to watching television. She had spent most of the afternoon getting Jason's room nice and tidy for when he came home next week, and she was taking a break.

About an hour had gone by when her cell phone rang. It was Marcus. Jordan looked at his name in her phone for a few seconds before she decided to not answer it. She put the phone back down and lay back on the couch as she was. She waited for the call to ring to voice mail, and she finally started to pay the show she was watching attention again. She tried to pretend that she couldn't care less that he called, but she could feel her curiosity wondering if he would leave a message. She didn't have a real reason not to answer, other than him possibly wanting to come over and her not wanting company. Besides, with Jason coming home soon, he wouldn't be able to come over much at all anyway. Things were going to have to change. She had put Jason through enough, and she didn't want to have him seeing different men come and go out of his mother's life.

A few moments later, her phone vibrated to alert her that there was a voice mail left. She picked up the phone and dialed the inbox.

"Hey, it's Marcus. I'm heading home from Brooklyn. I

wanted to see if you wanted me to stop and bring you anything over. Call me when you get this."

Jordan was so touched at his thoughtfulness, and although she was tempted to request some butter pecan Häagen-Dazs, ice cream, she tried to refrain from calling him back. His voice filled her mind some more, and she imagined him looking so fine driving on the highway in his lovely car. She was starting to prefer that he did come over, but she was debating with herself. She held out a few minutes longer, and then finally went ahead and dialed his number back.

"Hey, Marcus," she said as he answered the phone.

"Hey, babe," he replied.

"I got your message and wanted to take you up on your offer."

"Cool, I'm not that far. What would you like?"

"I'll take some Häagen-Dazs ice cream, butter pecan."

He laughed. "OK," he replied.

"Why you laughing?" she asked.

"No reason. I'll see you in a little while."

Jordan hung up the phone and leaned back on the couch. She had a subtle smile on her face, like a schoolgirl blush. She just didn't know what it was about him, but as much as she wasn't trying to like him, she was kind of feeling this guy.

33

The sunshine that was squeezing through the blinds was faintly lighting Jordan's office. She didn't bother to flick the switch when she walked in; she just headed straight to her desk to put her things down. Once she reached her desk, she plopped down in her seat. The office was still quiet; Jordan beat the rest of the staff in. She wasn't feeling too well through the night, so she got up a little earlier. Surprisingly, she had a fast ride in—not as much traffic as usual. She sat there for a bit with her head relaxed against the back of her black leather chair. The crisp scent from the plug-in air freshener was filling her nose as she sat in silence and practically in the dark.

The next few steps were to turn on her computer, put some things away, look through files, and start her to-do list. Her morning was on hold for a moment, and Jordan just sat there reflecting. A million thoughts were running through her head about all that she had been through in the past year, and that she would continue going through until she found some normalcy again. Her girls Dakota and Chrasey were usually an intricate part of her healing process with any problems, but in this situation they just hadn't been the cure. Jordan figured it was because she was used to feeling like the one who had it together. She had the healthier relationships and more successful career. Usually she felt like she was on top of the world, and her friends reminded her that she was too blessed to be stressed.

Thing was, this time, her relationship was nonexistent and her career wasn't looking too great. Omar wasn't paying her any alimony because she was making more than him at the time of the divorce, she was paying for their huge house by herself, and her money situation wasn't at its best. Since the issue with Jayon, she had missed about a dozen appointments, two that included potential new clients and others including influential clients. She had been trying to ignore all the problems she was having in her life, but they were getting to the point where she just couldn't ignore them anymore.

A high-pitched ring came from Jordan's office phone and broke her train of thought. Jordan leaned forward and noticed Tayese's number in her caller ID. Her secretary wasn't in yet, so she went ahead and answered the phone.

"Girl, what are you doing in the office so early?" Tayese asked.

"Just got here early, no reason. Why are you in the office so early?"

"I'm always in the office this early. Unlike you, I have a boss."

"Shut up," Jordan said with a chuckle.

"Guess who called me yesterday?" Tayese asked.

"Who?" Jordan said.

"Donovan," Tayese said, sounding excited.

"Donovan? For what?" Jordan said, trying to remain calm.

Jordan hadn't gotten around to telling Tayese about her and Donovan, and this didn't seem like a good time to tell her.

"He asked me out on a date," Tayese said.

Jordan's mouth dropped, not that Tayese could see it.

"Are you kidding me?"

Jordan didn't want to tell her, but she knew if she didn't she would have been as wrong as two left feet for letting her get excited over this man, who was clearly a dog.

"No, he called last night. He said he wanted just the two of us to hang out this Friday at the W."

What kind of friends had he mistook them for? Jordan was thinking. Did he think they didn't speak at all, or did he just think they were desperate and wouldn't care? Whatever he was thinking, Jordan was pissed off at the thoughts.

"Tayese, I didn't get to speak to you since it happened, but Donovan and I hung out at the W after dinner."

"What?" Tayese said.

"Yeah, that man thinks he must be some mack daddy."

"What happened? What was y"all hanging out for?" Tayese asked, sounding very curious and upset.

"We were initially just hanging out, and then I got into a fight with this girl, which is a whole 'nother story, and then we went upstairs. He had a room, and although I am so ashamed to admit it, I slept with him."

"What?" Tayese said, sounding in complete shock.

"I know," Jordan said. "To make it worse, he is trying to holler at you like we aren't friends."

"Are we friends, Jordan?" Tayese asked.

"What?" Jordan said, confused. "Yeah, we are friends."

"I don't know anymore. You knew I was feeling Donovan, and yet you hung out with him behind my back and slept with him."

"Tayese, that night I invited you and Eddie along. He asked me to dinner, and I invited you. How was that behind your back?"

"That was supposed to be business. Besides, you knew me and him were flirting at the table."

"Really, I didn't, Tayese. If you would have said something, I would've never slept with him."

"I told you at the club I was feeling him, and I made it quite clear at dinner that night, but that didn't seem to matter. You just trying to fuck everything in sight," Tayese said.

Jordan was shocked by her comment. She couldn't believe she said that.

"You calling me a ho, Tayese?" Jordan asked.

"I'm just calling it how I see it. You can label yourself. I got to go." Tayese said and hung up.

Jordan hung up the phone in total disbelief. She wanted to call Tayese back, and then she was tempted to call Donovan and curse him out, but she decided against either and chose to just sit back and relax for a second. Her heart was racing; she was so upset, it was taking her a minute to calm down. She understood that Tayese was upset, but what kind of friend was she being by taking it there over some man?

A few moments later, Jordan could hear someone talking outside of her office. Some of the staff were beginning to come in to work. Jordan still sat there in the dark, waiting for her secretary to come in and turn the lights on and get Jordan's day prepped for her as she normally did when she beat Jordan in. Jordan waited as she thought over her conversation with Tayese, and she tried to figure out if she should have done or said something differently. As mad as she was at Tayese for saying what she said, she was also feeling a little guilty.

34

Jordan didn't want to go home after work, so she went ahead and had Dakota meet her for a bite in the Village after business hours. Jordan walked into the quaint little restaurant that Dakota had suggested, and sat down. She looked around and noticed the eclectic mix of people. Several ladies in their midtwenties gathered around the bar with cocktails in their hands. There were a few men in suits meeting at a table, and a few gay guys sitting close to one another at one of the other tables. Jordan just observed the crowd as she waited on Dakota, who had said she was in a cab five minutes away.

Jordan pulled her BlackBerry out of her purse to check and see if she had missed any calls. She had a text from Shakai that read "Hey how are you? I was hoping we could meet for drinks tonight." The thought of dealing with another guy at the moment mentally drained Jordan instantly. However, she didn't want to be rude, so she replied anyway. "Hey, I'm cool. Hanging out with one of my girlfriends in the village. I'll hit you in a bit."

Jordan remembered how smooth and good-looking Shakai was, but after the incident with Donovan and Tayese, Jordan didn't feel like being bothered. She looked at her missed calls and saw Omar's house number was there. Jordan pressed TALK and dialed the number back. She wasn't sure if it was Jason calling or Omar, but since she had spoken to Jason when he got out of school, she assumed it may have been Omar.

"Hello," Elisa answered.

Elisa was Omar's fiancée. Jordan and her had a cordial relationship, but there was definitely no love their, either.

"Hello, it's Jordan. Can I speak to Omar?"

"Hold on," she replied.

A few seconds later, Omar came to the phone.

"Hey," he said, sounding a little out of breath.

"You called me?" Jordan asked.

"Yeah, I wanted to talk to you."

"What's up?" she asked.

"I was wondering if I could keep Jason for just another week or two. Not trying to change things up or anything, I'm just asking nicely if I can just have at least one more week."

"What is a week or two going to do?" Jordan asked.

"Nothing, really. Just give me a chance to enjoy him here a little while longer. Also, it's my mother's birthday, and we are going to have a little something here next weekend. I don't want people to notice and start asking me questions. I haven't really told a lot of people yet."

Jordan took a second to think about it.

"OK, Omar. But I want him for the weekend then, because I have been looking forward to him coming home. Bring him from school on Friday, and he can be back to you by Sunday to go to school for Monday."

"Cool, thanks, J."

"You're welcome, but I can only agree to one more week for now. We will discuss a possible last one after this weekend."

"Deal," Omar said.

"You explain to Jason that you asked me this and I agreed to just one more week, so he doesn't feel confused."

"I will. I'll have him call you when he is done with his homework if you want."

"OK. I'll talk to you later."

Jordan hung up the phone and thought about what a difference one week would make. It wasn't too much of a favor, but she already knew that two weeks wasn't going to work. She was more than ready to have her son back; she needed him more than she wanted him. Still, she didn't want to say no to Omar, because she would rather they be cordial with their son than get the courts involved. Besides, she had to give him credit for being such a great father. He could have been a deadbeat who cared less.

She sat there and waited for Dakota to arrive, and about five minutes later she did. Dakota stepped in dressed in a red wraparound dress with some black and red pumps. Her hair was in a fresh wrap, and her jewelry and makeup were flawless.

"How do you manage to look like that every day?" Jordan asked as Dakota approached the table.

"It's a gift," Dakota said, laughing as she knelt down to give Jordan a gift.

"Well, get me a gift certificate to that store," Jordan replied.

"Please, ain't a damn thing wrong with you."

"I can't take the time to do my makeup like that every day, and have my hair still lying perfect at 6:00 PM," Jordan said, laughing.

"It does take time, technically, but I'm just a little vain, so I can't help it," Dakota said.

"I hear you. Maybe I should care more and then I wouldn't be having the men drama that I'm having."

"What happened with you and Tayese?" Dakota asked, obviously dying to get the rest of the story that Jordan had only teased her about on the phone.

"Nothing, really. Just the guy I told you about from the W

hotel, apparently she was feeling him and she was quite offended that I slept with him."

"How did she know him?"

"He was the guy we had met at the club that night," Jordan replied.

"Oh, did she tell you she was interested in him?"

"No. We both agreed that he was good-looking, and that was it."

"Well, then she can't be mad at you. How were you supposed to know?"

"I guess she felt it was obvious and I should've known," Jordan said as she took a bite of the cheese and crackers at the bar.

"I guess, but she can't be mad."

"Well, she is, and in so many words she called me a ho."

"What?" Dakota said, laughing.

"That's not funny," Jordan said, not laughing along.

"Well, you *have* been screwing everything that moves lately."

Jordan looked at her in disbelief. "That's the same thing she said," Jordan said.

Dakota laughed as she too took a cracker. "I'm sorry, it's not funny, you're right. I was just making light of it. She'll get over it. He wasn't her man"

"I guess. It's just all so crazy."

An hour later, the two of them were working on their third cocktail. Jordan was feeling a bit nice from her Miami Vices, and Dakota was drinking martinis. They had been discussing everything from their drama at home to their drama at work. Some of the people that were there when Jordan arrived had already paid their tabs and left. Jordan was laughing and having herself a good old time, and she didn't notice how much time had gone by. She reached in her purse to get her BlackBerry and noticed that Shakai had texted her back. He was asking what was up with the plans for the evening. Jordan wrote him back and told him to come meet her where she was, and she asked him if he would drive her car home because she'd had too much to drink. She would've just asked Dakota, but she lived there in the city and Jordan didn't want to ask her such a big favor. Once Shakai wrote back that he would be there within an hour, Jordan put her phone back in her purse.

35

The morning sun was beaming through her window. She tried to close her eyes tighter to shut out the UV rays burning through her eyelids. She had wanted that big beautiful bay window in her bedroom, and several mornings after having forgotten to release the curtains, she regretted it was there. She tried to pry her right eye open to take a peek at the other side of her dreamworld. She began to notice that her head was throbbing, and she wasn't feeling too hot a second after she began slowly opening her eyes. She began to roll over when she jumped and opened her eyes suddenly. Lying next to her was Shakai, with the covers up to his chest and his eyes closed.

Jordan jumped out of the bed and stood there with her hand over her mouth. She looked down at him and just stared as moments went by and he lay there peacefully breathing. It was all coming back to her, how her night started last night, and she couldn't believe that she woke up without a care in the world. She was trying to piece the night together to remember how they ended up here, as well as what happened here. She just stood there looking at him. He was looking sexy as hell with his chocolate chiseled chest exposed. She finally walked away from the bed, toward the bathroom. She had thought about it and decided not to wake him just yet. She couldn't imagine what could make the situation more uncomfortable than waking him up to kick him out.

Jordan quietly walked to the bathroom to gather herself for a moment. Her head was still throbbing, and she felt like some vomiting could take place. She had never thrown up from drinking before, but she also knew that she'd never had a bad hangover, either. She didn't know what to deem this, but the way she was feeling and the body of a naked man in her bed told her this was her worst hangover yet.

Jordan turned the water knobs and began to wet her toothbrush. She placed toothpaste on her toothbrush and stuck the brush in her mouth to clean her teeth, when she felt a sudden push from her guts. Jordan threw herself over the toilet just in time to release the vomit she had hurled there. She held her stomach as she spit the last remains that was in her mouth into the toilet. She looked at herself in the mirror, and she was looking terrible. She rinsed her mouth out, then continued to brush her teeth. She didn't want to be in there too long. She had a houseguest to tend to.

She finished freshening up in the bathroom and made her way back to the bedroom. She heard a vibration coming from her dresser, and she walked over to it to see if it was her phone. When she got closer, it wasn't her phone vibrating; it must have been Shakai's. As she went to walk away, she did a double take. She looked at the phone again, and the name and number on the screen were Jayon's. Shakai was receiving a call from Jayon. Jordan could feel her heart beating a thousand times a minute. It crossed her mind to answer, but she knew that would've been crazy. Yet she was confused as hell. *Was she set up?* she asked herself. *Did the two of them plan this?* Jordan found it very hard to believe that Jayon would be a part of this situation with Shakai, so she figured maybe they were just friends. Still, it seemed a little odd and coincidental.

All Jordan knew at this point was it was time to wake Shakai up. For all she knew, he could sleep all afternoon. She sat on the bed beside him and nudged his shoulder. He began to open his eyes and eventually noticed Jordan sitting there.

"Rise and shine," Jordan said.

"Good morning," he replied as he sat up in the bed.

"Good morning to you," Jordan said, looking down at the sheets.

She didn't feel so confident sitting there in front of him, unsure of everything she said and did the night before.

"How you feel?"

"I just threw up," she answered.

Shakai began to laugh, as he reached out and touched her leg.

"You need anything?" he asked.

"No, I'm fine. I took some Excedrin already."

"Oh, OK." Shakai said as he looked at his watch. "Wow, it's time for me to get out of here. I didn't realize it was so late."

Jordan stood up so he could get out of the bed. Shakai got up and went to put on his clothes that were laying across the chair. Jordan watched him as more of her memory of the previous evening came back to her. She remembered that he met her at the restaurant and they took a cab to her car. He drove her home and obviously came in. He helped her to her bedroom, and she started to touch on him. She still didn't remember all the details, but from what she remembered, the sex was good. She didn't recall seeing any condoms, but she wasn't sure if he got rid of it. As she thought about it, she was feeling embarrassed at how aggressive she was when they got to the bedroom. She slightly remembered not wanting him to leave her there and beginning to undress him. As the thoughts filled her memory, she just shook her head as if she was going to erase her memory like an Etch A Sketch toy.

Shakai was done getting dressed and was placing his cell

phone on his clip. She watched him look at his phone and notice his missed call. She was kind of hoping he would call him back right then so she could hear what they said, but then again she knew she would be way too uncomfortable for that. She was relieved when she saw him place his phone back on his clip. Once he was done putting on his black leather jacket, she stood up to walk him downstairs.

Once they got to the front door, he turned to give her a hug good-bye.

"Wait," she said. "Did we use protection?"

He smirked, looking surprised that she'd asked that question at that moment.

"I had a condom in my wallet."

"Oh, OK. I was just checking. Sorry," she said as she extended her arms to hug him.

She watched him as he walked down the street. She didn't know if he was taking a bus or walking to a cab stand. She didn't want to ask because she wasn't willing to drive him to where he needed to go. She had a headache and was still recovering from her evening. Besides, she needed some alone time to think about what the hell she was doing with herself.

36

It's amazing how one moment life can be so great, and moments later the smallest thing can just wreck your entire day. Jordan had just spent the day with her mother, having lunch and helping her out with some things around the house. Days when Jordan was able to just spend time bonding with her mother, seeing eye to eye with one another, were always a great time for Jordan. She was so easily consumed by other things that she didn't always take advantage of time with her mother, who had done so much for the woman she was. Jordan's mother was strong, independent, and was the "take no nonsense" type of woman. Mrs. Moore's strength made her rough around the edges sometimes, and she could make a smooth conversation difficult to have if she was in one of her "not in the" moods. So any time well spent with her mother was a treat for Jordan, because she knew one day in this harsh life she wouldn't have her mother around anymore to help her grow and be there for her. Jordan wanted to make sure she didn't look back and wish she hadn't wasted a second.

So when Jordan left her mother's house, she was in the best mood. She was in such a happy place, feeling appreciative of all the small things in life. She had decided that she was done with this wreck she was becoming, and she was going to get it together right away. No more random men, no more slipping up at work, and no more emotionally abusing herself. She was feeling back on top all from one day with her mother. Her mother was good at reminding her who she was on the inside—that was the reason she envied her mother's strength so much. Jordan hadn't felt this carefree in quite some time. That feeling lasted about an hour and a half.

It came to a halt not long after she sat her black behind in Estelle's chair. One look at her head without the weave she had been wearing almost brought her to tears. Jordan was sitting there staring in the mirror, unsure what to do. Jordan wasn't attached to the weave; she had just started wearing weaves on occasion not too long ago. She would've chosen to wear her own natural hair anyway, but she had put the weave in out of convenience for her last vacation and become somewhat addicted to the convenience. What she didn't know was the new expensive Brazilian weave crap does a hurting to your own hair.

She sat there in Estelle's chair in shock.

"What am I supposed to do with this?"

"It doesn't look that bad," Estelle said back.

She ran her fingers through what was left of her hair. "I can't believe this."

"It's not that bad. You're just going to need a really good trim and a deep condition."

All she could think about is how terrible she looked. No longer a married woman, her looks were even more important than they had been for several years. She always kept herself up for her own self, but being a single mother who was trying to keep a love life alive, she couldn't afford to be looking busted.

"Estelle, I cannot walk around with my hair looking like this. I'm going to have to put the weave back in until my hair grows back in right," Jordan said as she spun around in her salon chair.

"OK, well, you are going to have to run to Barbie's and buy some hair and come right back."

Jordan didn't even take a second to contemplate the scenario; she hopped right out of the chair and grabbed her stuff.

"I'll be right back," she said to Estelle as she rushed out the door. She could hear Estelle laughing at the humor in the situation. Jordan was unable to laugh, because she was too upset about the condition of her hair.

Thirty minutes later, Jordan was sitting in Barbie's Hair World waiting on her hair to be woven. She sat down and pulled out her BlackBerry to e-mail her sister and tell her the disaster with her hair, when she realized that there was an e-mail from Jayon in her inbox. She opened it up and read a generic message that read, "Hey there, just seeing how you are doing." Jordan looked back at the message, confused. She hadn't spoken to Jayon in a while, and she wasn't sure when she was going to be ready to. A part of her did want to speak with him, but another part knew that she didn't have much good to say to him, so there wasn't much of a point.

She was back at Estelle's with her hair and her magazine, waiting to get her hair done. She looked back at her phone, and the last incoming message was still Jayon's. She read it again, as if there was so much to the text. She pressed REPLY and began to type a message back. "I'm fine. Yourself?" she sent. Unsure if she should have responded, she was feeling nervous about her decision. She hadn't had a pleasant conversation with Jayon in over a month. She tried to begin reading her magazine as if she wasn't counting the seconds that it took him to reply. Finally, her phone vibrated in her lap. She looked at it, and it was Jayon's reply. "That's great to hear. I'm doing ok. Would be much better if me and you could sit down and talk."

Jordan wasn't quite ready for all that, and she was surprised he jumped right to the point like that without warming up or feeling her out yet. It actually angered Jordan some that he thought it was just that simple. Had he forgotten what he had done to her? At that moment, she regretted that she'd even replied to him in the first place. "I'm not ready for that, Jayon. Good you're doing ok. Take care," she typed back and sent.

Jordan realized that she couldn't hold this heavy heart forever, and she had to eventually let go. She hadn't been to church, and her mother reminded her that she needed to attend, now more than ever. Jordan made up her mind that that was just what she was going to do. After she sat there for a bit reading her magazine, Jayon replied. "I understand, Jordan, but I am hoping soon we can just sit down and talk. That's all I'm asking. But I'll hit you up later. Have a good night." Jordan read it and knew that she wasn't responding, and he must have known as well.

A few hours later, Jordan was tired of sitting in that uncomfortable chair, and she was dying to stretch out. She was done with her magazine, didn't have a book on her, and was bored. She decided to call Marcus. The phone rang four times, and a man answered.

"Hello, can I speak to Marcus?" Jordan asked.

"You have the wrong number, and not to be rude, but can you have Marcus notify his friends? I've been getting calls all day for him."

Jordan looked at her phone to make sure she'd dialed the number that she had for Marcus all along. It read his name in her phone, and it was the number she had been using for him since day one.

"OK, will do. Sorry," she said.

She hung up the phone very confused, but she figured Marcus would just explain it to her later. So instead of dwelling on it, Jordan decided to watch the television show Estelle had on. It was something Jordan had never seen before, but it was better than just sitting there daydreaming.

Less than an hour later, Jordan's hair was done, and she was looking ten times better, and feeling much better too. She paid Estelle, hopped in her car, and went home to her empty house.

37

Jordan was actually excited to go out on this date with Marcus. He had called and suggested going to catch a movie. The new Will Smith movie had come out and Marcus apparently remembered how much Jordan loved Will Smith and suggested they go see it. It was Saturday, and Jordan had spent most of the day cleaning up. Jason was coming back home next week, and she wanted the house to be nice and sparkly clean for him. Hours had gone by, and Jordan had cleaned the kitchen, all three bathrooms, and her bedroom. She was about to straighten up in the living room and dining room when she got a phone call from Tayese.

She wondered if she should answer. She didn't really know what to say to her, even if she was calling to apologize. Jordan had been through a whole lot with her emotions, and having a friend who she once respected say the things that Tayese had said hurt Jordan. Although there may have been some truth to what Tayese said, as a friend, she could have said it differently. Jordan decided that she would speak to her at a later time and didn't answer her phone.

Jordan went ahead and finished cleaning up the living room and the dining room, then went upstairs to start getting ready for her date. She put on a sea green button-down shirt, some high-waist dark blue jeans, and her brown boots with the sea green buttons. She applied her Mac makeup and combed down her wrap, applied some Dr. Miracles hair oil, and in less than an hour she was ready and looking fabulous. Marcus had called and said he would be there shortly, so Jordan went downstairs to put on her brown leather jacket and wait on the porch.

Marcus pulled up in a black Range Rover—a car that Jordan hadn't seen before. Jordan walked toward the car with a smile on her face, excited to see Marcus. With all the dirt she had been doing, she wondered if he knew about her actions lately and if he would still be interested. She got in the car and sat down, and Marcus immediately turned the music lower. He didn't give her a kiss or hug, he just patted her leg and said, "What's up?"

"I'm good, sir," she said as she buckled up.

Moments later they were riding on the Cross Island Parkway listening to Common's new album. He had been telling her how good it was, and now was his chance to let her hear for herself. Marcus was bopping his head along to every beat coming through the speaker; you could tell he was loving the music. Jordan listened to the album carefully, and she had to admit it was pretty good. She had been a Common fan for years, but she had heard mixed reviews about his latest effort. She was happy to hear he was still staying true to himself.

Marcus pulled off the exit and drove down the road toward the movie theater. Jordan felt her phone vibrating and looked to see who it was. It was Donovan; he was calling from his cell phone. Jordan had been tempted to speak to him since her and Tayese's argument, but she refrained. Although she would never accept him as a client at this point, she tried to show restraint in cursing him out. When she thought about it, she figured he may be flattered if she cared enough to call. Just seeing his name on her phone, she wanted to pick up and give him a piece of her mind. But with Marcus sitting right there, she knew she couldn't go that route. So once again, Jordan let her phone go to voice mail.

The movie was good; Jordan really enjoyed it. She and Marcus walked to the car still talking about the movie, the stuff that was hot, and what confused them. It had been a while since Jordan had been on a real date, especially one where she was enjoying herself as she was now. Marcus suggested they go grab a bite to eat before they headed back home, and Jordan agreed. They drove a few blocks away to Benihana and went inside. Once they got inside, Marcus excused himself to go to the bathroom. While Jordan sat at the table alone, she decided to go ahead and check her voice mail.

There were few messages from her family, and then one from a colleague. The next message was from Tayese. She seemed to not be upset. However, her message was quite disturbing.

"Hi, Jordan. I was calling to apologize for what I said to you the other day. I understand that you're going through a lot right now, and you aren't all that happy. I, as a friend, should understand misery causes us to make mistakes. I spoke to Donovan, and he said that nothing happened between the two of you in the hotel that night. I don't know what's true. Maybe you just didn't want me to have him, or maybe he is lying. Either way, I forgive you."

Jordan couldn't believe she was making it seem like she was some basket case. She was so pissed off, and she couldn't believe that Donovan said that lie. The next message was from Donovan.

"Hey, Jordan. It's me, Donovan. I wanted to talk to you about my corporation papers, so if you can give me a call I'd appreciate it. By the way, I spoke to Tayese; she told me some of what's going on. There must be some kind of misunderstanding. Sorry about everything."

Jordan was shocked at the nerve of him to be so bold and leave a message like everything was all right. Jordan didn't even want to eat anymore; all she wanted to do was get home so she could call both of them and clear some stuff up. Marcus returned from the bathroom.

"Are you OK?" he asked.

At that moment, Jordan wished that Marcus was Jayon. If he had been, she could tell him exactly what was wrong with her. She could just get it off her chest because he was her friend first. She didn't know how Marcus would judge her or if what he would say would just make her more upset, so instead she just shrugged it off.

"Nothing," she said.

She wanted to rush home at first, but after a Malibu pineapple on the rocks and some conversation, she changed her mind. She figured why should she let the negativity ruin her night. These days she needed to sit back with some good company and enjoy herself without having to feel ashamed afterward.

The more time went by, the more charming Marcus seemed. He was funny, smart, successful, and tastefully good-looking. If Jordan didn't have so many reasons to not be interested in a relationship, he would surely be the ideal candidate. Jordan may not have been fully honest with herself, because she did have some feelings for Marcus. She just knew they couldn't be much of anything because she couldn't afford to let the relationship grow into much more. She wanted to focus on her son, she wasn't ready to open her heart again, and she definitely wasn't willing to trust again. Until she could get her heart and home in order, she was better off just keeping her feelings contained.

38

"J, you are a grown woman. I understand that, but we are really worried about you," Chrasey said.

Jordan couldn't even defend herself. She knew that they had every reason to be worried. Hell, she was worried.

"I'm fine, guys," she finally replied.

Jordan, Chrasey, and Dakota were sitting on the plush couch in Jordan's living room for the first time in a very long time. During the Jayon days, they didn't visit that much.

"Jordan, you are not being yourself lately, and I don't think that you are evaluating your actions at all," Chrasey said.

"J, listen. You know I am the first to tell you that you live once. Even I can say you're bugging out," Dakota said.

"So now even Dakota . . . queen of living in the moment, thinks I am having too much fun," Jordan said.

"I don't even do things like that anymore, Jordan. We are getting older, and we all have children to think about," Dakota replied, a bit defensive. Before Jordan or Chrasey could respond, she added, "And you're not having fun and you know it. You are just making yourself hate yourself."

Jordan lost it. Tears began to roll down her face. Chrasey hit Dakota in code for "What you had to go and do that for?"

"No, she's right," Jordan whimpered.

"Jordan, no one is saying that you are doing anything wrong. We just don't want you to—" Chrasey said.

"No, I am wrong," Jordan interjected. "I have really been trying to just let go, to stop caring so much, but the truth is I do still care, and I am playing myself."

"You are supposed to care, Jordan," Chrasey said.

Dakota saw the look on Jordan's face hadn't lightened up any, and so she tried to make her statement in another way. "Jordan, I know that being free can be fun. I did it for how many years, and if I wasn't too tired with Alijah, I'd probably still be running the street. But I know you, Jordan, and this isn't you. This is going to be something you regret. I know Jayon hurt you—" Dakota was interrupted by Jordan's reaction at that point.

Jordan was shaking her head and finally spoke. "You have no idea. I haven't even dealt with that yet."

"What do you mean?" Chrasey asked as tears fell from Jordan's face.

Dakota stood up to grab a tissue from the Kleenex box on the end table.

"I can't even think about him or what he did to me without feeling a pain in the depth of my soul, and so I don't think about it. I try to erase it like it never happened," Jordan said as she tried to dry her face.

"But you know what, J, you are trying to erase it by replacing it with other men, and you more than anybody knows that is not going to work."

"I'm not trying to replace it with men. I don't want these men or anything from them. I'm sick of men," Jordan blurted out.

"Jordan, you barely had men. You have been with more men these past few weeks than you have your whole life," Dakota said, laughing.

Her smart but true comment broke the tension, because all three of the ladies were laughing for a second. Chrasey began to rub Jordan's back.

"You are going to be OK, Jordan. You have everything you can ask for. Your love life just fell apart these past few years, and you are a little shaken. You are not the first, and you are not the last. You will be fine, with or without a man. All I'm asking is that you don't lose yourself just because you lost him," Chrasey said.

Jordan's eyebrows raised when she heard those last words.

"Don't lose myself just because I lost him," Jordan repeated. "That's deep," Jordan added.

"Don't tell her that. She already thinks she is Dr. Phil or something," Dakota said.

"Shut up," Chrasey said with a chuckle.

Chrasey stood up and headed out of the living room. "I'll be right back. Going to use the bathroom," she said.

Jordan remained and tried to pull herself back together. She was upset with herself for getting to this place, but at the same time she was happy she had her girls to bring her back to reality.

"I appreciate you guys coming over tonight," Jordan said to Dakota.

"Please, we had no choice. It was either this or find your raped body somewhere. You're playing with your life, and I can't have that. I've been down that road many of times, many, and I was built for it. You are not."

"I am too built for it; you see my weight's up, right?" Jordan said with a smirk.

"Please, girl, and you see you're over there crying like a baby too. You've never seen me cry over getting some pipe unless it was because it was good to me."

Jordan burst out laughing. "You are a nut," she said.

Chrasey was walking back in the living room at that point. "What's so funny?"

"Dakota was telling me how I'm not built for this behavior and she is."

"Jordan, you are not. You are thirty-four and had been with three guys before your little splurge. One before your husband, your husband, and one after. You think you're built to be jumping in and out of people's beds?" Chrasey asked while putting her hand on her hip.

Jordan just put her head down with a grin. She knew that they had a point.

"It's that damn Tayese. She got you thinking you're doing what you're supposed to do by moving on this way," Chrasey added.

"No, it's not her. I just don't feel like having rules anymore. For what? Where has it gotten me? Nowhere. I have been strict and moralized for nothing."

"For you, Jordan, that's for what," Chrasey snapped. "What's wrong with having your rules and morals strictly for yourself?"

"They are for me. They can't be for no one else, because no one agrees with them but me. You both have told me to give my stuff up many of times, said I hold on too tight. No one applauds it; I get knocked or get judged. So it's only for me."

"So then, that's it. Let the men come and go, but you do what you are happy with," Chrasey added.

Dakota was just sitting back listening. She knew she had been a home wrecker and was recovering from promiscuity herself. She wasn't going to sit there and be too hypocritical.

"Did you know that Jayon told me once I think I'm better than everyone?" Jordan asked Dakota.

Dakota started to laugh. "I think you told me that story."

"I commented on this girl we knew who'd had sex with this guy within a few days of meeting him. He got all defensive, saying how it was unnecessary that I would just say that about her for no reason and all this; and then he said 'you think you're better than everybody.'" Jordan's neck was turning with each word as she used a "can you believe him?" tone.

"You *are* a little bougie," Dakota said.

"Whatever. We all have an opinion, and we are entitled to them. Somebody in the church thinks they are better than me because I don't go to church three times a week and I got a divorce and so on. It's no different. We all try to be the best we can in an area. It can be morally, workwise, or overall. Either way, if you are trying to be better, you think that you are better than someone in some area. That's each person's own opinion."

"That's true, but can we let this go?" Chrasey said out of nowhere.

Dakota looked over, confused as to what was wrong with the topic.

"Jordan will go on about this forever. She was pissed off when he said it then, and she has never let it go. I don't want to hear about it anymore," Chrasey said to Dakota.

"Forget you too," Jordan said to Chrasey. Then she looked over to Dakota and added, "I used to tell your butt you were a slut too."

"Whatever. Well, now you are one too," Dakota jabbed.

Chrasey started laughing, and so did Dakota. After Jordan gave Dakota her evil eye, she began to snicker as well.

"I hate you both. Supposed to be making me feel better, not worse."

"Hey, you want to be grown. You want to screw your neighbor in a day, sleep with clients, meet people in cabs and bring them home. You a big girl now; you can take it," Dakota said.

"Leave her alone," Chrasey interjected.

"Listen, I am not proud of my recent behavior, I am not.

But I can't say I regret it, either. I know it's pathetic, but it has been the one thing that has kept me from going over and popping Jayon's tires and egging his house."

"Honestly, you probably would've been better off doing that. It would've just been out of your system and you could have taken time to cope and move on. This way you're going about it is only prolonging the whole situation. You are giving Jayon a lot more power than he deserves."

Once again, touching on the topic of Jayon brought Jordan to tears.

"I walked away from my marriage for him. I loved that man with every piece of me. I would've done absolutely anything for him, and he wasn't my husband nor did we have a child together. I just loved him, for who he was. I loved him since the day I met him," Jordan poured out.

"We know," Chrasey said.

"I have heard everything from 'he is just a man, it doesn't matter he didn't love you' to 'that girl probably didn't mean a thing to him,' but you know what, it doesn't matter. I didn't ask for much at all, but I gave all that I had. If he was capable of cheating on me—not once but twice—risking bringing me an STD, and lying to me in my face over and over again, I could never forgive him. It just hurts so badly."

"I know. No one thought Jayon was that type of guy."

"That's my point. There's no way to tell, so why bother. It's easier to just love them and leave them than stick around to get hurt."

"Jordan, stop it. You are doing it again. You can't think you're getting Jayon back with this. He doesn't know nor does he care. He is doing the same thing, but he is OK with it. You, you need to stay your butt home and take care of Jason. You are going to get hurt if you keep this nonsense up," Chrasey said, seeming frustrated.

"I am going to stop sleeping with these guys. I will. I admit that it's not helping anything, because no matter how good the sex is, I still feel just as awful the next day," Jordan said.

"J, deal with this Jayon thing. Move past it. Talk to him, burn his memories, do what you have to do. But you can't just internalize all that pain and anger, because you, as you see, are only hurting yourself, and he doesn't deserve that. He was a good friend to you once, but he is not worth all this drama," Dakota said.

Jordan finally just took it all in and didn't respond. These were her girls anyway; she knew they were only telling her what was best for her. It just always seemed easier than it actually was, to just move on and let it go. She had moved on, but letting it go wasn't quite as easy. Sitting there on that couch, Jordan knew that her whirlwind of one-night stands and rule breaking didn't prove anything. It didn't prove that Jayon lost a good thing; it didn't prove she could live without him; and it damn sure didn't prove she was a strong and successful woman who didn't need anyone. All she was doing was showing just the opposite, and she realized then, with her friends giving her a dose of real talk, that in order to move on she had to gain her self-esteem back and say a big fat "f— you" to Jayon. That was exactly what she planned to do.

39

Enough was enough. Jordan walked inside her house and all she could see was her reflection in the mirror in the foyer. She didn't even want to look at herself, so she quickly looked away. She walked directly into her living room, dropped her purse on the couch, and went upstairs to her bedroom.

She was still devastated by what had happened today, and she had just been waiting to get home and be alone. This was one of the few nights she was happy that Jason wasn't home yet. She just dropped on the bed. There were clothes and different objects on her bed that didn't belong. There were lotion bottles, cocoa butter, and panty hose she decided against when she was getting ready in the morning, and she just scooted them over as she sprawled out on the bed. She just lay there staring at the wall and all the black-and-white photos hanging up beside her bed. She looked carefully at each one and tried to remember what made her decide to choose those very pictures. One was of a black woman holding a child, and Jordan instantly thought of the way she thought having a child would be what fulfilled her life the most. She started remembering how happy she was when she got pregnant, how she felt like her life was finally about to begin. Then as she thought about how much Jason had grown, and how much her life had changed since he was born, she remembered her scare last year. She thought about when she thought she was pregnant last year by Jayon, and all the emotions that ran through her body at the time, and the emotions he pretended to have.

The beep from her alarm clock broke Jordan's train of thought. She looked over at her Sony CD alarm clock, and it was 9:00 PM. It beeped every hour. She thought to herself that she should get up, get undressed, and call her son to tell him good night. She wasn't pleased with herself; the charade had finally come to an end. She'd told herself these past weeks that she was able to handle this, but on the inside it was killing her. She couldn't lie to herself anymore. She tried, but she knew that it wasn't working for her. Those nights lying alone in her bed became more and more difficult, realizing how she was throwing her self-respect away because she was too weak to deal with what happened with Jayon. In the beginning, she told herself it had nothing to do with him and everything to do with her. She told herself that she was tired of living by rules, that they got her nowhere but divorced and alone.

The more Jordan thought about it, the angrier she got at Jayon. She was mad at herself, but he was to blame for throwing her life into this whirlwind. Before he did what he did, well before he got caught, her life was as it should be. She still believed in herself and that her morals were valuable. She was working every day and living her life in hopes of one day enjoying marriage with him, her son Jason, and hopefully more kids. He claimed that they were going to get engaged this year, but he had been saying that for years, that he was ready to get married, and nothing ever came of it. Jordan just wanted to believe that they were meant to be, and when things were bad they would get better. She never considered that he might turn out to be like any other doggish man. Not her Jayon. Not the man she knew for so long.

She was done reliving it. She had been through this in her mind a million times. She couldn't make excuses for her actions. No man should be worth your self-respect. Jayon didn't deserve that much credit, enough to erase all the self-respect that she gained in her thirty-four years on this earth. Yet, she had sex with more men in the past month and a half than she had in all her years before then. She knew each guy was taking a piece of her with them, but at the time, the way she was feeling, she didn't want the pieces anyway. That was until today, when she realized that that was not the woman she wanted to be, regardless. It was about that time for her to truly face the situation like a grown woman with integrity, even if it was a bit late.

Jordan was still extremely upset that things played out the way they did. She knew her rule never to see a client on a personal level wasn't just one of her rules—there was meaning to it. She was never single long enough to think the rule through, but she had gotten it from somewhere. Jordan made that a rule when one of her old colleagues, Cheryl, told her about how it bit her in the butt, and now Jordan was going through the same thing. Her colleague's situation was a little different, but it still would've been avoided if she didn't date clients. This woman was seeing her client when one day she bumped into some woman who caused the guy to start pretending it was a business lunch. By the time Cheryl caught on, the woman had introduced herself as his wife. It was hard for Cheryl not to react in a surprised and displeased manner, which was probably what led the wife to snoop. Sure enough, three days later, the client called to say that he was going to hire another lawyer, and so were the three other referrals he had given her. Cheryl lost her boyfriend and four substantial clients, and she couldn't even call to curse him out, because it was unethical according to the bar in the first place. One complaint from his wife and she would have to appear before the American Bar Association and it wasn't worth all of that.

Jordan's mistake didn't affect her pockets just yet, but it was affecting her reputation, and at one point that meant more to Jordan than anything in the world. Darren had called the office today and asked if he could come by that evening, but since he requested an evening meeting, Jordan lied and said she was busy and out of the office all afternoon until the next day. She didn't want Darren thinking her office was some late-night motel all of a sudden. She wasn't feeling him like that anyway. He was a fine, successful brother that technically would've been a great catch, but Jordan wasn't ready just yet to be looking at anyone for more than a little fun. Her heart was still broken, and her attitude toward men was still very much tainted. It was going to take more than looks and money to get her nose open wide. Someone was going to have to come real correct. She didn't think anything of her lie, until she was finishing up some paperwork and her assistant informed her that the next client was already there.

Gerome, Darren's partner, came walking in with his cell phone to his ear moments later.

"Yeah, she is here. She is just dodging you," he said as he walked in.

Jordan forgot that she had an appointment with him scheduled for six, way after the time she told Darren she would be gone. Gerome ended the phone call quickly, as if that's all Darren was waiting to find out.

"My man said you're dodging him, and there's nothing to be afraid of," Gerome said as he sat down.

Jordan could tell that Gerome knew what had happened, and it made her feel real cheap to know she was the subject of someone's sex tales. She tried to carry on like there was nothing to it, but the way Gerome kept licking his lips and looking at her, it felt as if he thought it was his turn. She wanted to know what exactly Darren told him and how he portrayed her. It didn't really matter, though. Just the simple fact she did what she did with him, with no relationship at hand, on her desk, and hadn't spoke to him since, probably said enough. Wham, Bam, Thank you, Ma'am. The ma'am that Jordan never wanted to be.

The entire time Gerome was there for the meeting, Jordan felt like a piece of meat. He was treating her totally different, and the professionalism for the meeting was totally not present. He kept saying things like "you know what I'm saying," and "fo real though." It was like he was trying to have his club swagger on versus the normal business man persona he was usually in there with. He complimented her more than once, and all in all it was making Jordan uncomfortable. She wasn't sure if Darren told him to get a piece for himself and that she was easy and just to press her, or if he was trying on his own based on knowing that she gave it up to his boy so quickly.

When the meeting was finally over with Gerome, her assistant brought her messages in. She looked through them really quickly, and the message from Marcus was overshadowed when she read the message that Darren left that read, "I'm jealous." What was she thinking? She had to ask herself. This wasn't somebody that she could just avoid without considering the income that she'd be losing. For all she knew, Gerome may get upset because he couldn't get some action and still try to pull their account. She knew she wasn't about to have sex with either of them just for their account, but she also didn't know how much longer she could act normal when she knew what the two of them were thinking.

40

Jayon had reached out a few times in the past few weeks, but he hadn't reached out in over a week. Jordan didn't know what else to say to him, so she hadn't bothered to respond. She had so many things she wanted to say to him, but she didn't think it made sense considering he should have known how she felt about him. There were several times she laid in the bed and just cried. The life that she had known for years and years had vanished. Some of the things that she had done in the last month she could never take back, and that's what hurt more than anything.

It was the first time in days that Jordan didn't find herself wondering what Jayon was up to, if he was seeing someone, or if he was feeling any of the pain and regret that she was. She wouldn't admit it to herself that what got to her the most was the thought of Jayon wifing up Randi. She told herself it didn't matter and that she could have him, but the reality was that Jayon was a man that had once owned her heart entirely, and the thought of him being with another woman didn't sit well with her. She wasn't that strong. Not strong enough not to care about him at all. She heard from his cousin that he seemed to be going through it too, but she couldn't tell if his cousin was just saying that to make her feel better. The only choice Jordan had was to not care, to ignore all her thoughts of Jayon, to ignore all her feelings of pain, and to erase all her memories of joy with him.

While cleaning up a few days ago, Jordan had stumbled upon a scrapbook she had made memorializing their relationship. As soon as she turned to the first page, she paused. She wasn't sure if she was emotionally ready to take that ride down memory lane, but she did. She wanted, just for a moment, to pretend that things were still good, but by the time she got midway through the book, her face was drenched in tears. The smiles and laughs on their faces cut her deep inside her heart. And in every picture, when she looked into his eyes, all she could see and feel was deceit. Before she could finish looking through the book, she was filled with so much anger she had to close it. She went to the bathroom, wiped up her tears, and quickly threw her armor back on. She was upset with herself for even shedding another tear over that piece of feces, as she referred to him lately.

That was then. Today, Jordan was spending the day with herself and her masseuse. She had booked a spa day at Bliss, and she was looking forward to it something awful. She wished she had done this a month prior. Maybe she could have cleared her mind and handled her breakup with Jayon a lot better. Jordan didn't like to admit that she was heartbroken, she didn't want to give him that much credit, but she couldn't convince herself enough to make that pain go away. She was hoping, though, that a long day of pampering would help her.

By the time she got to the salon, there were already two people waiting in the lobby. Jordan was ten minutes early for her appointment, so she refused to wait any longer than her appointment start time. She didn't have the patience for any extra stress; she was there to relieve all the stress she came with. The lady sitting behind the counter could barely be seen, as she was being blocked by a bonsai plant on the counter. Jordan walked up to the counter to get her attention.

"Jordan. I have an eleven o'clock appointment," she said to the Asian lady behind the counter.

"OK, take a seat. Someone will be right with you," the lady replied.

Jordan looked at her watch as though to let the lady know that she was on top of the time before she stepped away. She sat on the blue plush couch directly across from the receptionist area to prevent her from being out of sight and out of mind. She'd heard about Bliss, and she knew it was popular and the appointments were hard to get. She wasn't trying to have to wait until after these two other women were done with their services. She was on time and wasn't waiting. She made sure she looked at her watch when the woman sitting beside her looked at her as if to also let her know that time was of the essence.

Jordan got distracted by her trivial concern when her BlackBerry vibrated in her purse. She was dressed in a brown Juicy Couture sweatsuit, so she was carrying her pink and brown Juicy tote bag, which had a cell phone compartment. Without looking, Jordan reached into the purse and pulled out her phone. On the screen was an e-mail from Jayon. She couldn't believe it. As soon as she was on to something else, here he was. It was like he knew when she wasn't thinking about him, and he had to remind her that he was still out there.

"Hey Jordan, I was thinking about you. I really wish we could talk. It's a shame two old best friends can't even have a cordial conversation. I'd love to talk to you, call me. Jay."

Jordan sat there staring at the phone, reading the e-mail multiple times as if she was looking for some cryptic message. She was surprised that Jayon still bothered to reach out to her; she thought he would have given up by now. He wasn't the type to show emotions, and he definitely wasn't big on showing weakness. Jordan was flattered in a small way that he cared so much that he hadn't given up on her. It made her feel like maybe he did truly love her all that time, that maybe everything he said wasn't a lie.

A short African American woman came from the back and stood in the entryway. She smiled at Jordan and reached her hand out.

"Hi, I'm Zakiya. I will be giving you your massage today."

"Thanks, I'm Jordan," she replied as she shook the lady's hand.

They walked toward the back of the spa, and Jordan looked around at all the soothing pictures on the wall and tried to let the sounds of the waterfalls begin to relax her. There were various spa products on all the shelves in the hallway, and Jordan was already expecting them to try to make her buy some. She had already made up her mind that she wasn't going to get talked into buying any products that she didn't need. She was trying to curtail her impulse shopping, especially since the other day one of her credit cards was declined when she thought she had the available credit. Jordan told herself when she left her other credit cards at home that she was there to get some pampering and relax, not to shop. She knew that although she was there to clear her mind, most of her massage was going to be spent thinking of what Jayon had said to her now that he'd suddenly reached out. Damn him, why couldn't he have sent that earlier in the week or later today. He just had to send it right at that very moment, when the last thing she wanted to think more about was him.

Jordan was undressed and lying on the table with her face in the open ring. There was warmth in the room that relaxed Jordan the instant she stepped inside. She knew once she was cuddled in her plush white robe that she'd made the right decision. Zakiya began rubbing her back and working out the kinks that she was masterfully finding. Before long, Jordan was thinking through her life, and of course the situation with Jayon and how it caused so much grief and so many changes. Jordan was tired—physically, mentally and emotionally. The past month and change had been such an emotional roller coaster that she felt like she had been through four years of letdowns all in one glimpse.

Maybe she was being unrealistic to think that she could just move on that easily. Maybe she was lying to herself all this time that she was so strong and didn't need any man. At the end of the day, everybody needs somebody, and Jordan was no different. She had been head over heels in love, and it was easier to shelter herself than admit that she was still just as vulnerable as she was from the start. She didn't even consider admitting to anyone that she actually considered forgiving Jayon. Most of her pain stemmed from him putting her in a position where she couldn't just forgive him and move on. Thing was, deep down, more than anything Jordan wanted her life back the way it was, back when she woke up with a smile on her face because she was in love with her best friend. She knew it was weak to still have feelings for a man who had betrayed her so much, and she knew that was the reason that she couldn't face her feelings, because her feelings were all wrong.

41

The crazy thing was that Jordan's every reason for never being the loose party girl growing up was all coming full circle now that she was a grown woman. She never wanted to be that chick that guys talked about what they did with her, and she never wanted someone she cared about to hear through the grapevine about any dirt that she did. She never really expected any of those things to really be a possibility at her age. Dealing with Gerome and Darren was one thing, but this was a whole different story.

Jordan had just gotten home and decided to check her voice mail on her cell phone. The third message was from Jayon, and she didn't even know that he called. The message said, "Word. You out there wildin' like that? You slept with my boys Darren and Shakai. What, you the jump-off now? Not a good look, J, not a good look at all."

Jordan wanted to throw her cell phone at the wall she was so mad. What the hell part of the game was this? Jayon could sneak around for months and she didn't find out, she gets hers for a couple of weeks and her ex finds out just like that? Besides, who was he to say it wasn't a good look? He had no say whatsoever. She wanted to call him and curse him out for even leaving that message, but she knew she wasn't able to change the focus that easily. At first Jordan was happy he knew. The spite in her wanted him to know that he no longer had her heart. But deep down, she didn't want him to find out that much, not to where she was looking like a jump-off.

Jordan was still sitting on her couch in her nightshirt, thinking about it, when her phone rang. She looked down and it was Jayon. She looked at the phone while it rang two times in her hand. Jordan thought about how he called her a jump-off and, instantly upset, she considered not answering. At the same time, she figured that there was a chance that hearing his boys talk about her that way may not have been too fun. For seconds she had debated with herself about answering the phone, and by the fourth ring, she went ahead and answered.

"Hello?" she answered.

"Hello, Jordan," he said.

He seemed surprised that she actually answered.

"What, Jayon?" she said.

"You have an attitude, Jordan? I should be the one with the attitude," he said, sounding pissed off.

The nerve of him, Jordan thought to herself. Did he forget they weren't together?

"You? Really? Jayon, I wasn't even going to answer your damn phone call. I don't owe you shit. We are not together."

"So that means you go around fucking everybody I know?"

"Jayon, don't flatter yourself. Shakai and Darren had nothing to do with you. I didn't know they knew you, and I would've never been with them if I had known that."

Jayon didn't seem to expect that answer. It's like he really thought Jordan went around interviewing people to see if they knew him before she got with them.

Jordan wanted to ask him how he knew them, but she didn't want to show her concern or any weakness.

"I don't have to answer to you, Jayon," Jordan said.

"J, for real. This isn't you. What are you doing?"

Jordan didn't know what to say to that at first.

"You are not only embarrassing me, you're embarrassing yourself. Shakai and Darren know each other too; that's how it got back to me. This shit ain't cute, not in the least bit," Jayon's voice went from concerned to pissed off again.

"Thanks for your concern, but I'm a grown woman. I know how to handle myself."

"Do you? Did you when you woke up hung over with Shakai in your bed and had to ask him if y'all used protection?"

Shit! What did this boy tell him? Everything? Guys talk worse than girls.

"Jayon, I have to go."

"What, you got someone else waiting on you in the bed?"

Jordan slammed the phone down. What the hell was she supposed to say to that? She didn't even know why she answered the phone. When Jayon and Jordan were together, he had this exasperating way of trying to ignore away a problem. Whenever she wanted to talk about an issue that was bothering her, he would rather not respond or discuss it. It drove Jordan crazy, but after years of knowing him, whenever he felt like shutting down, he would without giving any courtesy to how she was feeling. It was one of the issues in their relationship that Jordan wondered if she could tolerate forever. Now she was using his own trick. She had no desire to talk to him about this matter, and so she wasn't.

She could feel herself fuming on the inside. How dare he talk to her that way? She wanted to just give him a full-blown, raw cursing out, but she knew that in reality she was looking like a whore. She had been around long enough to imagine how the guys' conversation went, and Jayon was probably too embarrassed to jump to her defense. He damn sure wasn't going to admit that she was his girl just a couple of months ago. What man wants to admit that the female he once called his wifey was known as a jump-off, especially at their age. Jordan's mind ran through all the variations of how the conversation could've gone. She tried to remember every detail of what she did with them before, during, and after. She really tried to imagine what Jayon would have thought if he was right there watching. She had to assume that he had a clear picture in his imagination anyway.

What was she to do at this point but try not to let it beat her down? Reality was that there was no way to turn back the hands of time. She did have careless sex with two men that meant absolutely nothing to her, and she was now facing the consequences. She was tired of crying, tired of beating herself up; she just had to handle the news accordingly. She would no longer be accepting Shakai's calls, and Darren she would handle professionally and inform him that she would work on his case but assign him a new attorney to correspond with it. If Darren wasn't willing to do that, then he could hire someone else. She knew that she shouldn't mix business with personal, but this was too close to home, and she had to put it behind her as soon as possible.

42

It was like old times. Jordan, Dakota, and Chrasey were sprawled out on Jordan's couches having a good old time. For the first time in a long time,their topic of conversation wasn't Jordan. Jordan was feeling much better. Ever since her spa day, when she came to terms with the root of the problem, she had been handling her feelings better.

"I actually really like *The Tyra Banks Show*," said Jordan.

"Me too. I TiVo it every day," Chrasey replied.

"Please, she is trying to be like Oprah. I can't stand the way she tries to pretend she is so righteous," Dakota replied.

"Well, who better to aspire to be than Oprah?" Jordan said.

"True, and she doesn't pretend to be righteous. She is actually very honest about how human she is," Chrasey added.

"Exactly. I wasn't always a Tyra fan, but her show really made me gain a newfound respect for her as a positive black woman," Jordan said.

"Yeah, well, I turn the channel when she is on," Dakota said.

"That's because she condemns floozies like you," Chrasey joked.

"Well, then Jordan must not like her, either," Dakota stabbed.

Instantly, Jordan rolled her eyes at the comment. Jordan wasn't really up for any jokes about her escapades. She was honest with herself and decided to put it behind her the best she could. She admitted to herself that what had been eating at her so much was not how much she hated Jayon but how much she loved him. She reminded herself who she was, and she told herself that it wasn't too late to bounce back. She fell off track, she did some unthinkable things, but she was woman enough to face that and move on. For years, her friends teased her that when she was older she would regret not having had more fun and more sexual experiences. Some of those same friends would tell her that her recent actions were just her releasing her inner desires from years past. Jordan thought about that, and she didn't agree with that theory. She was hurt and was looking for someone to heal the pain, any male attention to make her feel adequate. In reality, Jordan had to realize on her own that she was adequate, and no man could fill the void that she had inside of her.

"Don't get all sensitive on me," Dakota said. "I was just playing."

"I know. I didn't really want to talk about it, but all those risky decisions bit me in the butt big-time, and I'm finally ready to go back to the Jordan Moore that I was," Jordan said.

"What happened?" Chrasey asked.

As if Jordan hadn't been feuding with herself internally on a consistent basis, the phone call from Jayon and the things he said hit home for Jordan even more. She felt so low at that point that she knew it was time to put an end to all her spontaneity. She was tired of living the life of someone else; she wasn't comfortable with the way she was being perceived. Casual sex isn't for everybody, and going from three sex partners to seven was emotionally draining. She actually regretted having sex with every last one of them, including Marcus, even though she liked him. None of them were worth her self-worth.

"Jayon knew two of the guys I slept with, and they knew each other as well, and he called me and made me feel like trash," Jordan said.

"You spoke to Jayon?" Dakota asked in shock, as if she paid no mind to the more important part of that anecdote.

"Yes, I did. On the phone."

"Was he mad?" Chrasey said.

"I guess so, but he seemed more so disappointed."

"Damn, how did he find out?" Dakota asked.

"Guy talk, apparently. Out at a bar talking to one of the guys, and they called up the other one to tell him, and it turned out it was the same girl, "Jordan replied.

"You the chick R. Kelly was talking about in that song?" Dakota joked.

Jordan shot her a look as if to say this is not the time for comedy.

"That is so crazy. Talk about a small world," Chrasey said, trying to break the tension.

"Tell me about it. As big as New York is, two guys I deal with in the course of a month know each other and my ex. It just felt like a sign if I've ever got one," Jordan said.

"Yeah, that's definitely a telltale sign," Dakota said.

"I was already feeling like it was time to slow down once I left the spa. I did some soul searching, and I felt better about moving forward, and then two days later, I got the call from Jayon. It was like the nail in the coffin for me," Jordan said.

"So what's that mean? You're going to be celibate?" Dakota asked with her face turned up.

Jordan took the pillow beside her and tossed it at Dakota's head.

"You make me sick," Jordan said as she laughed at Dakota's yucky facial expression.

"What? I'm saying, I don't want to deal with horny Jordan," Dakota said, laughing.

"Well, I'm not going to have any more meaningless sex. I may still deal with Marcus. He and I have been more than just sex. I kind of like him."

"Yeah, I can't wait to meet this Mr. Marcus," Chrasey said.

"Every time we are over, he won't come by," Dakota said.

"I asked both times, but I don't want to push it. He says that he is busy, and I'm not his woman like that, so I'm not going to push it," Jordan said.

"It's like he is hiding or something," Dakota said with a chuckle. "He can run but he can't hide. He will eventually have to pass our tests."

Jordan laughed. She knew that Dakota wasn't lying; they were a hard group of friends to come by. They asked all the hard questions, and they didn't hold any punches, especially Dakota. As she put it, they were too old to be wasting time or playing games.

"In time, you will meet him. He is a really nice guy. I don't feel like I know much about him, but I enjoy the time we spend together. He seems pretty successful, and the sex is good," Jordan said.

"Well, he passes my test, the three Ss. Successful, Sexy, and Single," Dakota said.

"Please, since when was single a requirement for you?" Jordan said.

Chrasey burst out laughing. "Good one," she said to Jordan.

"Y'all heifers are not funny," Dakota said. "If you're speaking of my ex, Tony was single when we *first* got together."

"Yeah, and he was a first. Maybe that has some odd connection to why y'all are still together," Jordan said, laughing.

"Oh, you are just on a roll, aren't you?" Dakota said.

"I'm joking with you. Just some fun jabs back at you for all those jabs you took at me," Jordan said.

Chrasey had stood up and went over by the bar to pour herself another strawberry daiquiri.

"Pour me some too," Jordan said.

Jordan and Dakota remained sprawled out on the couch, too comfortable to move. There were two empty glasses on the table, and a bowl of potato chips and pretzels. The tray that had once been filled with quesadillas was now empty with only some leftover sour cream and salsa. The ladies weren't drunk, but the place looked like they had been partying all night, and it had only been about two hours.

"When is Jason coming home?" Dakota asked.

"Next week. Omar asked if he could stay with him a little longer," Jordan said.

"That's sweet that it's so hard to let him go. He loves his son," Chrasey said.

"Yeah, with these deadbeat dads these days, Omar is all right in my book," Dakota said.

"Especially when Keith lies around and doesn't do anything with Quinton. I wish he cared as much as Omar about fatherhood," Chrasey said.

"They all have their flaws," Jordan said. "Every last freaking one of them."

43

Jordan stepped out her door and headed to her truck. She was dressed in a sharp beige suit with a black collared shirt and some black and beige pumps. She was heading to work a little late because she was trying to avoid the rush hour traffic. She had dropped Jason off at school a couple of hours ago and heard on the radio there was traffic on the Long Island Expressway, so she decided she would go in an hour or so later.

Jordan was placing her things in her backseat when she heard a horn. She looked over her shoulder and saw Omar parked across the street in his silver Lexus truck. Jordan was surprised to see him and shut the door to the car.

"Omar?" she said as she walked toward him.

As she got closer, she could see the solemn look on his face. She became concerned as she walked up to the car window.

"What's wrong, O?"

"Nothing. You got a minute?" he asked as he pressed the button to unlock the doors.

"Sure," Jordan said as she walked around to the other side of the car to get in.

Once she sat down and closed the door behind her, she

looked over in Omar's direction. He looked like he'd had a rough night and morning, but she couldn't tell from what.

"Omar, what's wrong?"

"Nothing. I just wanted to talk to you," he replied. His voice sounded tired and weak. He wasn't exerting any energy, as if he didn't have any. He didn't seem drunk or sick at all, just weary like he hadn't slept all night.

"OK, I'm all ears," Jordan replied.

"Jordan, I'm sorry."

"For what?"

"For everything. Everything I put you through."

Jordan was speechless for a moment; she didn't know what to say.

"For not being an understanding husband, for leaving the way I did . . ." Omar's voice cracked some. Jordan looked over at him to see if her ears were deceiving her. "For that night that I came over mad and made you have sex with me. I am so sorry."

Tears had begun to stream down Omar's face, and the sight of seeing him this way and remembering that horrid night made Jordan's eyes begin to water as well.

"It's OK, Omar, I forgive you. You were going through a lot, and so was I. We both did things out of anger and emotion, and I'm sorry too. It's the past."

"That's the thing, Jordan; it's not in the past. We have a son together. Me and you are forever. Regardless of if we never spoke again, me and you are forever. For that reason alone, I owed you and our relationship so much more."

Jordan was wiping away the tears that had fallen from her eyes. Omar reached into his glove compartment and took some tissue out. He gave her one and used one to remove the evidence of his vulnerable moment.

"I can say the same, Omar. We are human. I was told by

people I should've waited for you longer before I started seeing Jayon, or when you came back I should've left Jayon. Who knows what was right. We did what we felt at the time. We can't fix that."

"That's true, but I started this mess, so I can't be mad at how you reacted without looking at me. I just up and left, wouldn't respond to your phone calls for weeks. I even ended up getting engaged to another woman. I had a lot of fault in it, and I know that."

Jordan was pleased to hear Omar reflect in such a mature way, but she was confused as to why almost two years later he was saying these things to her.

"Omar, we are both at fault. I must admit though, I am confused. Where is this coming from?"

"I just wanted you to know that I'm sorry. I was up all night packing up Elisa's stuff 'cause we broke off the engagement last week."

Jordan's mouth dropped open. "Really, I didn't know."

"Yeah, it's not going to work. She was there when I was going through all that mess trying to let go of you, and I tried to create something that wasn't there. I tried to re-create something that was unique."

Jordan was sitting there in shock. *Wow, Omar is single again*, she was thinking. She hadn't conceived the idea of him and her in so long. They had gone so far and left so suddenly, she never thought they would or could get things back right.

"Omar, you sure you aren't looking for comfort in me to get you through trying to get over her?"

"No, Jordan. I knew you would think that, and that's why I didn't want to tell you we weren't together. I have been thinking this way for a while now; I just knew it wasn't respectful to Elisa to tell you."

"It wouldn't have been disrespectful to tell me sorry."

"Well, I told you sorry, but disrespectful to come talk to you and tell you how much sorrow I felt and how much I still loved you."

The words just rolled off his tongue, but to Jordan they were like bricks falling on her. She looked down right away, as if she was too afraid to make eye contact with him and see exactly what he was saying. He didn't say "still in love with you," so she figured she could brush it off.

"I'm not only telling you this because I am no longer with her. For the most part, I'm no longer with her because I felt this way. I realized that I'm better off never getting married again if I don't feel the love I felt the first time around, because if that didn't work, nothing short of that will."

Jordan knew that he was right about that. It had crossed her mind before. She didn't know Elisa well, but Jordan knew that she was everything Omar wanted in a wife, and Elisa wasn't anything like her. She wondered just how much he would be willing to substitute, and when the substitute version would not be enough anymore. It was a thought, but after a while, the longer it lasted, she just figured it would be what it was. She figured that he was just settling, making the best of a bad situation. Now here he was sitting in front of her house deciding to stop and look at the big picture.

Jordan knew she couldn't be too judgmental about it, because she had just been through the same thing. She had spent months in denial as she tried to cope with the pain from her and Jayon's breakup, and it wasn't until after she stopped and looked at reality she realized how she was doing things all wrong. She understood, and she respected his honesty and willingness to be vulnerable and tell her. She knew Jayon would have never exposed his emotions like this if he was in the same situation, and she had to be impressed by Omar's manhood to do so.

For a few moments they just sat there silent. They said nothing to one another, and they looked out of their respective windows as if they were each trying to find the right thing to say next.

"Jordan, I didn't come over here so you and I could make some drastic change in our relationship. I just felt like this was the best time to tell you," Omar started back.

"Eleven o'clock in the morning on a Wednesday before work?" Jordan said with a laugh.

"No, just now, period. I knew if I didn't just do it while I was thinking about it so hard, I may not ever, so I just came over here. But what I meant was, now while I'm single and you're single. So if there is a chance that me and you can fix things, we better do it now. I waited too long last time; I didn't want to do that again."

"Jayo . . . I mean, Omar; you have been broken up a week."

Jordan really tried to pretend that slipup didn't happen. She tried to keep going, but his facial expression and looking away showed that he heard it loud and clear.

"I'm sorry, Omar, that was a mistake. Trust me, he is like my worst enemy, so don't be bothered by that slipup."

"Well, that's right where I'd want him, as your worst enemy," Omar said.

When Jordan saw the smirk on his face, she laughed at his ability to make light of a touchy topic.

"My point is, Omar, you just left Elisa. You and her may work things out. And even though I know that me and Jayon are over, I'm not ready to give my all to a relationship. Not right now. I need some me time."

"I'm not looking for a relationship, Jordan. Don't misunderstand me. I'm looking for me and you to be adults and raise our child and focus on what we started."

"That sounds like a relationship," Jordan said and laughed.

"No, I don't mean that way."

"Well, look, Jason is my first priority right now and forever. I want another child one day, but that may never happen. I would've liked to grow old with someone, but that may not happen, either. But right now, I've been through so much emotionally these past few years, I don't want to commit to anything but myself and my child."

"That's what I want to hear."

"Who knows, if you stay single, and I stay single we can try this again. I am willing to do that. I did vow till death do us part. Our little break won't hurt nobody."

Omar laughed. "Little break? Yeah, right."

"Well, in the scheme of life, it was a little break."

"That sounds fair to me," Omar said. "That's all I want right now. I'm hoping we can rebuild our friendship and hopefully one day pick up where we left off."

"We will leave it in God's hands."

"Are you seeing someone?"

Omar caught her off guard with that question. Apparently he could tell from her facial expression that she was, because he didn't wait for her answer.

"I guess that's a yes."

"No, that's not a yes," she said with a slight grin. "Nobody, really."

"I thought you just said that you weren't checking for nobody right now, you needed 'me time,'" Omar said, putting quotation fingers up.

"He is not someone I'm checking for. He is just some guy that I've been hanging with, just as friends. He is more my friendly neighbor."

"Well, you know how that 'friend' stuff goes," he said.

Jordan realized that she couldn't use that anymore. Friends

equated to something a lot worse in Omar's eyes. Jordan could never be trusted with a friend again.

"You know what, Omar, I never told you this, but I remember one time when we were going through the drama over Jayon and I asked you to be honest with me. I asked you if you thought I was messing around with him when me and you were together, and you said no. That made me not only respect you more for your honesty, but I thanked you for saying that. You could've said yes just to make me feel like crap, but you were honest about it, and I never told you how much that meant to me. It was one thing that we were going through all that, and the guilt trip was nauseating, but if you would've thought that I was cheating on you because that is what it looked like, I would've been even more devastated."

Omar didn't respond. He seemed like he was thinking about it.

"You want to go grab a bite?" Jordan asked.

"I thought you were going to work," Omar said.

"I was, but at this point it's becoming more senseless. Especially since I was picking up Jason from school today and he has an early let out today."

"You sure?"

"Yeah, but I do have to stop at the law office on Merrick Road to consult a client in like two hours if I'm not going in."

"What do you mean?"

"I told this attorney I couldn't make it because I would be in the city all day, but if I'm not going to the city, I have to at least do that. I can't just blow a full day's work off."

"All right, so where do you want to go?"

"I haven't been by your restaurant in a while," Jordan said.

"OK, then there we will go."

Jordan and Omar pulled out of the parking spot across the street from her place. It seemed obvious that things were falling back in order. Jordan wasn't expecting her and Omar to have a healthy relationship anytime soon, but the timing couldn't have been better for them to get on one accord. Jason would be home this weekend, and the better off her and Omar were, the better off Jason would be.

44

It had been a long week, and Jordan was absolutely exhausted. Although exhausting, it had been one of the best weeks Jordan had emotionally in a long time. The week before she had gone to the spa to relax, she did some soul searching, she spent some healing time with her friends, she spent some nights with Marcus, and it was the first week in several that she caused no regrets for herself.

She was sitting in her office working on some files; she was also back on top of her work. Last week she had done all the research needed for Darren's legal matters, and she was planning on having one of her associates work with him moving forward. The files that she was working on all needed to be updated since they'd been neglected the past few weeks. Jordan felt stronger than ever, feeling back in her zone, handling her responsibilities and being in control of her life. The feelings that had been eating her up for weeks were no longer surfacing, and she felt capable of truly moving on, in a healthy way, without the need to seek assurance and compromise herself.

Jason was due home in a few days, and Jordan was happy but also fearful. She didn't know if Jason held any resentment in his heart toward her for letting him go in the first place. She was hoping if not yet, one day he would understand her reasoning and that she honestly felt he needed his father's influence. Jordan would always feel a level of guilt for the decision she made, but she knew her heart was in the right place when she did it. And although that wasn't enough to justify it, it was all she kept telling herself.

Jordan reached for the can of cashews that were on top of her desk and took a handful out. She began to chew some as she flipped through the pages in her file. Her home office was pretty tidy except for some files piled in the corner and some law books that she hadn't put back. There was a time where Jordan spent all of her free time in her home office, to get work done, to clear her mind, or to get a break from Omar for a while. It was a place of serenity for her; it was a reminder of all that she had accomplished and what kept her humble and grounded. Once her and Omar split, it was more of a reminder of what she'd become, and she was less interested in letting her home office be her place for peace instead of the bedroom. She realized the poison in that way of life; she just realized it too late.

The volume on the television was turned very low in the office so that Jordan could concentrate on her work. She knew she could easily be distracted by the talk shows. Jordan put down the file that she was working for a few minutes to take a sip from her water when she heard knocking. She froze to make sure she was hearing things correctly, and then she picked up the remote and pointed it at the television to mute it. A second later, she heard her doorbell. Jordan put the documents on the desktop and stood up to head toward the front door. As she walked through the dining room, and living room, she tried to recall if she was expecting any packages. She hadn't recalled anything by the time she reached the door.

Jordan reached the foyer and peeked through her curtains

to see who was standing in front of her door. There were two men dressed in suits standing there talking to each other. One was Caucasian with brown hair and a mustache, and the other was a black guy with a faded haircut. They both looked like they were in their mid to upper thirties, and they appeared to have very reserved demeanors. After looking at them thoroughly, Jordan decided to crack the door open.

"Hello?" she said as she poked her head through the door.

"Hello, I'm Detective Charles and this is my partner, Detective Adams," the black man said as he flashed his badge. "We are with the FBI, and we just had a few questions for Jordan Moore."

In Jordan's line of work, she dealt with her fair share of law enforcers, but she never had any of them at her front door for questioning. She opened the door all the way and stepped in front of it.

"I am Jordan," she said as she looked down at his badge more carefully. "Can I see your badge as well?" Jordan asked the other officer.

He removed his badge from his right coat pocket and displayed it for Jordan.

"What is this about?" Jordan asked.

"You are under arrest for conspiracy of fraud, you're being charged as an accomplice to the Baron Jones crimes," Detective Adams said as he removed his cuffs from his belt clip.

"What?" Jordan yelped. "Who is Baron Jones?"

"Baron Jones, Marcus Shields, Tyrone Spencer, Phillip Watts . . . whichever name you would like to refer to him as," Detective Adams stated in a sarcastic tone.

"Please place you hands behind your back," Detective Charles said.

Before Jordan could say anything more, Detective Adams was reading her Miranda rights. As if Jordan didn't already know that she had a right to remain silent, the detective continued through the whole speech. Jordan was in disbelief, she had never been arrested before and she didn't even know what to say. All she could think about was what in the hell did Marcus get her into.

45

The room was empty all except for one long table and five steel chairs. Jordan had every intention on contacting a criminal attorney; for the meantime she decided she could handle it herself. She had no desire to prolong her stay any longer than necessary by waiting for an attorney to show up. They had driven her down to a federal office building in midtown Manhattan.

The same detectives that picked her up, entered the room that Jordan was waiting in.

"We wanted to ask you questions about a Baron Jones," the black officer said.

Jordan's eyes went up in the air as she thought for a second.

"I don't know a Baron Jones," Jordan said.

"Well ma'am, you may know a Marcus Shields," the Caucasian officer said.

Jordan instantly looked at the black officer with confusion in her eyes. Jordan's brain was roaming a mile a minute. What the hell was this about, she asked herself. What does Baron Jones have to do with Marcus and why did they need to question her about him, Jordan couldn't make sense of it.

"So, please explain to me how I can be of help about this

Baron guy, I've never met him," Jordan said as soon as she sat down.

"Well, Ms. Moore, Baron Jones is a man from New Jersey who takes on various identities and has committed identity theft over twenty times in eight different states already. He preys on women who he pretends to start a romantic relationship with, while in the meantime he is really gathering all the information that he needs to assume the person's persona," Detective Charles explained.

"How does he take on the identity of a woman," Jordan asked.

"With the woman victims he just gains all their information so that he can use their credit and purchase items in their names. With his male victims he has at different times used their names when he relocates to different places."

Jordan was beginning to assume what they were going to tell her next but she had to hear it for herself.

"So what connection do I have to this Baron person through Marcus?"

"Marcus is Baron Jones, Marcus Shields is one of his stolen identities," Detective Charles said.

"Wow," Jordan said as she placed her hand on her face. "So why am I under arrest?"

"Your name and address has appeared on several purchases, a flat-screen television was delivered to your house that was paid for with a stolen credit card, and therefore is reasonable suspicion that you are an accomplice," Detective Adams said.

"I am an attorney, and have nothing to do with his scams. I had no idea that he was a criminal; he told me he was an investor."

"Well, Ms. Moore, due to his habit of preying on women it is likely that you could be a victim and not an accomplice. We have considered that."

"So, why am I under arrest?"

"We haven't charged you with anything just yet; we just needed to question you. You have received stolen merchandise, which is a crime."

"It's a crime if I knew it was stolen, and I did not," Jordan said.

"I am going to be honest with you. I was just notified before we came in that it appears that Baron was targeting you as his next victim, he has already made purchases with your credit cards we believe," Detective Charles said.

Jordan instantly recalled her credit card declining a couple of weeks ago, and that strange UPS slip she received on her door the other day.

"He has had accomplices in the past, so we had to do some investigating on you before we could determine if you were a victim of his or an accomplice," Detective Adams said.

"I can't believe I was a suspect," Jordan said.

"We just had to verify some things before we were able to contact you. We have had our eye on Mr. Jones for years; we have finally located him and was able to assemble enough evidence to put him away for a long time."

"He lives around the corner from me, how would he expect to get away with this?" Jordan asked still in disbelief.

"His residence is just for deception. Once he is complete draining his victim he disappears in an instant, before they know what happened. He leaves the residence behind and anything else that he needs to abandon, they're not purchased in his name so it doesn't matter to him. He is already working on his next location and plan by the time he leaves. He needs a residence to look more authentic when he is settled."

Jordan sat there with her hand on her mouth. She was looking down at the floor trying to make sense of it.

"We may need you to testify if the situation calls for it," Detective Adams said.

"That's fine, but about what?" she asked.

"How you guys met, what tactics he may have used to get closer to you or gain access to your information, things like that. We need to show that this guy is a deceiving criminal," Detective Adams stated.

"That's fine," Jordan said. "I am assuming no charges will be pressed against me."

"Yes, Ms. Moore. We will finish looking into this matter, but you are no longer a suspect at this time," Detective Charles said.

She said she was fine testifying, but she knew she wasn't interested in stating on record that she was intimate with this man that she obviously didn't know.

"We just wanted to make you aware of the situation. We arrested Baron this morning from his home around the corner. Since he is a flight risk, he will likely not be released, but there are no guarantees. Therefore, just be careful, place fraud alerts on all your accounts and social security number, and request statements from all your accounts to dispute any suspicious activity," Detective Adams said.

"We are really sorry to be the bearer of bad news, and we apologize for all this inconvenience," Detective Charles said as he stood up.

"Am I free to go?" Jordan asked.

"Yes, Detective Adams will walk you out" Detective Charles said.

"Thanks," Jordan said as she, too, stood up.

Detective Adams held the door open for Jordan to walk toward and through.

"Should I change my locks or take any security measures?" Jordan asked.

"That's probably not necessary since Baron is not likely to be a physical threat. However it is a precaution that you can take if it will make you feel safer; we can't guarantee what is going to happen with his bail or what he is capable of." Detective Charles said.

He reached in his pocket and removed a card from his business card holder.

"Call me if you have any questions, and we will notify you if there are any major updates."

As she took the card, for the first time she realized just how handsome Detective Charles was.

"Thanks, I will definitely be in touch" Jordan said.

He was about six feet two, muscular build, a low faded ceasar with a whiskery yet neat goatee. He was chocolate brown skinned with dark brown eyes and nice pouty lips. He seemed to notice her scanning his features, because he smirked and broke eye contact. At that moment, Jordan had to mentally slap herself on the hand. Here she was in the middle of some drama due to some man, and she was already checking out another one. She had to tell herself, even though she didn't see a ring on his finger, she had no business even thinking about it. Jordan was no longer looking for Mister Right, at least not any time soon. So as fine as Detective Charles was, she wasn't going to use that card unless it was absolutely necessary, she told herself.

46

It was a long and expensive cab ride back home, and Jordan had time to let it all settle in her mind. The expensive gifts, the variety of cars, the array of credit cards she noticed in his wallet, everything that didn't add up. Jordan walked in her house and she walked straight to the living room and took a seat on her gray plush couch. There was part of her that just wanted to call someone and tell them about what just happened but at the same time she wasn't ready just yet. So instead of making any phone calls she sat there and tried to think over all of her dealings with Marcus, and all of the things that did seem suspicious and she ignored.

She remembered finding it odd when he didn't have a job but yet he had all these luxurious things. Marcus stayed dressed in designer clothes at all times, drove more than one car, had a well-furnished beautiful home, but never had anywhere to be. Maybe Jordan should've seen a red flag, but she believed him when he said he was an investor; that wasn't far-fetched. Hell, how was she supposed to know he was investing in people's identities?

The next few hours went by and Jordan had finished calling all of her credit card companies and accounts. She requested detailed statements from all of them, and asked them all to place a security alert on all the accounts. A piece of Jordan wanted to speak to Marcus, hear his side of the story. It was still hard to believe that the man that she had spent so much time with, that was so charming and she had such a connection with, was all just a figment of her imagination. She knew that chances were that even when Marcus was able to he probably wouldn't call her. Jordan knew that she could never tolerate a criminal even if he wasn't targeting her as a victim, because she was an attorney, but she had to admit that she was a bit disappointed that he was the only guy she had been seeing and now he was gone too. Jordan just had to face it that she was unlucky in love.

As Jordan compiled a folder in her home office with all the new codes and information she received concerning her accounts the past few hours, her home phone began to ring. She rushed from the office to go out to the living room, and with three rings having passed and no time to look at the caller ID she answered.

"Hello?" she said.

"Are you OK?" the voice replied.

It was Jayon.

"I'm fine, what do you mean?"

"Turn to Channel Nine, that guy is on the news," Jayon said.

Jordan picked up the remote control, pointed it at the television and turned it on to Channel Nine's five o'clock news, while Jayon remained silent. Once the screen appeared, Jordan saw the image of a news reporter standing in front of Marcus's house. She was reporting on his scheme and his victims, and showing the quiet neighborhood that he lived in. After Jordan heard most of it, she finally said something back to Jayon.

"The FBI came to my house today to notify me. I'm fine," Jordan said.

"That's crazy, they showed his face and I was like I know

that guy from somewhere but once I saw your neighborhood I remembered he was the guy from that night."

"Yeah, that's him. Once again the victim of fraud."

Jayon delayed in responding, clearly caught off guard by Jordan's aggression.

"I didn't call expecting you to allow me to console you; I just really wanted to see if you were all right."

"I'm fine, as good as I'm going to be under the circumstances," she replied.

"Did he do anything to you?"

"So far it seems he made a few purchases with two of my credit cards totaling about $3,000, but that's all that I have noticed so far."

"Wow," Jayon said. "You should get fraud alerts placed on your accounts."

"I'm one step ahead of you. That's what I spent the afternoon doing."

"Oh, good. Well I hope everything is OK, but if you need anything let me know." Jayon said.

In one sense she knew that he was the last person she would choose to depend on, but still it felt kind of good just having a friendly conversation with him again.

"OK," Jordan replied. "Take care."

"J," Jayon said real quick before Jordan could hang up. "I wanted to apologize for the things I said the other night."

"That's fine, thank you. I'm sorry as well for putting you in such an uncomfortable situation," Jordan replied.

"That's cool, when I thought about it I couldn't be mad at no one but myself, for losing you. Besides it's not like you knew they were my friends."

Jordan didn't reply. She didn't know what she was supposed to say to this. It was uncomfortable enough as it was without talking through it.

"Well, Jordan I know this has been a rough couple of months for you, and I know that I have caused a lot of turmoil. I just want you to know how sorry I am," Jayon began.

Jordan almost cut him short before he could start singing his song but then she realized that she did need to hear this.

"I can't make excuses for what I did, because there is none. I was wrong and selfish, and it's something I will have to regret forever. There is no doubt in my mind that you were the best woman for me, but I was too immature to treat you the way you deserved," he continued.

Jordan could feel herself tearing up from the emotions that were gushing through her body. She sniffled some, and hoped that Jayon couldn't hear that he had gotten the best of her.

"I know it's a sign of insecurity that I felt the need to cheat and seek other attention, but I never claimed to be perfect. I know that I let you down, and it kills me inside thinking about how you feel about me, but I truly hope that one day you can forgive me because my life just isn't the same without you. I know you may never trust me with your heart again, but at the very least I hope I can have my friend back."

By now, tears were streaming down Jordan's face. She didn't want to face the Jayon she once knew, it was easier to hate the Jayon she now knew. Hearing him open up to her just brought back all the feelings she had as his friend and his girlfriend. She realized that he could've been lying, he could've been trying to sweet talk her, but it didn't matter. At the end of the day, he was right. She would never trust him with her heart again and it just felt good to hear his explanation and apology.

"Thank you, Jayon, I appreciate you telling me that," Jordan said.

"No need to thank me, you take care, J, it was good talking to you."

"You too."

"Talk to you later," he said.

As soon as Jordan hung the phone up, she wondered how soon or how late would later be. She tried to assess if she was ready to have consistent interaction with Jayon. After she thought about it more she told herself one day, but today was not the day.

47

All the locks were changed at Jordan's house, and it had been over a week since she heard anything more about Marcus. She watched a couple more news reports on his arrest and printed some online information, but aside from that nothing new. She spoke to all her friends and family about the matter, got their advice, and even spoke to some attorneys who specialized in fraud. Overall, Jordan was over it. She had been through worse betrayals, she felt. She was just thankful she never let this man completely in her heart. The feelings for him she had she constantly tried to subdue, and the more fooling around she did, the less she was concerned about gaining his heart. So the news, although it was surprising and hurtful, didn't crush her. Jordan was already on to bigger and better things.

Jason was home, and he had been home for a few days now. Omar stayed over in the guest room the first few nights, just to make Jason more comfortable. Omar and Jordan agreed that they would coexist a lot better for the sake of Jason. He asked to sleep over the house a few nights a week to be closer with Jason, and not cause any more confusion in his life, at least until or if there was a good reason not to. Neither of them held any hard feelings, and they were both single, so there was no reason they couldn't function more like a family. According to Omar, it was worth a try. For all they knew, it was possible that it would grow into more. Still, in the meantime, they would help each other raise him and keep him happier at the same time. Jordan was content with the plan as well. She had her son, he was happy, and she had the only husband she ever had living with her from time to time, giving her that company that she secretly yearned for.

Jason had just gone to bed an hour ago, Omar was downstairs in the living room, and Jordan had just hung up the phone with Chrasey and Dakota. She was lying in her bed just looking up at the ceiling. Her television was on low, and the scent from the Glade candle burning on her nightstand was filling her nose. She was still emotionally confused about having her life back. Her son was in his bedroom sound asleep with his Batman night-light on, Omar was downstairs watching television, and she wasn't home alone. It didn't even matter that Omar wasn't her husband. He was the father of the one man that meant the world to her, and at least she knew that he wasn't a cheating and lying Jayon or an identity-stealing Marcus. She, for the first time in a long time, felt like she could let her guard down.

Jordan had finally come to terms with reality: No matter how much she liked it or not, God was only going to give her what she could handle. Just a few weeks prior, she would've never thought that she would feel the way she did on this night, carefree and genuinely happy. She knew that Jason would be home, but she didn't expect to be at peace over Jayon, not worrying about being alone, and she damn sure didn't expect to be watching movies with Omar on her couch. Jordan knew in her heart that God was good all the time. She realized that only time heals, and that there is no man that can rush God's hands of time. The things we stress over one day are menial and humorous another day. Life is unpredictable, and Jordan was ready to accept what God had in store for her.

A few days ago, Jordan considered calling Detective Charles, after she took twenty minutes to make up an adequate reason to contact him. After building up the courage, she realized that there was nothing gained from starting something new with another strange man, regardless of how good his profile appeared. Jordan asked herself where would it lead, and she knew honestly it would lead to another notch on her belt and nothing more. Her heart wasn't ready for new love, and neither was she.

A READING GROUP GUIDE

PLAYTHANG

Janine A. Morris

ABOUT THIS GUIDE

The questions and discussion topics that follow are intended to enhance your group's reading of this book.

DISCUSSION QUESTIONS

1. How much of who we are or trying to be as people is because of striving to be "impressive" to the people we are trying to attract?

2. When you reach a certain age, or have children, or are in a situation that makes your choice of mates less plentiful, should you be more forgiving of your mate's flaws or infidelities?

3. If you found out your partner was cheating with someone who knew about you, would it be petty to lash out at the person with whom your mate was cheating?

4. After a breakup from a serious relationship, is it okay to get into another relationship as soon as someone worthy presents themselves, or is it best to date around for a while, or spend some time alone?

5. Is it unacceptable to just throw caution to the wind and live in the moment after you reach a certain age?

6. Is it inappropriate to have sex with more than one guy in a week? If so, what is an appropriate amount of sex partners to have in a short time span?

7. Is it wrong to date someone that another single friend of yours could possibly be interested in if they never flat out asked you to back off?

8. Is it easier said than done to be a strong person and not emotionally fall apart after a breakup?